THE MATE INVESTIGATES

By

Gareth Dawkins

First Published 2025

Copyright © 2025 by Gareth Dawkins

All rights reserved. No part of this publication may be reproduced, distributed, or transmitted in any form or by any means, including photocopying, recording, or other electronic or mechanical methods, without the prior written permission of the publisher, except in the case of brief quotations embodied in critical reviews and certain other non-commercial uses permitted by copyright law.

Forward

I first became aware of Sir John Astley through George Plumptre's fascinating book 'The Fast Set (The World of Edwardian Racing)'. Sir John, or 'The Mate' as he was widely and affectionately known, appeared a particularly appealing character. Far from the most successful of racehorse owners, he never gave up trying and unlike many of his counterparts was always generous with his time and money in helping those less fortunate than himself. None more so than the stable lads, who were far from well renumerated in most cases.

Whilst researching for an article on the former Lincoln Racecourse, I found that The Mate had written a two-volume autobiography entitled 'Fifty Years of My Sporting Life at Home and Abroad'. Some of the attitudes expressed in the books inevitably need to be viewed in their time, it is however an entertaining read and confirmed The Mate to be a most endearing character. Of personal interest, he lived in Lincolnshire, where I too have lived much of my life.

A few years ago, whilst out walking with my wife, the idea of writing about The Mate came into my head as did the title 'The Mate Investigates'. From there I simply (!) needed a plot and further characters to make my initial idea real. The central plot of the book is fictional as are many of the characters. Others such as Henry Chaplin and all the members of the Danebury Confederacy were prominent figures in Victorian Horse Racing circles. The aristocratic rivalry that accompanies the story was one of the most explosive events to rock Victorian Society in the 1860's.

I hope that you will enjoy the result and for those curious to learn more, there are a series of short biographical notes on the characters both real and imaginary at the end of the book.

Gareth Dawkins (January 2025)

Preface by Joseph Lewis

I am, like so many before me, hugely indebted to Sir john Dugdale Astley Bart., or as he was known to the Victorian public at large 'The Mate'. A man truly a friend to all, from the Ticket Collector at Slough Railway Station to His Royal Highness the Prince of Wales!

Being diminutive of stature I was sent, aged twelve, to Newmarket to become a stable lad for the trainer Richard Marsh. Like so many other Lads, I dreamt that I too would become a leading jockey like Fred Archer.

By my late teens I had progressed to riding the stables horses on the gallops at Newmarket. On the morning of 17th April 1886, I was asked to ride work on a three-year-old colt called Catastrophe and never was a horse more aptly named.

Something spooked Catastrophe that morning and before I knew it, he had bolted across the gallops, my six five stone frame providing no opposition to half a ton of athletic horse flesh. My recollection remains vague, due to the mighty bump I took to my head when Catastrophe crashed into a noticeboard at the end of the gallops.

It was my extreme good fortune that this violent incident was witnessed by Sir John, who was sitting nearby on his cob conversing with Lord & Lady Zetland in their carriage. On seeing what had happened, Sir John galloped over and must, I think, have feared the worst. My arm was broken, and my left thigh snapped in two, the bone clearly visible through my trousers!

Lord and Lady Zetland readily agreed to their carriage being used as a makeshift ambulance and by the time I reached the local Rous Memorial Hospital, Sir John had organised for two doctors waiting ready to operate. At first glance the doctors assumed I had died but on discovering I was still clinging to life they operated, re-setting my arm and amputating one of my legs. Even then I was not out of danger, with the shock being so great, it was only by means of vigorous pressing on my chest that I started breathing again.

Five months after my accident, I was able to return home to London to live with my widowed mother. During that time Sir John had raised a fund from his friends to put me through college to learn typing and shorthand to equip me for a new career. The Duke of Portland even had a replacement cork leg made. Whilst I am very grateful to His Grace, I prefer to rely on my crutch, and I can now get along at a fair old lick!

For those of you not familiar with Sir John, he was born in Rome on the 19th of February 1828, the eldest of ten sons and daughters of Sir Francis Dugdale Astley Bart. and his wife Lady Eleanor. He grew up on the families Wiltshire estate where, from the age of sixteen, he started shooting, something to which he admitted to 'taking to like a duck to water'. It has been suggested that Sir John was the first to coin this now very popular phrase!

After Eton, Sir John spent a year at Christ's College Oxford as a 'Gentleman Commoner', which he described as 'a few trifling privileges and the chance to pay double for almost everything connected with the University'. Apparently insisted upon by the Dean of the College, in the hope that the extra cost might persuade his father from sending another troublesome Astley to Christ's!

His time at Oxford came to abrupt end when, on being asked to recite lines from Euripides he mistook two famous warriors, for a man and woman ardently making love! He was advised that he would be best to go down from Oxford, a suggestion with which he readily concurred!

On leaving Oxford, Sir John found he had totted up bills in the region of £400 on entertainment, an amount his father might be seriously inconvenienced to pay, requiring him to borrow from the family's solicitor. As Sir John put it himself 'thus laying the foundation of an amount of indebtedness from which I have never recovered'

In his younger years, Sir John was a fine athlete especially when it came to the 100-yard dash. He enjoyed running both for the sport and the chance to win money! In the mid-19th century, running matches were the subject of very serious wagering, attracting large crowds and reported upon by the sporting papers of the day.

At one time, very much as a precursor to owning a string of racehorses, Sir John managed his own string of human athletes. In fact, Sir John was very imaginative in the creation of betting opportunities, including a wining bet on which of a group of nuns in Rome would be first up the Spanish Steps!

Needing to earn a living post Oxford, he joined the Scots Fusiliers Regiment seeing service in the Crimean War. In 1858, at the nuptials of a brother officer, Sir John espied a fine young lady by the name of Eleanor Corbett, with whom he was much taken. On further enquiry, he established that Miss Corbett would be attending a ball in Sleaford the following week, to which he contrived to get himself invited.

Amongst Sir John's formidable array of talents, ballroom dancing was not one. He did not however let that deter him from asking Miss Corbett for a dance. Despite continually stepping on her dress, whilst desperately attempting to complete a quadrille, he clearly made a good impression and had, within just a few months obtained her hand in marriage.

He left the army in 1859 and came to live with his new wife at Elsham Hall the home of her father Thomas Corbett. The Hall was set in an estate of several thousand acres of gently rolling countryside, just outside the market town of Brigg, not far from the Humber Estuary.

At the time we start our story, Sir John had taken over the running of the Elsham Estate as Trustee for his son Frank, to whom it would pass on his majority. The estate was in a poor way, and he oversaw improving the farms, repairing 25 cottages and building two school rooms.

Sir John succeeded to the Astley baronetcy in 1873 on the death of his own father, leaving him with another badly rundown estate to try and rescue. Using typically bold tactics, he bought £4000 of sheep for the home farm, having persuaded the auctioneer to accept his bids, despite admitting to having no money to pay for them! Fortunately, he was offered a loan by a bank manager who heard Sir john, on Andover Station, telling of his urgent need for money! At the end of which, Sir John managed to turn a profit!

Perhaps his most unlikely endeavour came in 1874 when he succeeded his father-in-law as MP for North Lincolnshire. As Sir John wrote himself, 'I now become a Legislator – oh dear was there ever such a parody on that exalted title'. At his first public speech from the back of a wagon in Crowle Market Square, a local stepped forward to ask his view on Sir Wilfred Lawson's 'Liquor Bill'. Unsure as what that might be, Sir John answered that 'he did not know about Sir Wilfred's Liquor Bill but did know that mine was a deuced sight too high this year!' The remark caused much hilarity, given the Bill was an attempt through Parliament to further the cause of the Temperance Movement. Sir John did not enjoy being an MP and admitted to being mightily relieved when beaten at the 1880 General Election!

In amongst all his other endeavours, he still found time to organise large sporting events such as the Astley Belt, which saw competitors from both sides of the Atlantic compete in the then popular sport of Pedestrianism. Essentially a competition where the participants would walk hundreds of miles around a track for six days!

Sir John's real interest however was the Sport of Kings, both for the love of the horses and the hope of profitable wagering! He ran his own racing operation from 1862 until 1883 but was badly hit in 1881 when, he heavily backed his best horse Peter to win the Manchester Cup. Failure to pull off the gamble cost Sir John £12,000 and proved to be a hammer blow to his already shaky finances, leaving Sir John, in his own words 'cruel hard-up'!

Whilst no longer able to afford his own string of racehorses, Sir John remained a regular and popular visitor to the races and continued with his various good works, for which he sought no personal recognition. Albeit the stable lads of Newmarket, for whom he had raised £25,000 for a building of their own, named it the Astley Memorial Hall in his honour.

Sir John passed away on 10th October 1894, following an enjoyable day's racing with friends at Kempton Park Racecourse. On returning to the families London residence, Sir John took to his bed with a fever. Staff called for his doctor, but his condition worsened, and he passed away the following morning, mourned by family and friend from near and far.

I like to hope that Sir John's last days wagering was a successful one and at the time of the telling of the tale within this book, he was very much alive and as ebullient a character as ever, a cigar more often than not clamped between his lips.

Chapter 1 – The Mate Drops a Big Surprise into the Conversation!

'I feel like a bloomin' maggot in a nut' Sir John exclaimed, not for the first time, of his enforced sojourn at Elsham Hall, brought about by his valiant but ultimately failed attempt to beat the bookmakers at their own game.

It had been over a long lunch, at his London Club, where Sir john had been entertaining those gathered with stories of his colourful life that, at the conclusion of one of those stories, a friend asked.

"Why don't you write a book John! You are constantly complaining of poverty, why you would be a rich man, if you would take the trouble to put on paper the amusing stories you have just been telling us".

"It's all very well to talk my dear Charlie" Sir John replied "Any fool can tell a story, but it takes a learned man to write a book. How could I write one when, barring Bradshaw's Rail Guide, I never study any books!"

"Go on" he responded "you take a tip from old Charlie, and you will make a pile"

After taking time to ponder Charlie's suggestion Sir John sought help from his erudite friend Mr Dick Thorold of London, who agreed to edit the book and arranged a publisher, the esteemed firm of Hurst & Blackett.

Aside from the hope that his life in the world of sport and service to his country, would provide a measure of entertainment to his readers, it was Sir John's fervent hope that once again the adorable 'monkey' comprising £500 in fresh new bank notes would take up residence once again in its old quarters of his trouser pocket. For too long the only occupants having been 'nonsies' and 'flimsies', five-pound notes in Sir John's often quaint use of the English language.

All of which had led to my receiving a letter in early 1892 from Sir John, asking if I would come up to Elsham Hall and use my newly acquired skills to type up his memories for onward transmission to Mr Thorold. The completed version of which, came to form Volume's One & Two of 'Fifty Years of My Life in the World of Sport at Home and Abroad'.

I have taken the liberty of quoting from Volume One for Sir John's own thoughts on his writing style: -

'I am afraid I have been somewhat prolix at times and may have wearied my readers with many trumpery incidents, some few of which I have found very difficult to commit to paper in an amusing form; though over a pipe and a glass I have found them tickle the risible faculties of my hearers!'

For my part I found that in his occasional self-admitted rambles from the subject at hand, Sir John possessed a fund of facts as well as amusing anecdotes, that I have tried to include where possible in my narrative.

A week after my arrival at Elsham, we were sitting in Sir John's study, having not long finished his time in the Crimea when he announced' I think the moment has come for me to tell you how I came to be involved in horse racing, my very favourite sporting endeavour and one of life's greatest frustrations'!

'Whilst coming to live at Elsham had many merits, it could be a trifle dull at times and both Mrs Corbett and I agreed, we needed to rent a place in London for the summer season.'

'Once ensconced in our modest new London home, we found our only problem was that it was damn hard to make ends meet in 1861 on £1700 per annum! (I'm not sure Sir John had quite taken on board the irony of that statement to those from a different background!) 'It was this realisation that made me hit upon the notion of combining my urgent need for more money, with my love of racing'.

I had made money from wagering on my own racing chickens in the army, so I reasoned I should be able to make money from betting on horses! With rumour and gossip rife in racing circles, my thoughts were that I would be best placed to make money by backing horses in my ownership – that way I could be sure the horses were fully primed ready to win their races and not have that information shared far and wide!'

'My first issue was to raise the necessary capital. I had some £8000 from the sale of my Colonelship in the Fusiliers and a little extra from a fortuitous 40/1 touch on Caractacus, that most unlikely winner of the 1862 Derby. I would like to have asked my father-in-law for some 'investment capital', but the old boy was dead set against horse racing and the alleged sins with which it was associated.

With no help coming from Elsham and my own dear father having the same view on racing as Old Man Corbett, I had to come up with another idea. After a bracing walk across Elsham Wold, I devised the perfect plan - insure my life at a premium of 3% then borrow against the capital raised at 5% - ingenious if I say so myself!

Having raised my stake, I needed to find myself a trainer who, aside from skill and knowledge, was also honest! To this end, I decided upon Mr Dick Drewitt, of Lewes in Sussex. Another advantage of employing Drewitt was access to George Fordham, to my mind the finest jockey of his generation, despite his odd habit of clucking like a chicken whilst riding!'

'I opted for a modest start and for 1862 bought myself a horse called Hesper, who won me a selling plate, the lowest level of handicap race but if you know when your horse is hitting form, an excellent medium for a good touch.'

'I traded a few more platers and by the end of that first season, I had accumulated £11,097 in stakes and winning bets and was feeling damned pleased with my strategy. For 1863 I increased my string to ten horses. Over the next few years, I had some ups and lots of downs but in 1866 I finally managed to win a big race, The Cambridgeshire Handicap at Newmarket with Actea. Dr Shorthouse owner and editor of the Sporting Times, knowing my propensity for a wager, called it a well-planned coup. Well planned alright but given I was under the financial cosh at the time, I only managed to clear around £5000 in winnings!

At this point, Sir john threw into the conversation one of his more than occasional discourses from the subject. These discourses seldom aided early completion of the task at hand but often proved to be fascinating, particularly on this occasion!

'By the way, Joseph with my dear lady wife out doing good works in the village and not here to hold me steadfast to recording my memoirs, I'll tell you about how my involvement in racing led to me became a Detective? Something even more unlikely I'm bound to admit, than my totally undistinguished stint as the Honourable Member of Parliament for North Lincolnshire"! he chuckled expansively.'

'I'd definitely be very interested to hear about that Sir John' I replied, my interest already piqued.

'The story revolves around my good friend Harry Chaplin, whose name had been thrust, none too willingly, into the public domain due to the actions of his onetime friend and latterly bitter rival Harry, Marquis of Hastings. A rivalry which both shocked and fascinated Victorian Society.'

'My friend Harry was born in 1840, in Rutland, where his father the Reverend Henry Chaplin was a vicar. Aged just 18, he inherited, from a childless uncle, the family seat of Blankney Hall, to the south of Lincoln, together with its substantial estate.'

Harry Hasting's background was even grander. Born Henry Weysford Charles Plantagenet Rawdon-Hastings in 1842, his father was the hunting mad George, 2nd Marquis and his mother the free-spirited Barbara Yelverton, known as 'the jolly fast marchioness' for her love of both foreign travelling and gambling in continental casinos!

When the 2nd Marquis died in 1844, aged just 35, his twelve-year-old son Paulyn inherited the families' estates. Worse was to follow when Paulyn died in 1851, leaving little Harry to inherit both the title and family fortune at just eight years of age.

With his mother abroad most of the time, Harry was left in the family home, the Gothic fantasy Donnington Hall in Leicestershire, with his elder sisters, all of whom spoilt him outrageously. With the Marchioness passing away in 1858, Harry was left at sixteen with no parents and no adult guidance.

Both Harry's, like me, attended Eton then Christs College Oxford. The Marquis made little impact at Oxford, either academically or socially, despite being possessed of a high level of charm, when he wished. He was described as a handsome fellow with large brown eyes but a weak mouth.

Harry Chaplin on the other hand, whilst a rather thicker set young man than Hastings, cut quite a dash at Oxford. A good scholar and leader of the social set, he was awarded the nickname 'Magnifico'!

The Marquis had meanwhile discovered a distinct fondness for alcohol, and it was said he breakfasted on fried mackerel and caviar, washed down with a bottle of the finest claret! He also, discovered horse racing and gambling, clearly enjoying both the thrill of the bet and his growing reputation as, 'the great plunger'! All of which gave him a following amongst other young men, of a similar character.

After leaving Oxford, Hastings started 'investing' heavily in racehorses, with the object of busting the betting ring wide open. His trainer of choice was John Day Jnr of Stockbridge. One of the most successful trainers of the period Day enjoyed a reputation for laying horses out for a big touch.

In 1864, both Harry's became smitten with Lady Florence Paget, known to her admirers as the Pocket Venus. Whilst of diminutive stature, the Marchioness was a lady both beautiful and considered to be of perfect proportions, hence the 'honorary' title

Her grandfather the 1st Marquis, 'old one leg' as he was usually known, was a Major-General who, when struck in the leg by a cannon ball at the battle of Waterloo, apparently turned to the nearby Duke of Wellington uttering "By God Sir, I've lost my leg", to which the Duke answered "By God Sir You have'. Whilst I never met the Marquis, I did in a rum kind of a way meet his amputated leg some years later when visiting the village of Waterloo in Belgium, where it resided as a tourist attraction! Most macabre!'

Harry Chaplin appeared to be gaining the upper hand in the wooing stakes, and on 20th June during a ball held at the Mayfair home of the Duke & Duchess of Abercorn, Lady Florence accepted Harry's proposal of marriage. The wedding it was announced would take place in early August.

Lady Florence's decision seemed to have been accepted in all good grace by the Marquis. Indeed, on 15th July he was a guest in Harry's box at Covent Garden to see the world-famous soprano Adelina Patti sing Gounod's Faust. I don't know much about opera, but I'm told she had a mighty pair of lungs!' Sir John chuckled.

All seemed well until the following day, when Lady Paget decided to go shopping, for some final wedding essentials, unusually without her maid in attendance. On arriving at the Vere Street door of Marshall & Snellgrove's high class department store, Lady Paget calmly walked through the store and left by the back door, where she duly eloped with the Marquis! Making their way by carriage to St George's Church in Hanover Square, where they were married!

Suffice to say the elopement scandalised Society, the charms of the libidinous and heavy gambling Marquis clearly proving irresistible. Harry Chaplin meanwhile received a note from Lady Florence, apologising for her conduct and saying that she did not feel worthy of him.

Whilst my friend Harry did not have his former friend's myriad vices, he was equally drawn to the Turf. After a sojourn in India out of the public gaze, he returned to England and the world of racing. Doubtless spurred on by his rivalry with Hastings, a contemporary said of him 'he bets like he is mad and buys horses as if he were drunk'!

To bring stability to his reckless racing affairs, Harry placed the management of his horses in the hands of Captain Jem Machell, a fine judge of horse flesh and an astute reader of form. Machell, of whom more anon, was a fearless gambler who at the time of our story had, still aged only thirty-five, built up a considerable fortune both for himself and his aristocratic clients.

One of Captain Machell's first actions as Harry's racing manager was, in June 1865, to buy him a fine-looking yearling, at the Middle Park sale In Newmarket for the sum of 1000 guineas, the under bidder being one Harry Hastings!

The yearling, duly named Hermit, showed early promise as a two-year-old, winning a good race at Stockbridge, where he beat Vauban, one of the favourites for the 1867 2000 Guineas. Thereafter both Harry and the Captain began backing Hermit for the following years Derby.

Not everyone, me included, believed that Hermit would stay the Derby distance of one mile four furlongs. Another of this view was Lord Hastings who, word had it, stood to lose as much over £100,000 if Hermit won. Whether that was because of a genuine view on Hermit's stamina or simply an irrational dislike of Mr Chaplin no one was sure. As the Marchioness was heard to remark at the time 'Harry is betting against Hermit as if he is dead!'

Chapter 2 – A typically wet and windy Lincoln start to the Racing Season!

Easing back into his favourite armchair Sir John declared, taking a puff on his newly lit Partagas Cuban cigar' Enough of all this background'

'Our tale starts on Thursday 28th March 1867, and I had travelled down that morning to Lincoln, by train from Barnetby, for the first morning of the three-day Spring Meeting. As so often the case, Spring was a complete misnomer, the weather being cold, wet and windy'

Despite the inclement conditions, there was the usual sense of anticipation for the first major meeting of the Flat Racing Season, with the feature race, the ever-unpredictable Lincolnshire Handicap, to be run on the Saturday.

The course, located on the Carholme, just to the west of the city was already busy when I arrived at noon, the usual mix of mountebanks, pin-prickers and confidence tricksters mingling in with the public at large. I made my way to the top floor of the County Stand, to join my chum Harry Chaplin in his box. A large room with its own balcony, the box afforded capital westerly views towards the mile start adjacent to the road to Sheffield. Looking north over the course, and just visible through the rain, was the cities Medieval Cathedral, once the tallest building in the world, at 524 feet, until the steeple collapsed!

As ever our host had laid on an excellent spread with slices of cold meats from his estate; pies; pasties, bowls of nuts and assorted chutneys. All to be washed down with fine wine, sherry and steaming hot mugs of tea and coffee.

'Wonderful to see you John and so pleased you could make it today' Harry called out as I entered the room.

'Delighted to be here Harry and hopefully a good season ahead. You have the favourite for the Derby whilst I'm aiming to win a selling plate at the humbler surrounds of Brighton!'

'You know as well as I do Mate' he said with a laugh' the smaller tracks often provide the best opportunity to land a bit of a touch, well away from the prying eyes and gossip of Newmarket'

'You're too right there Harry!

'Ah, the vicissitudes of racing' Harry responded' isn't that what attracts so many of us, that and the sheer love of the thoroughbred, even if neither of us will be riding our own racehorses this season!'

'Given the size of the spread you've laid on Harry, that will never be the case'!

'There are few things in life Mate that give me more pleasure than being able to share my good fortune with those I hold dear'.

'A splendid sentiment my friend and if you don't mind, I think I will tuck into some of that excellent game pie I spotted on arrival'

Also present in the box was my good friend Sir Carlton Scroop, owner of a fine estate in the Lincolnshire Cliff village of the same name, plus a fair old slice of the east end of London and a fine collection of Jade. All of which made him a very wealthy man.'

I had known Sir Carlton since we'd both been at Oxford and belonged to the famous Bullingdon Cricket Club, as had Harry Chaplin. Whilst we all shared a common love of the great British summer sport, an equal amount of Bullingdon Club time was given over to general merriment. Albeit I considered Wisden Cricketer Magazine's description of the Club as 'ostensibly a cricket team, it uses cricket as a respectable front for the mischievous, destructive and self-indulgent tendencies of its members' a little unfair!

Whilst I'd been an effective if agricultural swinger of the cricket bat, Sir Carlton had been an elegant timer of the ball who still retained that same elegance in his appearance. Unlike yours truly, who had put on many pounds from his prime running weight of twelve stone, Sir Carlton had kept his trim six feet figure. As I commented upon whilst devouring my first plate of game pie and accompanying pickles!

Sir Carlton's wife had sadly died in childbirth and despite being one of England's most eligible men he had never re-married. Although there is always time, take the Reverend John King, owner of the Ashby Estate, adjacent to Harry's Blankney Estate, who upped and married the kitchen maid at the age of 72!

'Good to see you Carlton, first time since we rode together on that bracing day in February with the Yarborough Hunt. The biting wind coming in from the North Sea made me think of winter nights in the Crimea!'

'I seem to remember John your father-in-law having a few problems that day' Carlton replied in jocular fashion.

'Yes, another case of his myopia getting the better of his enthusiasm. I found the old boy at the end of the hunt berating his mount for a bumpy ride – I hadn't the heart to tell him the bumps were the result of the horse making his own mind up to jump the hedges his master had failed to spot!'

'I admire the old boys pluck and hope to still be out in the field when I'm that age'!

'I'm sure given your youthful bearing you'll be out jumping your contemporaries for years to come' I replied whilst giving Carlton an encouraging slap on the back.

'We'll see John' he laughed; his admirably white teeth visible. I'd definitely got the rough end of things when it came to style and elegance I reflected, tucking into a wedge of pork pie this time.

'Apologies for now Carlton but I picked up a whisper for the chances of that canny trainer Issac Arkwright's runner in the opening race'

'Good luck John and see you later'.

As it transpired, I would have been better not listening to whispers from the world's worst tipsters – also known as jockeys - and saved my £5!

The principal race of the day was the Brocklesby Stakes, named after the Earl of Yarborough's magnificent estate to the west of Grimsby. It proved to be an eventful race, victory going to a horse wearing the white and crimson colours of the elderly Earl of Glasgow.

I can think of few owners who, aside from yours truly (!), had more runners with less overall success! Unlike me, for whom money has come and gone with alarming alacrity, this was never a problem for the Earl who, in a rare moment of philosophical reflection on his racing career, noted that 'no one is unlucky who has an income of £150,000 per year!

After racing was over and I had said my goodbyes, I climbed the very aptly named Steep Hill, pausing for breath outside one of England's oldest homes, the 12th Century Jews House, on my way to the venerable White Hart Hotel. Located betwixt the Cathedral and Castle the hotel was handily placed for the Assembly Rooms, where a ball was to be held on Friday night to celebrate the start of the Flat Racing Season, at which I would be joined by my good lady wife.

I had been intending to have a runner on the Friday but with the horse having gone lame on the Lewes gallops, I had scratched my entry and took the opportunity to get the train over to Nottingham to attend to some business matters.

I was back in Lincoln in good time to meet Eleanor on her arrival from Elsham. After a wash and brush up at the Hotel, we took the short walk along historic Bailgate, to the Assembly Rooms. The city's most fashionable meeting place since the 1740's, dinner was to be enjoyed in the magnificent, marbled hall. Present would be some of the foremost and also most colourful members of the racing fraternity.

And talking about colourful there were few more so than the Duchess of Montrose, or as she was known, for a variety of reasons, 'Carrie Red'. The politest being a reference to her habit of attending the races dressed entirely in matching crimson from her hat to her shoes.

We passed her walking to the Assembly Rooms, holding onto the arm one of Lord Hasting's acolytes Viscount Bowlhead. Less than half her age and a rather timid individual, I didn't doubt he had been ordered by the Duchess to attend as her companion, since he looked none too happy with the situation!

'Once there, we joined Harry at his large and convivial table, where the talk was about the following days Lincolnshire Handicap. After about twenty minutes of animated chatting and imbibing Harry, who was sitting to my right, gave out a large harrumph!'

'Is everything alight Harry' I enquired with concern.

'I'm afraid John, it's definitely not alright! Harry responded with a pronounced look of distaste spread across his face 'See who is now sitting next to Carrie Red!

I turned round and saw that slumped in the previously vacant seat was a louche young man, already very sozzled. Namely Harry, 4th Marquis of Hastings.

'Fully understood Harry' I said, trying not to stare too obviously.

Next to the Merry Marquis was 'the Pocket Venus', and next to her was Hastings best friend Lord Coggles, together with his intended Miss Mavis Enderby. Also on the table were the other members of Hastings coterie of close friends, including Lord Zeals, who I had recently heard described, in my view accurately, as 'a supremely loud, chortling mound of blubber under an unruly mop of blonde hair!

'Good manners require me to welcome Hastings to my county' said Harry through gritted teeth' and ask after the health of the Marchioness.

'I'll join you Harry, happy to share the burden!'

With which we made our way through the crowded room to the Hastings table. The Marquis had clearly been on the sauce all afternoon and the same applied to most of his guests, especially that uppity young man Tobias Bracklesham. Ironic really given his family had made a colossal fortune from Brackelsham's Tonic, much loved by the Temperance crowd. Its terrible taste and lack of alcoholic content quite enough to put me off for life!

'Welcome to Lincolnshire Henry, I hope that you, the Marchioness and your friends are enjoying the counties many charms?'

'Oh, it's quite, quite charming Harry' the Marquis slurred back 'I must make a note to give Monte Carlo a miss next year and head straight for Lincolnshire!' Which on cue produced a loud chortle from cheerleader in chief Zeals.'

'As I am sure you are aware, I have a runner in tomorrow's big race and thought I would come up the night before to get in some pre-race celebrations.'

'I do hope' he added, heavily laden down with irony' that Woldsway gives you a very jolly run for your money. I'm informed by my trainer Mr Day, that Oculato is trained to the last ounce and ready to run the race of his life'

Wisely choosing not to rise to the bait, our Harry merely replied 'Let's hope that all the horses and jockeys have a safe run to the finishing tape'

'Oh, how wonderfully sincere a thought, quite what one would expect from the son of a country parson'! The Marquis sneered before adding' Still intending to run Hermit in the Derby? His pedigree is against his lasting the distance and not entering him in the Guineas, hardly a powerful show of confidence'

'I don't see that as your business Henry or any of your friend's, but I can assure you I remain as confident as ever in Hermit' With which we set off for our table.

I should add that the Marchioness was looking very embarrassed and may well have been regretting already, the choice she had made in the matrimonial stakes. Lord Coggles looked none too happy either but seemed resigned to being unable to prevent his best friend from acting in such an undignified manner.

There remained however time for one last drunken sneer, this time from Tobias Bracklesham 'Not been shopping at Marshall & Snellgrove of late have you Chaplin!'

As we walked back Harry muttered 'From next year I'm going to throw a house party, so I'm only surrounded by those whose presence I actually desire'

Sadly, the episode with the Marquis cast a cloud over the rest of the evening, albeit the Assembly Rooms had managed to produce a thumping good Turbot, and I was mercifully not required by Mrs Astley to attempt any form of waltz or gavotte!

We finally made our way back to the White Hart at about 2.00pm, where I once again needed to feign sleep, in anticipation of Eleanor's expected enquiry as to how my betting year had started – poorly to tell the truth but not something I was keen to dwell upon at that moment!

Chapter 3 – A day of constant uncertainty, its the Lincolnshire Handicap!

Eleanor had returned to Elsham early on the Saturday morning, whilst I had partaken of the White Hart's fine breakfast of eggs, bacon, sausage, kidneys, black-pudding, kedgeree, toast and marmalade, which I hoped would be enough to sustain me until luncheon.

I was joined on my perambulation down Steep Hill to the races by my good friend George Payne, once described as a 'true English gentleman, light-hearted, high-spirited, the pink of chivalry and the soul of honour'. He had inherited a substantial fortune when just seven years of age, after his father was shot dead in a duel by the brother of a young lady, he was alleged to have seduced. Despite having worked his way through a large part of his fortune, George still retained his amiable disposition and sparkling wit.

As we walked, we talked our way through the merits of the runners for the Lincolnshire Handicap, at the end of which George concluded 'Frankly Mate, with nineteen horses rushing towards a first furlong kink, better suited to half that number of runners, in my view its anyone's race'

'Agreed George and wise words as ever' albeit it would still not stop either of us having a bet on the race!

On arriving at the course, we stopped a moment just outside the gate to listen to an evangelical preacher warning us of the evils of gambling. I think it was fair to say that we were both aware of the perils but very unlikely to mend our ways!

I remarked to George that some years before, I had seen the 'Lincolnshire Thrasher' give a very similar speech. An uneducated farm labourer from Tetford in the Lincolnshire Wolds, The Thrasher had discovered late in life, a gift for rousing evangelical fervour but I'm afraid I didn't heed his warnings either!'

When deciding what to back, I am always interested to see which owners had travelled a long way to see their runner when who should come into view but James Merry. Seldom has the name Merry been less aptly bestowed! Uncouth and mean of visage, Merry inherited a large fortune from his father, an itinerant tea peddler, who had acquired a very damp bog for his sheep, underneath which it transpired lay one of Ayrshire's largest deposits of ironstone. Something Merry Snr had the wit to exploit to his great good fortune.

James Merry had only a limited love for his horses but a much greater love for money and that most revolting of 'sports', cock fighting, allegedly keeping 1000 of the poor blighters for that express purpose.

Walking beside Merry was his odious side-kick Norman Buchanan, whose sole interest in life appeared to be accusing perfectly decent chaps of being crooked and working against his employer's interests. Also present was former Black Country boxer Tass Parker, less odious than Buchannan, but when needed willing to physically enforce his master's wishes, particularly anyone touting the chances of Mr Merry's horses before Merry himself had had the chance to put his own large wager down!

Merry managed a growling grunt as he strode by, Parker remained stone faced his flat Black Country voice seldom heard, whilst Buchanan true to form, felt the necessity to make a suitably unpleasant remark.

'No runners today, Mate, I'd have thought in your own county you'd like to show off your fine collection of selling platers to your grand friends.'

I decided to be extra friendly on the basis this would probably only rile him more 'Even if I don't have any runners for your delectation, it's always nice to welcome a true Scottish gentleman such as yourself to our fair county'

'Fair county! it's cold and more rain to come no doubt' he sneered. After a little more of this we walked on, George remarking, with a shudder, on Buchanan's continuing odiousness.

Before the morning was out, I'd also seen Jem Machell, with Harry's trainer William Bloss, to saddle Harry's horse for the big race. Whilst I knew our Harry would I am sure, intensely disliked public rivalry, seldom mentioning it in conversation, I had few doubts getting the better of the Marquis and his runner would add to any triumph.

With George having to pay heed to a call of nature, I found myself alone but only for a moment. Feeling a gentle tap on my shoulder I turned to find it was none other than David Coggles. Standing about five feet ten inches tall, slim build, wavy mid-brown hair and trim moustache, from a distance it was sometimes difficult to tell David and Viscount Bowlhead apart.

'Good to see you David' I said with genuine pleasure.

'And you too Mate, I wanted to apologise for Harry Hastings and Tobias's behaviour last night, it was uncalled for, and I know it's not Harry's true character'

'Many thanks David, you have nothing whatsoever for which to apologise. I think I'll have to take your word for it about the Marquis's true character, since I've personally not seen too much evidence to support that notion, but I admire your loyalty'.

Unlike Hastings, Coggles did not attend Christ's Oxford, going instead to Kings College, Cambridge. He had however attended Eton with Hastings and as far as one could see, in amongst the sycophants and well-heeled bounders with whom Hastings mainly surrounded himself, his only true friend.

I had known David from childhood, having served in the Fusiliers with his father Buffy, Earl of Utterby, owner of an estate centred around the charmingly named village of Burton Coggles, to the south of Grantham.

Of David's relationship with Miss Enderby, at times David seemed every bit the devoted consort and at others not fully aware of Edith's delightful presence. Hopefully however there was a happy ending in sight.

With George having returned from toilets which he described as, if anything more odious than Norman Buchanan, we bade David goodbye and repaired to Harry's box where mien host and a gathering of around twenty others were present. The spread was even larger than on Thursday, with the addition of the finest French Champagne, albeit the grey clouds hovering above were hardly reminiscent of Nice at the height of summer.

Before long I found myself reminiscing with Sir Carlton over our days playing cricket for the Bullingdon Club.

'Do you remember John, the time you got a golden duck against that hard drinking crowd from Woodstock and had to down a yard of the truly terrible local ale before ridding the first mile home blindfold?'

'In view of the strength of the beer I'm surprised I can remember anything' I replied.

'Good days John'

'Good old days indeed Carlton'

Without wanting to appear indiscreet I decided to ask Sir Carlton 'Is it ten years now since your Mary sadly passed away'

'Yes, ten years next month'

'I am sure Mary would understand if you ever thought of remarrying both to provide some company and indeed a son to take over the title'.

''The title will go to my younger brother Jasper'

'I thought he was a confirmed bachelor?'

'He is indeed and one devoted to art and living what seems to have been a twenty year 'grand tour' of Europe, but I live in hope for him' he laughed.

'In any event I do hope someone nice appears on your horizon'.

'I can see people on the horizon but sometimes it's difficult to move them into the foreground' he replied with an enigmatic smile.

Come three o'clock, we made our way down from the box to the paddock to view the runners. Here we picked up the news, doubtless a relief to Harry Chaplin, that The Marquis had become 'unavoidably' drunk and was understood to be deep in a game of cards and goodness knows what else in his suite at the White Hart. It did not however stop that asinine dandiprat Zeals booming a few ill-judged comments in Harry's direction.

Standing adjacent to the Hastings crowd was the Merry party. Merry himself was in an intense conversation with his trainer James Waugh and jockey John Osborne, he of the enormous mutton chop whiskers and the popular epithet 'The Bank of England Jockey' in recognition of his integrity!

A little closer to where George and I were standing, by the paddock rail, I could hear Bracklesham and Bowlhead, expressing a withering assessment of the Merry horse, albeit one gained the impression Bowlhead was merely following the lead of his friend.

'Mr Merry doesn't take kindly to rude comments about his horses' Buchanan sneered'. Tass and I like to protect Mr Merry's interest because he's too much of a gentleman to be doing that himself' a comment which caused me to snort out loud!

To which Parker added in his flat West Midland accent; 'we'll not be forgetting what has been said here'

'I'm all a quiver' Bowlhead rejoindered in an apparent but rather unconvincing show of bravado, doubtless knowing Parker's fearsome reputation'

As George had predicted, the Lincolnshire Handicap threw up a big surprise when the John Dawson trained outsider Vandervelde got up to win in the final strides at 33/1. Both the Harry's runners had picked up plenty of support but dropped tamely away before the business end of the race

On returning from our vantage point to the unsaddling enclosure, I nodded my commiserations to Harry Chapline who had, as expected taken defeat with the greatest equanimity. The Hasting's party looked crestfallen, particularly the Marchioness, doubtless all too aware that each large loss put another dent in the declining family fortune.

I popped over to congratulate the winning owner, the Hungarian Prince Gustavus Batthany. A hugely popular figure in the world of racing, both his horses, with their scarlet clothing and the stable lads with their dark blue liveries looked appropriately princely.

After racing was over, I made way back to the station for what turned out to be a far longer train journey home than I had hoped. Having missed my connection at Gainsborough Central, I passed the time with the stationmaster, a former pugilist known locally as the Gainsborough Gorilla. A game fellow indeed, given he lost more bouts than he won. A quieter life on the station seemed to suit him better!

'And now Joesph, with it having passed noon and with Eleanor's brother, the Reverend Corbett coming over for lunch, it is time for a pre-meal snifter. Only way I can get thought one of his sermons on the alleged merits of the Temperance Movement'!

Chapter 4 – The Racing Season moves onto the Newmarket Guineas Meeting where The Mate makes a new acquaintance from the world of detection!

Later that afternoon, we returned to Sir John's memoirs and a section concerning Captain Thomas Webb, the first man to swim the English Channel, for whom he had organised various commercial swimming events.

'Ah Webb, a stout fellow but given to worrying a lot!'

'Another fascinating recollection Sir John to add to the many others thus far' I remarked.

'What I think you mean' Sir John responded with his customary chuckle' is a mildly interesting anecdote but can't we return to your tale of detection!

I tried to protest' Oh no Sir John not at all'

'No need to apologise Joseph, it is more interesting! We'll pick up again four weeks after the Lincolnshire Handicap, with the first major event of the Flat Racing Season, the Guineas Meeting on Newmarket's historic Rowley Mile Course, featuring the first two of the years five Classic races.

The meeting was spread over three days, the 1000 Guineas for the fillies on the Thursday and the 2000 Guineas for the colts on the Saturday. Estate business required us to miss the filles race, meaning Eleanor and I did not get to Newmarket until the Friday evening'.

'As per usual, we put up at the Rutland Arms, a fine old place, always full of friends and acquittances. That night we enjoyed a most convivial dinner hosted by George Payne, who I'd not seen since the Lincolnshire Handicap. Present on our table was George's lifelong friend Colonel Jonathan Peel, younger brother of Robert Peel, of Metropolitan Police fame, who was accompanied by his delightful wife Lady Alicia Jane, daughter of the 1st Marquis of Ailsa.

Also present on our table was ex-Inspector Charles Field, the renowned Scotland Yard detective and apparent inspiration for the character of Inspector Bucket in his friend Charles Dickens Bleak House. By now in his 60's, he cut a portly figure, not that I can talk, with a husky voice and a habit of wagging a corpulent forefinger to emphasise what he was saying.

The son of a publican from Chelsea, Field informed us that he had worked his way up to Chief of Detectives, before retiring in 1852 to become a private investigator. Much feted by the press, he had a great penchant for self-publicity and for dressing up in disguises, in my view a clear symptom of his original desire to be a thespian!

Conversation over dinner was wide ranging and whilst Field was not at all displeased with the sound of his own voice, he had some good stories to tell. Most particularly the case of Dr William Palmer, or as he was better known 'The Rugeley Poisoner'.

Fields had been sent by the Prince of Wales Insurance Company to investigate the death of Palmers unfortunate brother Walter. A confirmed alcoholic his brother had been feeding him several bottles of gin a day, having taken the precaution of insuring his life for £84,000! From his investigations, Field found that the brother was not the only 'friend' or 'relative' who Palmer had tried to insure for a very large sum of money. He was eventually arrested and convicted for poisoning yet another friend, with strychnine.

I'd met Palmer at Shrewsbury races back in 1853 and can testify that he was just as inept at gambling as murder!

Whilst Field was keen to learn about the world of racing, his interest in the rivalry between the Harry's seemed much greater. Piqued by the 'discovery' that I was a good friend of Harry Chaplin's.

Field was however denied the chance to meet Harry who, with Hermit not entered for the 2000 Guineas, had decided to give the whole meeting a miss. The same was not however true of Harry Hastings, who was there in force with a typically large entourage.

The Marquis was in high spirits from the start on the Saturday, with his colt Rhapsody, just getting up to win the opening race, the Six Mile Bottom Stakes. He apparently picked up several thousands in winning bets, albeit given the sums he bet it was generally going to be either a big win or a big loss!

Come the middle of the afternoon, the sun was shining across the open expanses of Newmarket Heath and The Parade Ring was filled with the good, the great and indeed not at all great amongst the owners, trainers and jockeys.

Eleanor and I were standing by the Paddock railing adjacent to the Duke of Beaufort, owner of the 5/2 favourite Vauban. Whilst not the most frequent attendee at the races, there were few more charming and popular men on the Turf. I asked him once if he was able to furnish me with any idea as to why the eponymous sport was named after his home Badminton House, to which he admitted to having no idea at all!

Standing next to the Duke's party was Yorkshire ironworks owner Major Elwon, whose horse Plaudit was 7/2 second favourite. Plaudit's jockey was Jem Snowden who would have been one of the greatest of jockeys in the land but for his love for the bottle. I was told that on one occasion, Snowden refused to ride a horse normally fitted with blinkers, on the basis that it was best if one of them could 'bleedin' well see where he was going'. The horse duly won!

Also present were the ubiquitous Merry party, there to watch Marksman, well fancied at 100/15 and Sir Joseph Hawley one of the most successful racehorse owners of the era. Distrustful by nature, he would lecture anyone he met on the evils of gambling, whilst scooping a reputed £80,000 when Teddington won the Derby in 1851!

Further down the Paddock was the Marquis and his group, there to see his runner Uncas, a 200/1 outsider. Entered either out of extreme optimism or simply because his owner liked being represented in the Classics.

Standing to the left of the Marquis was his trainer John Day Jnr and to his right Tobias Brackelsham, accompanied by his swain Lady Amelia Irthlingborough, youngest daughter of the Marquis of Irthlingborough. Lady Amelia had, until the previous year, been engaged to David Coggles. They had seemed to me to be very happy together, but affairs of the heart were not my strong point, and with both now engaged to others, presumably all was well that had ended well.

Just beyond Brackelsham was Lord Zeals, resplendent, in the most garish green, orange and purple waistcoat. It was difficult to decide what was louder, the waistcoat or Zeals himself! An Old Harrovian, he met Hastings at Christs and like the Marquis was said to consider a bottle of Bollinger for breakfast as de rigueur.

Claude Zeals was the younger son of the Earl of Tenterden, owner of a fair chunk of the North Downs to the east of Maidstone and a rather charming house modelled, apparently, on a Roman villa.

And finally, there was Viscount Bowlhead, who had seemingly escaped the clutches of the Duchess of Montrose. Son of the Earl of Haslemere, he cut an altogether different figure to Brackelsham or Zeals. Diffident by nature, he appeared ill at ease at times with his brasher friends and all too easily put upon. Together with Brackelsham, he had formed the Frensham Confederacy, named after a well-known beauty spot on the Haslemere estate. To date the confederates had seen little success from the horses carrying their puce and amber diamond colours.

The only one missing from Hasting's regular crew was David Coggles, who was apparently under the weather. Miss Enderby was however in attendance and was kindly being looked after by my old friend Sir Carlton, a cousin of David through his mother, the former Lady Henrietta Barnack. So typical of Sir Carlton to step into the breach and not leave poor Mavis unescorted.

As for the race itself, Vauban, ridden by Fordham eventually wore down Mr Merry's Marksman, to the point that Jem Machell's Knight of the Garter passed him close to the line to finish a very creditable second at 20/1. Last I saw of Merry; he was storming over to the unsaddling ring – doubtless to explain to his trainer and his jockey exactly why it was entirely their fault and not simply a better horse had won!

Net result of the afternoon, Vauban was made a hot favourite for the Debry and despite not having run, Hermit's odds also shortened, it being an open secret that in a trial race Machell had arranged, Hermit had beaten the Knight over a mile carrying ten pounds extra weight.

At this point, spurred I think by the recollection that Guineas Day 1867 had been a particularly unprofitable days racing, Sir John decided that we should return to the more urgent matter of his book!

Chapter 5 – The Circus moves on to Hampshire and Lord Coggles fails to make any new friends!

When we returned to Sir John's grand tale of detection later the following day, he commented 'I believe we are in a period of what those writer chaps call scene setting but we'll arrive at the more dramatic stuff soon enough!

'I will await that with bated breath Sir John, conscious though of the continued need to keep your publishers happy'

'Quite so Joseph, I'll not be sorry when the book is complete, and my empty pockets can be filled again with the magical feel of a monkey or two!

'To resume' Sir John began' the week following Newmarket saw the opening meeting of the year at Stockbridge, one of my very favourite racecourses. A pretty little town nestled in the rolling Hampshire Downs, it sits astride the Test, truly one of England great angling rivers. In mating season, it is almost possible to reach down into river where it passes through the Town and pick out a magnificent trout, without need of a rod or waders!

Reunited once again with my steadfast friend George Payne, we caught the early Waterloo train to Andover, from whence we took the 'Sprat & Winkle Line' to Stockbridge Station, and from there a trap to the Grosvenor Hotel, centrepiece of the town's one main street. After dropping off our overnight bags at the hotel and partaking of a quick spot of luncheon with an agreeable bottle of claret, we made our way to the course, about a mile to the east of the town, under the lee of the giant Iron Age Hill Fort that is Danebury Hill.

By the late 1860's, Stockbridge had grown into a training centre to rival Newmarket itself, with fine gallops across the Hampshire Downs, and at the centre of things, the Day's, of Danebury, the towns first racing family.

No doubting their brilliance as trainers but it was also said of them, that they treated the interests of their clients as a minor inconvenience, when set against the betting interests of them and their special friends!

Leader of the clan 'Honest John Barham Day, either as a nod to his regular church attendance or an ironic comment on his scruples, lost his first major patron Lord George Bentinck after his son William wrote to his lordship advising him to back a particular horse with maximum confidence. He also wrote to a friendly bookmaker advising him the horse had no chance of victory. Unfortunately, Day's skills of deception were not matched by the same level of skill in putting the letters in the correct envelopes!

Come 1867 and Danebury was under the control of the aforementioned John Day Jnr, trainer to not just the Marquis of Hastings and the Duke of Beaufort, but also one Henry Padwick, a major figure in the story about to enfold!

Of medium to heavy build with receding silver hair and a manner redolent of someone for whom helping his fellow man was his sole raison d'etre, Padwick was by day the epitome of respectability, a solicitor in Horsham, his money lending business hidden behind the cloak of his legal activities. Along the way he had picked up some powerful friends, such as Lord Jersey who he had helped when his MP son Frank hastily left England for foreign climes, not overly anxious to pay back the £100,000 in gambling debts he had amassed.

Padwick had entered what became known as the Danebury Confederacy with his cohort Harry Hill, a very bent bookmaker, John Gully the former prize-fighter and his son in law Tom Pedley who had married one of his daughters from the 24 children his two exhausted wives bore him.

The protégé of Bristolian boxer Henry 'The Game Chicken' Pearce, Gully became Champion of England after defeating Bob Gregson, steamboat captain and self-proclaimed 'poet laureate of the ring'! In retirement Gully become a publican and then bookie and highly successful racehorse owner before becoming like yours truly, another unlikely Member of Parliament!

By 1867 the confederacy had cornered the market in extremely high interest money lending to the aristocracy, with a strong rumour that their next tasty target was Harry Hastings! Come late 1866, with my own 'investment strategy' not working as I had hoped and accepting, that I could not keep insuring my own life ad infinitum, I made a very big mistake and took a loan of £2000 from Padwick, which had, by May 1867 increased, at an unholy rate to £3000!

Meetings at Stockbridge were of especial interest to the Confederacy for the Grosvenor Hotel, was home to the Bibury Club the nation's most exclusive racing club. The Member's Room was a grand salon projecting out from the front of the Hotel on four large Doric columns.

Formed in 1798 by Major-General Thomas Grosvenor, the Bibury was, in earlier years at least, very secretive as to its membership, but included no less than three Dukes Dorset, Somerset and Wellington and a future Prime Minister, Lord Palmerston.

Many of the Club's current members were keen to avail themselves of funds for the occasional large or even monumentally large wager. They were however not necessarily as keen for their families, estate trustees or the wider world to know of those activities. All of which was of major interest to the Danebury Confederacy, particularly the brains behind the operation Henry Padwick. Before long and very much hidden from public view, they had become in effect 'private bankers' to the Bibury Club.

The confederacy's modus operandi, used by others but never to the same devastating effect, was, for Padwick to go to the Banks offering to pay interest of 10% on their money. With lending rates at the time being little more than 1.5% this was of immense interest. As I now knew from personal experience the loan rates the Confederacy applied were considerably above 10%, becoming much worse the more embroiled one became in their web! Padwick was aptly known as 'The Spider'!

Padwick was an excellent host to the many aristocrats, or more accurately 'Flies' who flocked to take advantage of open house at his opulent homes in London and Horsham, where the tables creaked with every delicacy one could imagine, together with the very finest wines.

With kind offers to help on financial matters, the Jeunesse Doree seemed completely unaware they were crawling further and further into a web from which there no escape.

The horribly igneous part of the plan was that, in return for lending large sums of money to their aristocratic clients, the Confederacy would take securities over their landed estates. These securities were then offered to the Bank for the very loans the Confederates were making to their aristocratic clients.

Occasionally victims were allowed to 'pay off' some of their debt by introducing the Confederacy to friends who might require their services, but this only tended to appeal to those, who felt no compunction in selling their friends down the river!

As for the day's proceedings, main race of the day was the Fullerton Stakes which went by a head to the George Clement ridden Wild Moor. The winning owner and recipient of a rather splendid trophy was the Duke of Hamilton. Over six foot tall, with a neck befitting a bull and weighing nearly 20 stone he was, despite his size, a fine huntsman, a crack shot, and apparently very handy with his fists!

Like others in our tale, the Duke inherited young, in his case when only eighteen. It did not take him long to start working his way through his fortune on gambling and owning a string of racehorses, albeit with less wine, women and song than Harry Hastings!

The Duke, like Hastings, was of the opinion that Hermit's distances limitations would preclude him from winning the Derby. Rumour had it that Machell had laid him £10,000 to £30,000 against Hermit winning the Derby. Either an easy way for Machell to win a tidy sum or potentially ruinous for the Duke!

I had noticed on the way down in the Sporting Life newspaper that David Coggles had a runner in the penultimate race of the day, the one mile two-furlong Nether Wallop Handicap. I managed to catch a word with him before the race.

'Good luck David with Knight Templar'

'Many thanks Mate, albeit our hopes are not high, but I have a few other matters to attend to in Stockbridge in any event'

'Has Mavis joined you for this glorious day in the Hampshire sun?'

'I'm afraid not, she has family affairs keeping her in Lincolnshire this week, but I will see her soon and my apologies Mate, but I need to get to the Parade Ring' and with a friendly wave he was away!

George and I found ourselves a good spot to watch the horses make their way around the ring and spotted Lord Coggles together his trainer Ben Land; his cousin the Hon. James Hydestile with whom he jointly owned the horse; James's sister Christina and her friend Lady Amelia Irthlingborough.

After a slow start, Knight Templar came from the very back of the field to win by a head, to the surprise and delight of all connected with the winning horse. It was nice to see that whilst no longer courting David and Lady Amelia appeared to remain on good terms, even if their romantic attachments had taken them in different directions.

With racing having finished we hailed a cab back to town. After a pre-prandial snooze and a wash and brush up, we dined at the Grosvenor and as befitted the location, enjoyed an excellent baked trout, washed down with a most agreeable Chablis. After which, George begged forgiveness saying the healthy country air had induced a rare desire to go to bed early. Rather than going to the lounge, where I would doubtless have found other racing chaps with whom to converse, I decided instead on a stroll along the High Street to enjoy my final cigar of the day.

I had only walked a short distance from the hotel, when I became aware of a most lively conversation, taking place in the gloom between two of the streetlamps about ten yards ahead. On moving forward a few steps I realised that it was none other than Henry Padwick and Harry Hill. Padwick, conservatively dressed in a black and the bulky figure of Hill, sporting a boater with a bright yellow scalloped Petersham Ribbon, and a very tightly fitting waistcoat, so gaudy it might have failed to find its way into Lord Zeals wardrobe.

My assumption was that they must be deep in conversation with one of the Confederacies many aristocratic clients. To my complete surprise however, the other person in the conversation was David Coggles, someone they had not sunk their mercenary claws into.

I am not a man who likes eavesdropping other chaps' conversations but, given I was standing in the shadow of a shopfront, and they had clearly not seen me, it seemed an inopportune moment to move. It was clearly a very intense conversation, and I quickly concluded, initiated by Lord Coggles rather than the Confederates. Quite possibly the 'other matters' to which David had alluded earlier.

'I've seen you insidiously sidling up to Harry' David exclaimed. I had no doubts he must be referring to Harry Hastings.

'I really don't know where you get your ideas from your lordship' Padwick responded 'My confederate Mr Hill and I are merely men of business, working on occasion for some of the finest families in the Nation. For my part I have provided advice to Mr Benjamin Disraeli, as well as standing for parliament myself'

'So have some of the best-connected rouges from the grandest families in the nation' Daivd rejoindered 'I've seen what has happened to others who have become tangled in your tortuous web, and I intend making sure Harry does not fall into your clutches whatever that might take!'

He continued, barely stopping for breath, 'I am sure that there are people of influence in the highest quarters in the land who would be very interested in learning the truth about you! Masquerading as an ever so humble servant of the gentry when in reality you are practising usury on a biblical scale! I know plenty I can assure you Mr Padwick and I'm willing to act if anything happens to Harry! I have in my possession a detailed dossier of evidence that would have with catastrophic consequences for you and your confederates if revealed'!

'I'm sure we can discuss this in a civilized way' responded Padwick, the picture of wounded innocence, almost as if accused of faking his giant marrow entry at the Village Fete!

David had however clearly had enough and had already started storming off down the street. I was not therefore sure if he heard Hill's growl' You don't want to do anything you'll live to regret your lordship, you never know who might be behind you one dark night!'

With that the dreadful duo crossed to the other side of the wide main street. I remained in the shadows for a last few puffs on my cigar, reflecting on what had been a disturbing scene and feeling a little guilty, that my own problems with the Confederates may have influenced me not to intervene.

The following morning dawned brightly and with George seldom the earliest of risers, I set out for a pre-breakfast walk. Before I had perambulated more than the 22 yards of a cricket pitch, I heard my name being hailed in friendly terms.

'Lovely morning Mate'

I turned to see David Coggles bounding up behind me looking in particularly good spirts, wearing a well cut dark grey three piece 'ditto' suit and bow tie

'An excellent one young David' and before I had a chance to say anything further, he thrust a well-padded envelope into my hand. I forgot to give this to you when we met last met in Lincoln. One framed photograph of you and my father mounted ready for the first Belvoir hunt meeting of the year!'

'Thank you so much for letting me have that' I continued' I am relieved to see you this morning in such good spirits'

'Why so' he asked quizzically.

I explained the circumstances in which I had come to witness his heated discussed with Messer's Padwick, Pedley and Hill adding' 'I sometimes wonder if the Marquis fully appreciates the efforts you make in protecting his interests? It took real gumption to say what you did. Racing would be a far better place without their presence. It was, however, what they said as you left that disturbed me.

For a moment I was not sure if he had heard Hill's threats' Oh, I'm not taking that seriously, all bluster I have no doubts.'

'Do you mind my asking David, if the dossier to which you referred actually exists or was it perhaps a cunning ruse to dissuade them from trapping Hastings in their ghastly web'

'Oh, it exists alright Mate and I'm taking precautions to ensure it does not fall into the wrong hands' he said with an oddly knowing look and a slightly surprising wink, not something I'd seen David do before. Maybe a new fad amongst the younger members of the gentry.

'I am pleased to hear that David, but you make sure to take care'

'I will Mate and please don't worry. Apologies now, I need to go and find James to make our way back to London with our unexpected trophy'.

And there ended a most interesting visit to Stockbridge. As George and I made our way back up the Spratt & Winkle line to Andover, I was left pondering what David intended to do next and how the Confederacy might react, if he made good on his threat, or whether they were already plotting their next move.

With the time having come round to nearly 1.00pm, Sir John announced that we both deserved a large slice of game pie and accompanying pickles, before mounting a major offensive, post luncheon, on his sporting memoirs!

Chapter 6 – The Mate finds time for a hearty lunch with Harry Chaplin and David Coggles forms the main topic of conversation!

After a further concerted attack on his sporting memoirs, Sir John announced late morning the following day, we had earned a further canter through the world of detection, and he had earned his first cigar of the day!

'In mid-May, I met with Harry Chaplin for lunch at the Clinton Arms Hotel on Newark on Trent's historic market square, where I am told Sir John chuntered' that awful man Gladstone gave his first political speech from an upstairs window some sixty years ago!

Over a particularly fine post lunch ten-year-old Gourry de Chadeville cognac, Harry chastised me once again, in the friendliest of manners, for not having more faith in Hermit's chances in the forthcoming Epsom Derby.

'I've told you before Mate' he jested' you are being an old fool on this one not being on my horse, for I stand to win big when Hermit triumphs and I want my friends to win too'.

As things presently stood, like Harry Hastings, I had taken the view that Hermit, despite his two-year-old form, lacked the stamina to win at Epsom and had therefore taken every bit of the 20-1 against him I could find to win £8000.

He also dropped into conversation that Jem Machell had had a very interesting discussion with David Coggles.

'Apparently' Harry recounted' David approached Jem at Newmarket saying that he felt it would be fairer to Hermit to withdraw him from the Derby and save him for the shorter distance of the St James Palace Stakes at Royal Ascot. I have always got on well with David, despite his terrible choice in best friends. I am however a little peeved about this. Jem had the distinct feeling that It was some sort of farfetched ploy to help Hastings avoid catching the most gigantic cold when Hermit wins!

'I am very interested to hear what you have to say about David, since it has a distinct link to a conversation that I witnessed recently'

'Very interesting Mate' Harry commented after I had recounted said conversation. 'Like you I admire his pluck in standing up to the Confederacy, who I've no doubt see Hastings as a very juicy fly, just waiting to get caught in the web they weave so effectively!

'Quite so Harry, quite so'

'All of which Mate' Harry continued' leaves us with something else very important to discuss'

'And what is that?' I enquired a little puzzled.

'Will it be another glass of the Gourry or finish the meal on a high note with a glass of the Maison Ferrand.'

'Capital idea Harry and I should say the Ferrand!

Chapter 7– Snow is in the May air; it must be Derby Day!

When Derby Day, the 22nd of May, finally arrived, the weather was truly foul, an unholy mix of sleet and hail. I made my way to London Bridge Station for 7.30am, where I met with Colonel Jerry Goodlake, my very best friend. Our meeting place was the vast seven storey cube shaped Terminus Hotel. After an appropriately vast breakfast, a veritable bulwark against the cold to come, we made our way onto the station. Knowing London Bridge to be the most sprawling of the capital's termini, we had allowed ourselves an additional ten minutes to find our 9.00am train.

Despite the atrocious weather, the station was teaming with humanity and the London & South Western Railway Company had laid on many extra trains. Even with all the additional trains, the roads from London to Epsom would still be jammed with cabs, barouches, open carts and fours in hand. I didn't feel inclined to put my own gallant horses through such a melee, the risk of crashing an ever-present danger to human and horse flesh alike!

On the train there was a high level of excited chatter and speculation on which horse would win the afternoons big race. The betting market had been thrown into confusion the previous week, when, it was reported that Hermit, had damn neigh collapsed on the Newmarket gallops with, it transpired, a broken blood vessel.

I had seen Harry again a couple of days later, at the Turf Club, and he seemed to be of the view that Hermit would have to be scratched from the race. Jem however, believed that the horse could recover and should take its chances, nonetheless Hermit's odds drifted out to 100/1. The Marquis, egged on I was told by Zeals, was strengthening his position against Hermit.

By the time our train pulled into Epsom Downs Station, opened in 1865 to accommodate the 70,000 or so of us arriving by train, there was snow in the air but even that had not dampened the already lively atmosphere. Jerry and I hired a cab and as we rounded Tattenham Corner, we had our first sight of the vast numbers already in attendance, a giant sea of humanity sweeping down to the stands in the far distance.

Interspersed amongst the thousands of good-hearted London folk there for a grand day out, were dozens of confidence tricksters and assorted charlatans, all willing and very able to relieve the unwary of their money

For entertainment there were booths selling beer, cider, pies and pastries of all descriptions, as well as acrobats, fairground rides and bear baiting. I love a good day's shooting but watching noble animals being humiliated for profit is very far from my cup of tea.

On our way down from Tattenham Corner, we stopped to partake of an ale with that grand Epsom character 'Jolly' Sir John Bennett. A flamboyant figure of a man Sir John sat astride his white horse, wearing the shiniest of black velvet jackets under a broad brimmed hat. It was his habit to halt every few yards to 'toast the health of the people', usually involving the people providing a free drink for Sir John at each stopping point!

On arriving at the entrance to the course, we swiftly made our way to the Grandstand. Inside, the building was dominated by a magnificent flight of stairs, leading up to the grand Salon where fashionable society promenaded between races.

Once ensconced in the Members Room with a warm coffee I had a look round to see who was in attendance. Aside from the normal crowd of racing owners and aficionados, the Derby inevitably attracted people from a much wider arc of society.

Sitting nearby was Sarah Russell. Wearing a long flowing robe with a slew of crystal talismans around her neck, she was better known as Madame Rachel, owner of a plush salon in Bond Street, with the words 'Beautiful for Ever' emblazoned above the door.

I knew the place from Mrs Astley having paid a visit. Star of the show was the 'Magnetic Rock Dew of the Sahara for Removing Wrinkles' brought, my Eleanor was told, to London from Morocco 'on swift dromedaries'!

Aside from the astronomic prices and the fact that none of the remedies worked, I had it on good authority that Madame Rachel indulged in both blackmailing her clients, as well as procuring hard up young actresses from Drury Lane to take a starring role in a friend's nearby brothel! All things considered we agreed it would best for Eleanor to steer well clear of the salon and its products!

As a complete contrast to Madame Rachel, I spotted the poet laureate Alfred Tennyson. I'm no great reader but will always stop and listen to the Charge of the Light Brigade, a charge in which I fortunately had no part. It inevitably reminds me of my own days in the Crimean Peninsula and the scar I have in my neck from where part of a cannonball passed through from one side to another!

From the world of racing, decked out as ever in red, was the Duchess of Montrose, this time with young Lord Ruyton Eleven Towns on her arm in place of Viscount Bowlhead I also spotted, clutching a large mug of coffee before hearing back out into the snow Jem Machell, with whom I managed to have a quick word.

'Good luck Jem, I hope that Hermit gives you a good run for your money'

'Thanks' Mate even if I know you don't share our confidence' he replied with good, humoured irony, knowing that I stood to win should Hermit lose.

After finishing my coffee, I decided to venture out into the cold and soon happened upon Miss Enderby. She was with her maid but no sign of David Coggles

'How are you my dear' I enquired doffing my top hat 'is David with the Marquis?'

'I've not actually seen him since last night. We were midway through dinner at the Spreadeagle Hotel, when David received a note and announced that he needed to go straight out and not to worry about staying up to await his return.' Whilst obviously curious as to what had prompted David to venture out into the Artic night, I did not dwell on it and with the Marquis and his friends, getting increasingly raucous, like the other ladies, I was keen to retire to bed as soon as possible.

Come the morning and I made my way down to breakfast but David, normally the earliest of risers was not present. On enquiring, no one seemed to have seen his arriving back at the hotel and he did not respond when I tapped on the door to his room. By this time, I was getting quite perplexed as to his whereabouts and spoke with Sir Carlton, who recalled something similar happening at a family event, where David had left on some pretext or other and not reappeared later the following day.

'I am certain he will appear very soon' she added, albeit not with what I would describe as total conviction.

'I am sure you are right my dear and do please let me know if I can be of assistance' I offered in a hopefully reassuring tone, albeit it did all sound a little odd. Inevitably however, with the general hustle and bustle of the day, the whereabouts of David Coggles slipped from my mind.

After leaving Mavis, I rejoined Jerry to go and inspect the horses for the first big race of the day the Headley Handicap. Favourite was, Merry's colt Scottish Charmer (a description I could in no way apply to its owner) followed in the betting by Lurgashall, owned by the Frensham Partnership.

I doubt it was what they would have wished but Bowlhead and Bracklesham once again found themselves, standing immediately adjacent to the Merry party in the Parade Ring. In a continuation of what had happened at Lincoln, there were choice remarks being thrown in either direction, by Buchanan and Bracklesham.

For his part, Parker seemed to be staring in a peculiar way at Bowlhead, albeit his granitic features tended to make it tantamount to impossible to discern any obvious form of emotion!

As for the race itself, this turned out to be a non-event. The Frensham horse whipped round at the start, catching jockey Maidment by complete surprise, pitching him over the horse's head onto the ground. Meanwhile Merry's horse was brought through by Grimshaw to a facile if bittersweet victory – a decent pot for winning the race but not at the starting price Merry had wanted for his own betting purposes!

Jem Grimshaw had also been booked by Merry to ride Marksman in the Derby. A highly competent and honest jockey, he was also known to be short sighted, albeit far less so than his myopic older brother Harry, who had failed to land a major gamble in the 1865 Cambridgeshire Handicap when, coming into the last furlong of the race, he had believed his horse to be about thirty feet behind the leaders and not the 100 yards he was in reality!

Time soon rolled on to 3.00pm and the twenty-nine horses contesting the Derby were being walked around the parade ring, whilst their owners and trainers stood shivering in the Arctic conditions. The horses looked both cold and bedraggled, none more so than Hermit. Seldom had I seen a horse look so unhappy with its surrounds, something the bookies in the ring had clearly taken on board with his odds drifting out even further. To my mind Vauban looked a much safer home for my money, especially with my favourite jockey Fordham in the plate!

What many of us did not know and he did well to keep it under wraps, was that Machel had Hermit back working, soon after the broken blood vessel. Very gently downhill at first and on the Saturday prior to the big race, he had passed a much stiffer trial.

Talking of Machel, he was in deep conversation with his jockey, young Johnny Daley. Whatever instructions Daley had received, it was clear that Jem was intent that they should be obeyed to the absolute letter or woe betide the poor rider. For his part. Harry looked admirably calm and collected, despite the weight of money riding on a horse that looked like he'd rather be at home in his box under several thick blankets. I noticed that Harry seemed to have jammed his top hat as far down his forehead as it would go, doubtless trying to keep out the cold!

Harry and Machel, were standing at the far end of the ring, as far I had no doubts as they could get, from the Marquis and his crowd, still minus David Coggles. The Marquis seemed to be in particularly good spirits, not I was sure based on any hopes for his runner 200/1 runner Uncas, but for the pleasure of seeing his bitter rival's dreams and money, disappear down the proverbial plughole, with Hermit's defeat and the substantial enrichment of the Marquis himself!

With the snow still falling, the horses made their way to the start on the far side of the Downs from the Grandstand. As with everything else on this foul day nothing was going to plan and it took no less than ten false starts, before it was eleventh time lucky, and the race finally started an hour late!

Fordham immediately took Vauban to the front, remaining there for the first mile and three furlongs until just a furlong from the finish, when Grimshaw brought Marksman through to take up the running. The story was however far from over and to the confoundment of myself and almost all the huge crowd, following Machel's orders to the letter, young Daley produced Hermit with a long late run to beat Marksman by a neck in record time. The horse doubtless keen to get back to the relative warmth of his box as soon as possible!

Fordham came in for criticism, unfairly in my view, that he had made too much use of Vauban, and Marksman's trainer James Waugh was openly critical of Grimshaw, suggesting he had missed the run of Hermit because he considered Vauban the only threat. Mr Merry was more concise stating 'that myopic bastard will never be riding for me again'!! Buchanan was joining in but not Parker, I had been told that as well as being a man of few words, like Grimshaw his eyesight was apparently poor so maybe did not want to join in this debate!

Whatever the merits of the race ridding, the ever-shrewd Machell had been proved right once again, leaving many people, me included, nursing very depleted wallets. As I made my way down from the Siberian outpost that posed as the roof terrace, I spotted the Marquis who, to be frank, looked white as a sheet and on the point of being profoundly sick. In all fairness to him, he was the first to give Hermit a congratulatory pat when he arrived in the unsaddling enclosure. Albeit there was a marked lack of eye-contact with Harry Chaplin who being the gent he is, did not seek to gloat at his rival's self-induced misfortune, however tempting!

Lurking in the background, as ever, was Old Man Padwick, speaking I was interested to see with Viscount Zeals, who looked remarkably jolly in the circumstances, I could only assume his losses were rather less gargantuan than those of the Marquis. I was not sure if, Hastings had yet to have recourse to Padwick's services, but the greedy old vulture was clearly circling ready. Not that I was too keen for him to look in my direction, given the twelve-monkeys I still owed him!

I did not catch sight of the Marquis again but was told that he had left shortly afterwards, together with his followers, for an evening out in Richmond on Thames, I somehow doubted Harry or Hermit would form one of the evening's toasts!

I was able to catch up with Harry as he left the winners enclosure and offered him my heartiest congratulations, on both his victory and winnings. Yet, on seeing me his first thought was of my self-inflicted misfortune.

'Let me know your losses on Monday and I will pay them John'

'I really cannot accept such a wonderfully generous offer Harry'

'As I told you last time we lunched, my happiness at this wonderful win will only be enhanced by the knowledge that my friends benefitted too, in whatever way!'

'Well, if you absolutely insist, I would be delighted to accept but I will make sure I pay you back as soon as I can and please let me know if there is anything, however big or small, that I can do to help you out at any time.' The moment when I could do Harry a good turn transpired to be rather closer to hand than either of us had expected!

Whilst he never did confirm to me the final figure, I am told that Harry netted something in the region of £140,000 in winnings from Hermit's success and the Captain a more modest £63,000! As for the Marquis it was estimated that he had lost more than £120,000 a vast amount to find before the following week's settling day with the Bookies

After the excitement of the afternoon, it was time for the unwelcome prospect of getting home. After a cold and seemingly interminable wait at the crowded Station, we finally managed to get on a train to London Bridge. By the time I reached home it had passed 11.00pm and I was ravenous. Mrs Crumpbucket, my housekeeper, kindly rustled up a light snack, comprising a couple rounds of Lobster sandwich, four large slices of bone marrow toast and some pickled oysters on the side.

Accompanied by a large warming brandy, I sat down to read the special evening editions of the sporting press. Suffice to say the headlines were full of the unexpected sight of Hermit coming through the snow to win by a neck!

To my no great surprise, not everyone was willing to share in Harry's joy, some clearly believing that Hermit's problems had been either exaggerated or indeed made up to improve his odds. Stuff and nonsense but prompted the sporting paper Bailey's to publish a parody of Lord Macaulay's poem 'Lays of Ancient Rome' describing Hermit's victory thus: -

> "Despis'd, abus'd forsaken,
>
> Predicted not to "stay"
>
> A byeword and a proverb
>
> The Hermit won the day!"[12]

I'd have to confess that I've not read any of Macaulay's works and one lifetime might not be enough to ensure that this will ever happen!

At which point Sir John turned to me and said, the moment I start drifting off into talking about poetry, a subject upon which I remain in a state of continued ignorance, it's time we broke for lunch. With Lady Eleanor out for the day, I propose a jaunt in the trap to the White Hart in Brigg, where we can enjoy a foaming pint of A. E Seargent's Dolphin Ale and individual beef suet puddings with boiled vegetables! I will admit the foaming pint of Dolphin held more appeal than the likely gargantuan sized pudding, doubtless more suited to several people rather than one individual!

Chapter 8 – The Mate receives a substantial shock with the delivery of the Evening Standard newspaper!

With the trip to the White Hart having taken rather longer and more pints of Dolphin than expected, on our return Sir John was hit by a rare fit of guilt and we ploughed on unabated with his memoirs for the rest of the afternoon. I had to wait until 11.00am the next morning and Sir John's first cigar of the day, before it was deemed time to restart his tale of detection and in the most dramatic of fashions!

'It was teatime on the day after the Derby' Sir John began' that I picked up a copy of the London Evening Standard' The front page shocked me to the very marrow, taking me right back to the conversation I had with Mis Enderby just prior to the Derby'

The paper reported that, with David having still not returned by the end of the day's racing, the police had been alerted to his apparent disappearance. Once the Downs were clear of all bar the most inebriated racegoers still unable to find their way to the station, the local bobbies were sent out to see what they could find. The Racecourse Management and local stables were also alerted but by the time darkness had fallen, no trace had been found of the missing Lord.

Come the next morning, the police had started to become very concerned, albeit the possibility that Lord Coggles had simply hailed a cab and left the district of his own accord could not be ruled out. Sadly however, this further search comprehensively destroyed the idea of any innocent explanation, with the terrible news that David Coggles body had been found in a ditch on the Burgh Heath Road, not far from the famous South Hatch Stables!

With no other details available, the paper had taken to speculating that Lord Coggles must have been the victim of ruffians unknown, possibly a mugging that had gone too far.

At this point this point, the investigation was handed over, to the Metropolitan Police., who it was understood would be sending down one of its best men, Inspector Richard Tanner. After the bad press the Met had received for their handling of the Railings Affair and the latest mass demonstrations in Hyde Park by those Reformist blighters, Sir Richard Mayne, Commissioner of the Police, was doubtless looking for a good result here!'.

Aside from the initial horror that such a monstrous thing should have happened, I felt a sense of guilt that I had been so wrapped up in Harry's magnificent Derby triumph and my own good fortune in terms of my losses, that I had ignobly failed to wonder if David was alright. Sadly, Sir Carlton's prediction that David would simply turn up, had proved to be very wide of the mark. My next thought took me back to that day in Stockbridge and the threats uttered by the loathsome Harry Hill.

I had just finished writing letters of condolences to both Buffy Utterby and Miss Enderby when, around six a clock there was an urgent knock at the front door and Mrs Crumpbucket, showed young Mr Chaplin into my study

'Are you alright Harry? I asked, 'You look none too bright for someone who has just won the Derby and in urgent need of liquid medication.' Without stopping to ask, I quickly poured us both a reviving dram of Royal Brackla Whiskey.

Once sat in the two green leather upholstered chairs I kept in my study, for chap-to-chap discussions, Harry began'

'Do you know an Inspector Fields former denizen of Police HQ at 4 Whitehall Place, London or as it is better known to us all Scotland Yard.

'Indeed, I do! Eleanor and I dined with him at the Rutland, the night before the 2000 Guineas. I found him entertaining company, clearly knows his stuff but a touch bumptious and a little too fond of his own legend.

'Well, here is the rub Mate. Field has been hired by Harry Hastings to carry out an independent investigation into the murder of David Coggles

'Not satisfied that the Yard's finest will get to the bottom of things' I ventured.

'Ostensibly yes and I also appear to be the focus of his investigation!

"Why on earth would that be the case!?'

'I hope I am wrong, but I am concerned that Hastings may be using his apparent concern for Coggles as a chance to either blacken my name or possibly get out of paying his debts.

At this point Harry pulled from his pocket a single sided letter and handed it to me to read 'I don't doubt John you will be struck by the irony of this?'

Dear Chaplin,

I cannot tell you how much I am obliged to you for your kindness to me. I would sooner cut off my hand than ask anyone to do such a thing, but as you say it will not inconvenience you, I shall take advantage of your offer for a short time. But you may depend upon my doing my utmost to repay you as soon as possible though you know as well as I do that however well off a man may be to get £120,000 in 24 hours is a rather hard job. I am just off to Paris as I am sick of being pointed out as the man who has lost such a sum. If you do not particularly want the "sister to the Duke" at the Hampton Court Sale I should much like to buy her, but I am afraid it is useless opposing her now.

With very many thanks, yours very sincerely,

Hastings

'What an extraordinary letter, asking forbearance on a major debt then at the self-same time talking about buying an expensive yearling!

'I should add John that I only agreed to what was requested with the greatest reluctance, overcoming a strong temptation to squash the letter into a ball and direct it towards the fire. Despite the way I have been treated by the pair, I saw little to be gained in putting the

Marchioness in an even worse position than her actions have put her now. Nor would I have beetled off to Paris with Buffoon Number One Viscount Zeals, as I understand to be the case'

'Quite so Harry and tells you much about the mark of the man. Aside from escaping one of his debts' I continued' and the pleasure he may take from impugning your good name, there can be no reason why Field or for that matter the Met themselves can have an interest in speaking you with about the murder?

Much to my surprise Harry paused before saying quietly' Yes John, I'm afraid these is a reason?

'I'm astounded Harry, what on earth can that be?'

'Going back to that fateful night before the Derby, like Hastings and his crew, Jem and I were staying at the Spreadeagle. Rather than bumping into them at dinner, we had arranged to dine at the Heathcote-Drummonds home The Durdans near to the racecourse'.

'Prior to our leaving, I was told that David Coggles wished to have an urgent word. I had few doubts it would concern Hermit. Given however, I did not view David in the same light as some of his awful friends I agreed and made my way to his room'

'I'll not bore you Mate with a verbatim account, but it was an appeal to withdraw Hermit from the race altogether, since my colt clearly had no chance of victory anyway'.

'I pointed out that if Hermit had no chance, surely no one need worry about his presence? It was at this point that David let slip the real motive for his request and it was as I had expected.

"I will be frank with you Harry, if Hermit were to somehow win, I have no doubts that Hastings will fall completely into the clutches of Padwick. They have been constantly at his side, with insidious offers to 'help'.

'Despite his being my closest friend' Coggles continued' I am not blind to Harry's many failings and fully understand your feelings towards him, but do you really want to see the Confederacy 'recruit' another victim. I know the Marchioness wronged you too, but would anything be served by her being dragged down with Hastings?

'I am fully aware' I responded' that behind Padwick's 'respectable' front lie some very nasty business methods and I am not keen on throwing anyone into his hands, even Hastings. I am, however, quite astounded that you would expect me to withdraw Hermi, a horse in which I have invested a large amount of faith and indeed staked more than £20,000 on his chances. I can hardly see the bookmaking fraternity simply saying, 'fairs fair Mr Chaplin, we fully understand, do have all your stake money back' I don't doubt I would also have received a very robust response from Jem!'

'David went on to say he did not trust everyone in Hastings immediate circle, I've no idea to whom he was referring. He also alluded to exposing Padwick and his cronies, but I gained the impression that was very much a last resort – heaven knows how many of the good and great of the nation would be embarrassed if that happened!'

'Whilst I did acknowledge' Harry continued' to Coggles that I had a grudging respect for his loyalty I felt it to be very misplaced. The conversation had all been a little tense with raised voices but nothing that could be construed as a threat to life and limb! Soon after that, Jem and I set off for the Durdans.

'The whole situation has not been helped by, my having developed a bad headache during dinner, probably the result of the earlier disagreement, and leaving The Durdans early. Returning by myself, to the Spreadeagle around 10.30pm. There was no one on the desk when I got back, just a note saying that the duty manager would be back shortly. All of which leaves me with no alibi for the period when David went missing.'

'And if that was not enough,' Harry added with a deep sigh' I managed to trip in the foul weather, tearing my coat and cut my forehead. You may have noticed I had my topper pulled down to try and hide it from public view'

'But that proves nothing at all Harry, merely a series of unfortunate happenchance's and a sad last conversation by which to remember David Coggles''

'You and I know that Mate' Harry responded' but others may not see things that way. Fact remains John, I was on the Downs at the time of the murder and had just been involved in a rather heated discussion, with the victim!

Returning to the events of the evening' Harry resumed 'I am told that the Hasting's party, already well fortified on the way down to Epsom, had embarked on a typically rumbustious dinner, doubtless celebrating Hermits expected defeat. Coggles, not one of the heavier drinkers in the group, was apparently rather subdued, quite possibly regretting events earlier in the evening.'

As you will be aware, mid-way through the evening, Coggles received a note which spurred him into immediate action. Biding a very hasty goodbye to Mavis, he headed off into the windy night, giving no clue as to who he was intending to meet or where and the rest of the whole sad affair you know already

I do indeed Harry and please don't worry, the police will be making every effort to find the real killer!'

'I am sure you are right' Harry replied but with noticeably little conviction and with that we bade each other our farewells.

Chapter 9 – A first introduction to Mr Lewis and an even more unexpected request from Harry Chaplin!

Late the following afternoon I was going through the entries for the following weeks Goodwood Races, when there was a rapid knock on the door. With both Mrs Crumpbucket and her husband, who acted as butler cum general factotum, on a half day, I went to the door myself and opened it to a tall slim young man of an eager disposition dressed in a well cut lightweight double breasted frock coat.

'Mr Astley?' he entreated with an underlying accent suggestive of someone who had spent their formative years in North Yorkshire.

'The very same' I rejoindered' and to whom do I owe the pleasure.

'My name sir is Oswald Osmotherley and I have the privilege of being articled clerk to Mr George Lewis of Lewis & Lewis. In this instance, London lawyer to your good friend Mr Chaplin.' I had met on occasion Harry's Lincoln lawyer old Walter Skellingthorpe, this suggested something more serious.

'I have been asked to give you this letter and to wait for your answer'

With there being no time like the present, I quickly tore open the envelope. Inside was a simple note from Mr Lewis, asking if I would be kind enough to attend a meeting at his office at 5.30pm that very afternoon together with his client Mr Chaplin.

Suffice to say I assured the young man that I would be there and wished him bon voyage on his journey back to the city. I just had time to polish off a couple of Mrs Crumpbuckets delicious crumpets before setting off for the meeting.

Rather than hailing a cab, I scurried up to Baker Street Station and availed myself of a journey on the new underground section of the Metropolitan Railway Line. I had thought when it had opened just four years before, that underground travel would never catch on but like a fair few of my racing predictions, this one was shown to be wide of the mark and the line had proved to be highly popular

With trains running every fifteen minutes, even off-peak, it was not long before one of the little green Metropolitan Tank engines with their huge external cylinders pulled into the station. This one I noticed being a Hornet built in 1862 by the renowned Vulcan Factory of Newton le Willows!

Within twelve minutes we had arrived at journey's end – Farringdon Station. A rather noisy twelve minutes but considerably quicker than by cab.

I made my way from the platform to the concourse, then it was up Cowcross Street, round Smithfield Square and I was soon at Lewis's office. A handsome new building in a classical style with a large Greek portico to the front, it was handily placed for clients awaiting trial at the Central Criminal Court, or the Old Bailey as it is better known!

On arrival I was shown into a meeting room, lined with row upon row of heavily bound legal tomes with titles such as the 1866 High Court Law Reports of the Admiralty & Ecclesiastical

Courts. A good read I am sure to those of sufficient intellect but otherwise there I assumed to overawe us non-legal bods!

I was soon joined by Harry, young Osmotherley and George Lewis himself. Slim and whilst still only 34, a man of obvious bearing, with a razor-sharp mind, Lewis had made his name prosecuting the directors of the failed Overend & Gurney Bank.

'Good to meet you Mr Astley and thank you for coming here at such short notice' Lewis began' and for the help I very much hope you may be able to provide'

'Think nothing of it, I am ready and willing to do all I can to help my friend Harry, to whom I am in debt for his many kindnesses' I said with an appreciative nod in Harry's direction.

'I believe that my client has already made you aware that the Marquis of Hastings has hired ex-Inspector Field to privately investigate the terrible murder of Lord Coggles?'

'He has indeed'

'Since you met with Mr Chaplin, he has now had a visit from inspector Tanner of the Metropolitan Police'

'Not to put too fine a point on thing' Harry interjected' I seem to have become the focus of their interest. The police are of the opinion that David's murderer was known to him and my lack of an alibi for part of that night is seen as being highly pertinent.

'David's death must surely have been the work of passing ruffians as the papers have speculated.' I expostulated.

'Would any 'self-respecting' ruffian have left David's body without relieving their stricken victim of the £500 he had in his coat pocket? Harry responded' and of the note David was sent, not a trace, suggesting it was removed by the murderer to cover their tracks'

Before I had a chance to express my complete outrage, Lewis intervened' I understand that you may have information that could be pertinent to the whole affair and hopefully set the police off in a different and more productive direction?'

'I assume Mr Lewis it is Henry Padwick and his cohorts to whom you refer' I enquired.

'It is, indeed, the estimable Mr Henry Padwick' Lewis replied cupping his chin in his hands and setting his face in a most knowing way' Despite his plausible front I am fully aware that many of Mr Padwick activities are not in step with Law Society rules or even the rule of law. I have other clients who have had substantial problems resulting from their dealings with the Danebury Confederacy. Understandably most would not wish to have those problems aired in public, something upon which the Confederacy rely.'

'I've no doubts in my mind the Confederacy lie behind what has happened' I responded' I cannot for one moment imagine Padwick or his cohorts carrying out the murder, but having tricked David into attending the assignation on the Burgh Heath Road, they have ruffians in their employ who may have been over zealous in their attempts to wrest control of the Dossier.'

'I believe Mr Astley that your conjecture could well be correct but my apologies for having to ask, have you ever had any personal dealings with Mr Henry Padwick.

'It is a matter of great regret, particularly in current circumstances, but I did go to old man Padwick for investment finance, not I'll admit one of my better strategies but fortunately my little problems are as nothing to others' I responded ruefully.

'On John why on earth did you not have a word with me if you had temporary cash flow problems'

'I really could not do that Harry; I was a bloody idiot to accept the blandishments of Old Man Padwick and did not want to involve my dearest friends in such matters, but I will not be doing that again'

'Make sure you mean it this time Mate' Harry added with a smile, mixed I was sure with a degree of frustration at my utter folly.

At Lewis's request I quickly ran through the contra temps I had witnessed between David and the Confederacy, and the threats uttered as he walked away. I also related the conversation I had with David the following day, assuring me the dossier existed.

'I would like to share with Inspector Tanner what you have observed Mr Astley but in the first instance, I would be very grateful if you could find a pretext for visiting Mr Padwick as soon as possible. I would not suggest asking him any questions outright but hopefully enough to provoke a reaction, which I can also share with the police.'

'I'll feely admit that as things stand, Padwick would not be amongst my first ports of call but helping my young friend Mr Chaplin must take precedence'.

'We also have another small favour to ask Mr Astley. **You are a popular figure liked and trusted across all strands of society**'

'Modesty forbids me from agreeing with your kind view Mr Lewis although I'll admit to being flattered!'

What I'd like' Harry took up the running' is that as well as speaking to Padwick, could you also see what you can find out about others who may have borne a serious grudge against David?'

'You mean like Field, a kind of detective?' Both Harry and Lewis looked surprised if not a little aghast at my self-applied description!

'Er quite so John; Harry responded 'but what I'm really after is for someone I trust to ask some questions on my behalf'

'I'd be delighted to assist Harry!' I asserted, with perhaps more confidence than I felt!

With the meeting finally ending at 7.00pm, it was agreed that I would provide my 'clients' with regular updates on progress in my new role!

Chapter 10 – Mr Astley selects a running mate, enter Jimmy 'The Flying' Tailor' Patterson!

Rather than returning home via train or cab, I decided I would benefit from a long walk. By the time I reached Trafalgar Square I was quite ravenous, not an unusual feeling in my case!

Help was however at hand in the form of a stall run by one Obidiah Framlingham, from whom I ordered a couple of large bloaters, together with a refreshing mug of saloop.

As I stood eating my fare, I pondered on the newly completed lions at the base of Nelson's Column. The lions looked magnificent and far from me to question an artistic genius such as Sir Edwin Landseer, but I doubt I was the first person to notice that the lion's backs seemed to bend the wrong way!

More important than my musings on the lions, I concluded that what I really needed was someone to assist me in my new role as a 'detective'. It needed to be someone both astute and completely trustworthy, and I knew just the man! **Jimmy 'The Flying Tailor' Patterson, as bright and trustworthy a man as one could hope to call friend.**

By lucky happenchance I had been needing to go and see Jimmy's employer, the esteemed gentleman's outfitter Mr Henry Hill of Bond Street. I resolved to make that happen in the morning!

To those who did not know him, Mr Hill was a most excellent a man. Willing on occasion to lend his clients funds, at a far more acceptable rate than his unscrupulous near neighbour in Carey Street Mr Harry Hill!

Come the next morning I made my way to Bond Street, which always makes me think of a cartoon I once saw, depicting an 18th century group known as the Bond Street Loungers, who would parade up and down the street wearing the most extravagant wigs! All sounded perfectly ghastly to me!

I was at Mr Hill's elegant premises, the upper floors having I am told having been home to Jonathan Swift, for his 10.30am opening time. After a quick canter through the usual pleasantries, I got to the muttons of the matter and explained to Henry what I was doing and how I thought that Jimmy, who was out that morning measuring up old Lord Gussage All Saints for a new suit, would be ideally placed to assist!

To my delight Mr Hill readily consented to 'loan' me Jimmy for the next two weeks and assuming Jimmy was agreeable, which he was sure would be the case, would ask him to meet me at 7.00pm that evening at the Olde Cheshire Cheese in Fleet Street, which he knew to be a favourite haunt of both Jimmy and me.

I think that in truth, he was relieved and indeed surprised I had not been going to ask for another 'venture capital' loan and that helped him to agree so readily!

I was back home mid-afternoon, after a quick spot of lunch at the Old Turf Club. Having not received any message to say that Jimmy would not be at the pub, I set off at 5.30pm and soon hailed a cab. With the journey going much faster than expected, I allowed the silver-tongued cabbie to persuade me it was my duty to stop and buy a quick drink at the Museum Tavern in Bloomsbury.

As with previous visits to the Museum Tavern, there was a portly gentleman sitting in the corner of the bar with a constantly refilled drink to hand and a large jar of pickled cucumbers, he seemed intent on devouring in its entirety. Every so often he would break off from debating the ills of capitalist society, to complain in a heavy Germanic accent how his boils were ruining his life. I'm embarrassed to admit, particularly as a former Member of Parliament, that it was not until many years later that I realised that said gentleman was none other than Karl Marx, a monomaniacal zealot if ever I met one, but at least he enjoyed a drink!

Following the impromptu stop, I arrived at my destination bang on the appointed time. The Cheshire Cheese, which was rebuilt just after the Great Fire of London, is entered via a narrow passageway to the side of the building. Inside it is a myriad of stairs and discrete wood panelled rooms and alcoves, ideal in fact for the conversation I now intended to have with Jimmy.

I'd barely had time to settle into an alcove with a pint of Barclays Russian Stout when standing in front of me was my friend Jimmy, all five feet seven of him, sporting the most elegant of topcoats, one of the perks no doubt of his vocation. Unlike yours truly, easily five stone over my peak running weight, Jimmy was still as trim and dapper as ever, with a neat thatch of brown hair and trim moustache.

Jimmy had been a fine runner in his younger years, when we could both cover the 100 yards dash in around eleven seconds, enjoying a few decent 'touches' backing ourselves on the old cinder path! Many a time we would strip down to our running spikes and silks on our trips around the country, making sure on our training runs to beat each other to confuse the prying eyes of any interested bookies or their touts!

After a quick trip down memory lane about our running days, I got down to the purpose for our meeting.

'As you know Jimmy, I am a good friend of that most splendid of fellows Harry Chaplin'

'A man to be admired indeed Mate' Jimmy responded and from the slight smile on his face I was guessing that unlike me, he had been shrewd enough to back Hermit.' I should imagine he is still celebrating his victory to the fullest.'

'You would like to have hoped that would be the case but sadly not'

'I'd not let a few jealous comments in the press spoil my enjoyment' Jimmy said with a laugh

'Nonsense like that is water off a duck's back to Harry, it's something a little more troubling I'm afraid'. I quickly explained what had happened and Harry's request for help.

'I have to admit Jimmy that detection is a little outside of my previous experience and having a nimble friend and cohort at my side would be just the ticket'

'I'm flattered you should think of me Mate and with Mr Hill's kind blessing I'm raring to get started'

Over a couple more pints of Russian Stout and two generous portions of the pubs renowned lark, kidney, oyster and steak pudding, I filled Jimmy in on the entire background, including the conversation I had witnessed and my ill-judged business arrangement with the Danebury mob.

'Well, what are your thoughts then Jimmy? I asked.

'First thought - the idea that Mr Chaplin is involved in murder is arrant nonsense but if I was the police, presented with evidence of someone having had a disagreement with Lord Coggles only a few hours before the murder; out on the Downs with no alibi and signs of physical damage, I'd feel pretty much obliged to investigate further. '

Notot what I wanted to hear but I had to concede that Jimmy was right.

'So, do you see Padwick and his merry men as the obvious alternative direction for the police?'

'I would say Mate, they look a very strong candidate and if I were a bookie I'd be quoting short odds on them. To my mind Mate, it must revolve around Lord Coggles dossier, albeit I rather doubt he would have taken it with him to his final assignation

Despite what David had said I was still not totally certain there was and added a little glumly' If it wasn't just a bluff to scare off the Confederates'

'Even if it's not come to light yet Mate, from everything you have told me about Lord Coggles, I'll give you very short odds it exists. At the risk of seeming even bolder, the Confederacy might not be the only people about whom he was keeping a dossier, given his desire to protect the Marquis from all possible threats'

'Now that's an interesting thought Jimmy. I suggest we discuss over another pint of Russian Stout and a further slab of pie! A suggestion which seemed to cause Jimmy, who settled for another Russian only, a degree of alarm!

At the end of dinner, we had agreed that come the morrow, as well as visiting the dreaded Padwick at his Mayfair office, I would also go and see Mavis Enderby. For his part, Jimmy would pay a visit to Epsom and see what he could find out.

'Well Joseph, I think we have reached an end of my tale for today. All this talk of beer has made me a little thirsty, but I think this time, we'll settle for a nice pot of tea and in the absence of pie, a couple of toasted muffins!'

Chapter 11 – The Mate takes his first steps in the world of detection with a visit to see Miss Enderby!

After a morning and most the afternoon battling away with 'My Fifty Years', Sir John decided that we had done enough to merit a further session on his tale of detection

'Mavis's father Ernest was a good friend of mine from the hunting fields of London, their estate being located in the small village of Bag Enderby, in the beautiful Lincolnshire Wolds. Come the morning' Sir john began 'I made my way to the Enderby families London home, in St George's Square, Pimlico. One of the many London developments undertaken by the master-builder Thomas Cubitt.'

I was received at the door by a maid and after introducing myself, I was shown into the salon. The room was filled with portraits of past members of the Enderby family. One looked a little like a Sir Godfrey Kneller that hung in our family home, albeit many of these portraits looked the same to me, whichever family!

After five minutes, the young maid announced Miss Enderby. Slim and tall, with what I believe is referred to as Titian coloured hair. Mavis always seemed to me if not demure but very self-contained, albeit one sensed that there was a far livelier personality waiting to burst forth. She was dressed in black but at first glance looked to be bearing up well in such sad circumstances.

'Hello, my dear I just wanted to come and see you to express my condolences at your tragic loss'

'Thank you so much Mr Astley for coming to see me at this sad and difficult time. I know that you were very fond of David and had known him since he was a child'

'Quite so my dear, I may have had doubts about his choice of best friend, but I respected his sense of loyalty and never saw him behave in the way of some of the Marquis's acolytes'

'Yes, the Marquis' Mavis responded in a rather pointed way' much of David's life seemed to be taken up trying to protect Lord Hastings from those he felt likely to do him harm, which as far as I could tell seemed to be the Marquis himself!'

'Has the Marquis been to see you my dear?

'I am not sure Mr Astley if you will be too surprised to learn the answer is no. As you may be aware already, the Marquis is in Paris and not returning to England until the start of Royal Ascot. Possibly not unconnected with the need to settle one or two rather hefty debts.

''I have been visited' she continued' by his new emissary, ex-Inspector Field, hired I understand to satisfy the Marquis's apparent desire to seek justice for David. I was however able to tell him no more than I had told Inspector Tanner, namely that as soon as David read the note, he declared that he needed to go out and not to wait up. Like the other ladies present, I was keen to escape the increasingly raucous dinner table. Beyond that sadly I have nothing I can add.'

I decided this was the right time to mention that I had seen Harry very recently.

'You will know therefore' Mavis continued' about David and Harry having had words?'

'I do indeed my dear'

'As I told the detectives, I was sure that David regretted those words but for whatever reason, it seems to be of particular interest to the forces of law both public and private'

'Together with my associate Mr Patterson I have been asked by Harry to carry out a few enquires on his behalf, with the aim of ensuring the police redirect their efforts as soon as possible'

Mavis paused a moment before saying 'A bit like a detective?'

Conscious of the reaction I had received from Harry and Lewis when I had self-applied that sobriquet, I suggested' more a case of aiding and abetting the forces of the law'

Smiling for the first time since I had arrived, she said 'you might in fact say it's a case of the Mate Investigates'

'Quite so' I laughed' and in my new role can I ask you who of the Marqui's merry men have been to see you?'

'Zeals is in Paris with the Marquis; Tobias Bracklesham has not been near, but I did receive a nice letter from Viscount Bowlhead expressing his sorrow and offering to do anything he can to help. I am really not sure what help he could provide but unlike the others, he is a nice young man just very easily put upon by those of a stronger character, which appears to be everyone!

Oh, and Sir Carlton' she added' has been a staunch friend to me and my family'

'He is a capital chap and always there when his friends need his help'

'Yes, he really is a splendid gentleman' she responded with what was clearly genuine admiration.

I made my exit promising that we would do all we could to help and concluding that Mavis was indeed a young lady of pluck and spirit.

Chapter 12 – A far less welcome visit to see Old Padwick in his Mayfair lair!

I had not written in advance warning Padwick of my intended visit and would have to trust to luck that he would be there. To give me a little more time to decide what to say I opted to walk up to Victoria; then a welcome stroll through the spring flowers in Green Park and finally to Berkeley Square with its grand trees and new fountain, created by a Mr Munro a part, I am told, of a group of artistic Johnnie's known as the Pre-Raphaelite Brotherhood!

By the time I reached the north side of the square, I had still not reached any conclusions as to how to deal with such a tricky customer, so it was back to thinking one's feet, dodging any cannon balls coming my way and on no account raising the subject of the outstanding loan!

In keeping with his image as friend and confidante to the aristocracy, Padwick's office was the suitably grand edifice of Number 48 Berkeley Square. The neighbouring property Number 50 was allegedly the most haunted house in London. Its sole resident, one Thomas Myers, had not been seen in years, spending all day locked inside moving from room to room uttering strange loud noises lamenting a lost love!

Whilst Padwick's property provided a grand front to the world, some of the 'gentlemen' who left by the tradesmen's entrance were far from grand. Not content with garnering as many mortgage deeds as possible from the aristocracy, the Confederacies other line of 'business' was placing bets on behalf of their clients, through a network of touts and middlemen who would come to Berkely Square for their instructions.

On arriving at Number 48 and presenting my calling card, I was shown by a gaudily attired footman, to Padwick's first floor office. There he sat behind a large mahogany Sheraton desk with, to even my limited knowledge of art, a large work by Mr JMW Turner on the wall behind him.

As ever, Padwick was charm personified, or more accurately an unctuous level of false charm personified, which I felt obliged to play along with on this occasion.

'How very excellent to see you Mr Astley, and to what do I owe the pleasure of this visit at the end of such an eventful week'. His accent redolent of one who had bestrode the playing fields of Eton or Harrow, which was far from the case!

'Yes, indeed Mr Padwick an eventful week.

'A most unexpected victory in the Derby for your friend Mr Chaplin, followed by the terrible murder of Lord Coggles. My colleagues and I had left Epsom before the last race, to avoid the worst of the crowds, and were unaware as to the tragic news until reading about it in the papers' the next morning'

'It is indeed Lord Coggles I have come to see you about. I have been to see Miss Enderby and promised I would speak with respected members of the racing community, to find out if anyone has heard any rumours that might assist in bringing his murderer to book'

'How coincidental that you should ask, since I had a visit yesterday from the redoubtable Ex-Inspector Field, asking me the very same question, on behalf of the esteemed Marquis of Hastings'

'How typical' he continued' that someone of your generous nature Mr Astley should wish to help. I fear however that I may prove to be something of a disappointment since I only recall meeting Lord Coggles the once'

'Would that have been at the recent Stockbridge meeting' I enquired innocently!

'I'm afraid not albeit I did see him in the distance with his cousin, I think it was possibly Royal Ascot last year and I believe I asked after the health of his father Lord Utterby

'Another of your clients? I asked again as innocently as I could, knowing full well that Buffy Utterby would rather appear on stage at Wilton's Music Hall singing 'Jingle Bells' than borrow money from Padwick!

'As a matter of fact, not, I did indeed offer to assist him any way I could, but he had no current need of my services, albeit as ever, I remain happy to help. I am sure you are aware of my record in assisting members of the nobility when they have need of my legal services or advice'

'Your desire to help the good and great shines forth' I replied trying to avoid gritting my teeth' 'Perhaps your friends Mr Hill or Mr Pedley have had more recent conversations?'

'You would indeed need to ask them, albeit I know them both to be very busy gentlemen so I would imagine not. I do however hear' he continued rather archly', that your friend Mr Chaplin and Lord Coggles may have had a vigorous discussion on the night of the latter's demise?

'A case of young men letting off steam'.

'Indeed Mr Astley, I am sure that must be the case' he replied, leaving an obvious air of doubt in his response.

I was rapidly concluding that short of challenging Padwick outright about that night in Stockbridge, which I had been asked not to do, I was going to get nothing from him. My aim now was to bring the conversation to its speediest conclusion and be on my way. That was until Padwick uttered the words I had been praying to avoid 'Whilst you are here Mr Astley, I would be delighted to have a small word about the little matter of the £3000 still owing?

'Quite, absolutely at the top of my agenda!

'So good to know that keeping to our little arrangement is never far from your mind?'

'Of course, not my dear Padwick' how on earth did I ever get involved with this awful man (oh I remember lack of bank credit!)! I had in mind say, six equal instalments spread over the next twelve months'

'Let's say instead the whole £3000 in a single instalment by the July Goodwood Meeting or earlier if you prefer'' Before I had the chance to respond he drew the meeting to a close with an ingratiating smile' so nice to have seen you today Mr Astley and do pass on my best to Mr Chaplin when you are next able to see him.'

I had few doubts that Padwick had guessed I had come to speak with him on behalf of Harry, rather than Mavis but for now, I was merely grateful to get back out into the fresh air of Berkeley Square!

Chapter 13 – A Meeting at the Lamb & Flag, Jimmy recounts an informative visit to Epsom!

On arriving home, I penned a quick letter to Mr Lewis informing him of Padwicks denial about meeting David Coggles, after which I devoured a late lunch of Mrs Crumpbuckets excellent pig's trotters, followed by a generous portion of Syllabub. After an afternoon nap it was a quick wash and a slice of Victoria Sponge, to keep me going, before dashing out to meet Jimmy.

Before leaving, a rapid response arrived from Lewis to say that he would be speaking to the police straightway. There was also an invitation to be at his office for 3.30pm the following day to see him and Harry.

For our meeting, Jimmy and I had agreed to meet at another of London's historic hostelries, this time the Lamb & Flag in Covent Garden, or as it was known in the days of bare-knuckle fighting 'The Bucket of Blood.'

At the bar as I entered was Mr Charles Dickens, holding forth to what I had no doubt to be assorted friends from the press, all eagerly guffawing at each bon mot. I decided to make my way to the quieter first floor where I found my compatriot, clearly of the same mind.

'Good to see you, Jimmy!'

'And you too Mate' I hope that a pint of Horseshoe Brewery Porter' he said pointing to a full glass on the table' is to your fancy'.

'Correct as ever Jimmy!' Albeit whenever I think of the Horseshoe, I remember being told how in the Great Brewery Flood of 1814, 27,000 gallons of the stuff flooded the brewery and neighbouring houses, forcing people to stand on tables to avoid getting washed away by a torrent of beer!

Before I side tracked myself again with another of my little stories, we quickly settled down to reviewing the day.

I recounted to Jimmy, my visit to Miss Enderby and her evident sadness that David Coggles life appeared to be dominated by the Marquis. And of most relevance to the task at hand, Padwicks denial of having met David in Stockbridge, let alone the threats issued against him.

'Hopefully Mate when Mr Lewis has spoken to Inspector Tanner, it will not be long before the police are shifting the axis of their investigation away from Mr Chaplin and onto Padwick and his associates. Notwithstanding our hopes for tomorrow' Jimmy continued' I thought that it would be a help to us both to start recording our findings in a systematic way'

So, saying, jimmy brought out of his pocket a brand new leatherbound notebook, titled 'Case Notes'.

'A capital idea Jimmy' I responded' and maybe one as 'lead' detective' I should have had myself!

'I just wanted to save you another job' Jimmy kindly added. 'In the meantime, Mate, I will give you a quick rundown of my first day investigating'.

'Please do Jimmy, I am all ears!'

'I was in Epsom by lunchtime and there was really only one place I could go first'

'The George?' I ventured' its renowned for its Battalia Pie!

'Delightful as I sure that pudding is Mate, I felt the Spreadeagle would be more pertinent to our investigations.

'Quite so Jimmy, quite so'

'I needed to find someone who worked at the hotel willing to have a discrete chat over a drink. In the spirt of all good subterfuge, I decided to take on the persona of crusading journalist Tommy Cornelius trying to get to the truth of what happened that night, rather than one seeking to help Mr Chaplin.'

'Prior to lunch I made my way to the bar and by serendipitous chance, found myself in conversation with one Thaddeus Belvedere, Duty Manager on the night of Lord Coggles disappearance. I explained the undercover nature of my quest and how it was his civic duty to help my investigations and how, in turn, it would be my bounden duty to recompense him for his time. With his ready agreement, I arranged to meet him post lunch in the Amato public house in Chalk Lane, which provided the necessary level of discretion.'

'My new friend turned out to be rather verbose and always keen to use a multitudinous number of words when one might suffice. To summarize, Belvedere has no idea from whom the note to Lord Coggles came, but he did see him leave the hotel at about 9.00pm on his fateful last journey'

'He did not see Mr Chaplin arrive back but admitted that they were short staffed that night and there were periods when the front desk was unmanned, which accords with what Mr Chaplin said.'

'Of most significance, he did let slip that, a couple of gentlemen, applied in the loosest sense, had come to the hotel yesterday asking about an apparently missing dossier! They left no names and appeared generally shifty of characters. They did however leave an address at 48 Berkley Square and confirmation that it would be financially worth Belvederes' while if anything came to mind or hand'

'Excellent work Jimmy and sounds very like the kind of gents I observed entering Padwick's Palace this morning by the tradesman's entrance!'

With Jimmy having politely, declined my suggestion that he join me in a portion of the venison pudding, a house speciality, and following more discussion about the case, we said our goodbyes. Jimmy generally seemed to look quite alarmed at my culinary suggestion – clearly not a lover of good British suet!

Before leaving it was agreed that I would make Jem Machell my next port of call whilst Jimmy had what he called, a couple of ideas he wanted to follow up before meeting me at Mr Lewis's office.

And with that, Sir John declared all this talk of good food had made him hungry and a break for lunch would be our best course of action. To be followed by a whole afternoon on his book as restitution!

Chapter 14 – A meeting with Captain Machell!

After the promised afternoon session and the whole of the following morning, Sir John declared that we had made sufficient restitution and could return to matters investigative.

'Come the morning' Sir John commenced' I had been able to establish that Jem Machell was in London and had arranged to meet him at the Old Turf Club at 11.30am.

Prior to leaving I was left with a choice of going through a bundle of bulky envelopes of what were quite clearly Estate Papers, sent down from Elsham, or as I chose, 'devour the morning's copy of The Thunderer where David's murder was inevitably still headline news. The presence of the £500 on the body had now seeped out to the press, causing speculation that the killer must have been known to David, which for Harry, I did not see as welcome news.

The Times also featured an interview, sent by telegram from Paris, with the Marquis of Hastings. As one would have expected, the Marquis confirmed his distress at the murder of his dearest friend but as ever, sounded distant from the normal affairs of man. He could not however resist trumpeting the important role being played by the ubiquitous Inspector Field, who was apparently following up on various important leads as well, from what I had seen, granting interviews to his friends in the press with merry abandon.

The Marquis also confirmed that he would soon be finished with his 'business' in Paris and would be coming back soon to do all he could to help bring the murderer to justice.

I had few doubts that the 'business' to which he referred was connected to the looming settlement day with the bookies. To this end, the article also mentioned that Hastings had reached agreement to sell the families Scottish estate. Whether Harry Chaplin would be seeing any of his £10,000 I was seriously doubted, more likely another letter explaining why repayment had to be delayed just a little longer.

I set off to walk to the Club at 9.30am and was there in comfortably inside the hour.

The Turf Club is now on the corner of Piccadilly and Clarges Street, in 1867 we were in nearby Bennett Street. Founded in 1861, the original intent was to call ourselves simply The Club, but it transpired we had been beaten to that title by Dr Johnson for his personal dinning society!

I arrived to find Machell already waiting for me in the library. A big man of erect bearing with a large walrus moustache, I could see just poking out of a waistcoat pocket the little book in which he kept details and valuations of all his assets, including his horses. Like Jimmy and I, Jem had been a keen runner in his youth able to cover the 100-yard dash in little more than ten seconds. Such a good athlete was the Captain, it was said he could jump up onto a mantlepiece from a standing start, not something I was going to try and emulate!

Jem had kindly ordered a pot of coffee for us both, a sure sign he had arrived early, given the time it took our staff, almost all of whom looked as if they were old enough to have served alongside the Duke of Wellington at Waterloo in 1815, to bring orders from the kitchen!

With pleasantries exchanged, Jem's first question was' and to what do I owe the pleasure of this meeting Mate?'

'It's all to do with the sad demise of David Coggles. Harry may have mentioned already but Scotland Yard, have been taking a completely wrong-headed interest in him.'

Jem nodded confirmation that he was indeed aware.

'To which end, Harry has asked if I could make a few enquiries on his behalf, speak to a few chaps and see what I might be able to find out.'

Despite his obviously best efforts, Machel was unable to stifle a loud guffaw' Apologies Mate but of all your many great talents, criminal investigation is not one of which I had been aware!'

'I'll admit it's not quite my usual hors de combat, but Harry convinced me I might be able to help' I responded trying hard not to feel a little put out.

'You could almost say The Mate investigates' he quipped with no attempt this time to hide his obvious amusement.

'That has been said before' I responded a little stiffly' I have also drafted in my old friend and running associate 'Jimmy 'The Flying Tailor' Patterson to help'.

'Now he is a bright chap' Machel responded none too flatteringly to yours truly 'shrewd move on your part I'd say Mate.

'Funnily enough' he continued' you're not the only one who has come to see me on this subject. Ex-Inspector Field called round yesterday, seemed to be almost preening with delight when telling me he had been appointed by that paragon of virtue the Marquis of Hastings'.

'That's no great surprise to me Jem, blessed man seems to get everywhere. Cutting to the quick, the reason I believe Harry asked me to help, is that I witnessed a conversation between Lord Coggles and the Danebury Confederacy, rather than for my detecting skills!' I went on to explain what I had seen, including the threat from Hill to David, if he were to expose his dossier of information on the Confederacy to public view.'

'Ah yes, that does make more sense!' Machell responded' and I assume that you wanted my view on whether they might be capable of murdering Coggles'?

'In a nutshell, yes'?

'Whatever else one might say about Coggles, it took guts to stand up to them. I don't think that Padwick or his cohorts would want the public knowing what really goes on behind grand front doors of 48 Berkely Square. Whether' he continued' they would resort to murder who knows but they have a lot to lose so yes, I would see them as strong suspects.'

'Jimmy is of the view that as such an assiduous chronicler as David, may have turned his pen of moral righteous on others who he viewed in a similar light'

Intriguing thought' Jem replied' and I suspect any such dossiers are likely to be related in some way with Coggles obsession with protecting the Marquis of Hastings from all comers.

'Agreed, albeit I am hoping that come this afternoon, Lewis will confirm that the police are of the same view too and my brief sojourn as a detective will come to an early end! On a change of tack, I wondered if you'd be able to collect all your Derby winnings from both the bookies and those of a more noble lineage?'

'Not sure if you are trying to practice your investigative skills on me or not' he laughed' but I'm going to assume it is to his Grace the Duke of Hamilton that you refer, even if Graceless might prove a more apt description!

'It is indeed!'

'Not to put too fine a point on it, I have been 'leant' on from the very highest quarters (which I was taking it to be Bertie, Prince of Wales) to cancel the bet. He doesn't want to see a Duke financially embarrassed in front of the public! I'm expecting at least a baronetcy for my generosity' he added with a hollow laugh.

At that point, Jem leapt to his feet, almost as if he was about to launch himself onto the nearest mantlepiece and announced.

'Always a pleasure to see you Mate but I need to be on the next train back to Newmarket. Let me know if you ever need any help'

I thanked Jem for his time and thoughts. I could not really imagine why I would need his help but always best to have a one-man battalion in reserve.

After Machell had left, I opted to remain in the Club for an early luncheon. On entering the dining room, I was delighted to spot Sir Carlton.

After expressing my condolences at the sad loss of his cousin, I asked if I could join him for chef's latest suet creation, something of a standing joke amongst Club Members and maybe a consequence of a public-school education!

'That would be excellent and let us share a bottle of claret in memory of David' Sir Carlton announced.

'And a swift resolution to finding who really committed this foul deed' I replied.

I spent the next ten minutes explaining everything I had just told Jem, with in Carlton's case a welcome lack of guffawing at the attribution of the word 'detective' to yours truly!

'I cannot believe they would even consider that about Harry' Carlton exclaimed when I had finished' quite preposterous.'

'I could not put it better myself but there you have it I'm afraid'

'I am a little concerned' Carlton added in an apologetic tone' that my recollection about David's habit of wandering off may have somewhat underplayed the seriousness of the situation. I was at the Spreadeagle myself that evening but dined in my room to avoid the noise from Hasting's parry.'

'I'd not trouble yourself there Carlton, I know that you merely wanted to ensure that Mavis did not get too worried, and I know from seeing her, that she appreciates your kindness'

'Yes, she really is a very sweet girl'

'Aside from keeping your ear to the proverbial ground, can you think of anyone who might want to have done David harm'?

'I know he was none too keen on some of the company the Marquis kept, then again, I'm not either!' As for the Danebury Confederates, not a bunch with whom I would wish to mix but I'd still be of a mind to think, that it was an attack by unknown ruffians that got out of hand with tragic results. Rest assured John, if I do hear anything I will let you know and do please tell me if there is anything I can do to help'

'Many thanks Carlton and I knew that would be the case!

We devoted the rest of lunch to the all-important question of what to back at the forthcoming Royal Ascot Meeting. Carlton, despite his great wealth, only had a few horses in training. Probably why he had experienced no trouble in hanging onto his large inheritance, unlike yours truly trying to enhance his wealth with a much larger string of horses!

By the time we had finished lunch, time had marched on to nearly 3.00pm. With no cabs in sight, time running short and rain in the air, I reluctantly caught a London General Omnibus Company two horse bus. The lower deck was completely full, necessitating an undignified climb up the iron rungs to the upper part. Then a very wet and uncomfortable ride on the 'knifeboard', a single seat fitted lengthways along the roof!'

Best I can say is I arrived on time, albeit not in the happiest of states. I was duly ushered into the Library to join Jimmy, Lewis, Harry and young Osmotherly.

After the normal felicitations and the immediate ordering of a large pot of coffee, Jimmy swiftly and efficiently ran through his neatly written up notes of his visit to Epsom and my meetings with Padwick and Miss Enderby.

'Most informative gentlemen and thank you so much for the logical summation of all action to date' Lewis responded. To my relief he seemed impressed with what had been achieved, to which Harry added his own vote of thanks.

Having meant to exercise patience, I was unable to resist asking. 'I hope Mr Lewis you will not mind my getting to the muttons of the matter but are you able to confirm, that on hearing my evidence, the police and for that matter old Field will be changing horses and galloping off with alacrity after the real villains.'

To my disappointment however, Lewis hesitated for a moment, before continuing. 'On being asked if they had been involved in the conversation you witnessed, all three denied having been there, saying they were at the house they keep in Stockbridge to better 'service' their Bibury Club clients. Furthermore, their domestic staff were also willing to swear on any bible to hand that, their employers had been an evening of quiet reflection in the house'

'They said what'! I could not help shouting' does the word of a good honest Englishman count for nothing!

'I fully understand your disquiet Mr Astley and it was not the reaction I was expecting. Knowing you to be a man of the utmost integrity I have no doubts as to the voracity of what you have told us. Unfortunately, with the Confederates all vouching for each other and no one to corroborate what you saw, the Police are not willing to take this line of enquiry any further nor, sad to say, the existence of the dossier and any bearing it might have on the case!

'The only person who could corroborate is David Coggles and he is dead, quite possibly at their hands! I expostulated before pausing a moment to take a deep breath and calm down' Apologies gentlemen for my anger but I am shocked.'

'Your frustration is fully understood' Lewis responded in a reassuring tone' and I would I am sure feel the same.

'If it is of any consolation, Inspector Tanner was personally unimpressed by Mr Padwick, particularly his keenness to drop the name of at least one Earl into each sentence. Something Tanner described as being akin to drowning in an ocean of obsequiousness'

'I propose' Lewis continued' that we concentrate our efforts on investigating the Confederates further and establishing any other enemies Lord Coggles may have had and whether they too, are the subject of dossiers.'

With everyone in agreement, Jimmy volunteered to take up the cudgels with the Confederacy, a relief to me given the £3000. For my part, I would investigate the Hastings crowd, starting with the obnoxious Tobias Bracklesham. To which end, Lewis offered to arrange a meeting for me the next day, with one Lionel Truscott, who he believed could be of help.

Throughout all this Harry had stayed unusually quiet but at the end announced 'Gentlemen, whilst I have nothing to hide, I see no purpose in courting attention. I therefore intend keeping low-profile pro tem. I have plenty to keep me occupied with Estate business and agreeing with Jem our strategy for runners at Royal Ascot.'

'It is very reassuring to know' he continued' that I have you fine gentlemen representing my best interests, and it will not be long before the police have turned their attention elsewhere. This is England and justice will out!' And, with that rousing finish, we agreed to meet again very soon.

Post meeting, Jimmy and I decided that an investigative team discussion was needed, and we returned to Ludgate Hill Station, where Messer's Spiers & Pond had recently opened a new refreshment bar. For those not familiar, with these fine gentlemen, they had previously run the Shakespeare Grill Room in Melbourne, serving gold miners seeking a reprieve from a daily diet of Kangaroo and Wombat!

With an order placed for tea and a selection of their excellent buns, it was down to business with young Jimmy opening the batting.

'I think Mate, it would be very helpful to have an inside track on police thinking'

'Sound logic Jimmy but maybe easier said than done' I replied, already certain that Jimmy would likely have a plan in place!

'I've no doubts Mate you'll remember Percy Proudfoot who ran for you in that five-mile match with Dangerous Dan Dismore's man O'Leary across Hackney Wick?

I did indeed remember Proudfoot. He'd run a blinder to win a handy wager, managing to avoid various nefarious characters Dismore had stationed around the course to nobble him. Post race I found him hiding under a blanket in the back of my Brougham. Transpires he had accepted £50 from Dismore as well as myself! In my case to win the race and Dismore's to lose! Out of 'loyalty' to yours truly he had won! We had quite a hairy journey back into town, making sure to avoid Dismore's ruffians catching up with us!

'And how might he be able to help' I asked incredulously.

'After his little adventure that day, Proudfoot decided it would be safer, to lead a life of greater moral certainty and joined our friends the Peelers, where he could put to good use his obvious understanding of the criminal mind. Even better he has been assigned to work with Inspector Tanner on the Coggles case. After a gentle reminder about the Dismore incident, he came round to the view that he owes you a good turn Mate. Assuming it was not too presumptuous I have arranged for us to meet Sergeant Proudfoot tomorrow 12.30pm at the Fortunes of War public house in Cock Lane, just off Smithfield Square?

With that agreed, we parted company and rather than another unpleasant session on the Knifeboard or get persuaded into another impromptu drink by a silver-tounged cabbie, I made my way home via the Metropolitan Line.

On arriving home, I was pleased to find both a letter from Lewis confirming a meeting with Truscott and that Mrs Cumpbucket had been simmering her excellent Turbot Casserole awaiting my return!

Chapter 15 – The Mate meets Mr Truscott!

I was up early the next morning and restricted myself to a light repast of kedgeree, bacon, sausage, egg and a beef marrow fritter, together with a large pot of tea and some rolls and preserves.

As kindly arranged by Lewis, I made my way to Stockwell, where Truscott resided, via Battersea Bridge, by then the last of the dangerous old wooden Thames crossings. Truscott's home was a sizeable modern stucco faced villa, not quite Pimlico, but perfectly pleasant, nonetheless. I was granted entry by a maid and taken in to see her master, a gentleman of I would say about 65 with wispy grey hair artfully wrapped around his head to suggest a greater amount of follicle growth than the reality. He had in his hand Lewis's letter of introduction.

"Ah, The Mate' he commenced 'I remember wining a few pennies on your 1845 one-hundred-yard race against Captain Trumpington'

'Always happy to do a fellow punter a good turn in the eternal battle against our old enemies the bookies'

I understand from Lewis' he continued, ignoring my attempt at humour 'you want to know a bit about the Bracklesham's, particularly young Tobias and his friendship with the Marquis of Hastings.

Yes indeed' I confirmed' any background you can let me have, would be much appreciated.

He squirmed around in his leather armchair until apparently comfortable, which I took to mean there was a fair amount of background to come. And I was proved correct from the opening salvo!

'To start from the beginning, it was 1825 and I had landed my first job as a very junior sous chef at Crockfords newly opened gaming house.'

'Ah, Crockford' I exclaimed', of whom it was said that by the time he closed his Club in 1840, he had won all the ready money of the then existing generation'

'That's about right' Truscott responded with a less than delightful phlegm filled wheeze. 'To entice his high rolling clients against any daft notions of going home before they had lost all their money, he hired London's most famous chef Louis-Eustache Ude to provide them free food and drink all night. I remember Ude telling me the £1200 a year Old Crockford paid him, was four times more than he received as chef to Napoleon Bonaparte's mother!

I soon became friends with the junior bottlewasher, one Archie Bracklesham. Noticing that, Club Members were inevitably left feeling much the worse for wear, as well as poorer, whichever morning they finally surfaced Archie spent his days 'experimenting' with potential pick-me-up potions. When given a glass of the final mixture many of them appeared to revive, either with the energy to return home to contemplate their losses or else, to Crockford's delight, remain at the Club and lose more money!'

'Aside from Archie no one knew what was in the drink, but people seemed convinced it worked, and he was equally convinced, it could be sold profitably to the public at large.

Problem was he lacked the capital to put it into production. As luck would have it, Crockford had a soft spot for Bracklehsam and together with John Gully of pugilistic fame backed the enterprise'.

Within a few months 'Brackelshams Tonic' was selling like the proverbial hot cakes. It was not long before the Brackleshams had left their modest abode in Brixton for a new home in Belgravia, with a county estate in Hertfordshire to follow.

When Crockford passed away in 1844, his fourteen children could not decide what they wanted to do with their share of the business and allowed Archibald to buy them out, giving him majority control of the company. Not sure what happened to Gully's share when he passed away, whether to one of his 24 children or someone else.

Like so many financially successful men Archie, egged on by the ambitious Mrs Brackelsham, was keen to gain social acceptance. They had achieved some success already with their daughter Elizabeth's marriage to the Honourable Freddie Fleetwood son of Lord Mangotsfield. Tobias meanwhile was sent to Rugby and from there to Christs at Oxford where he became a part of the Hastings set'

'For many years I managed the bottling plant' he continued with barely a pause for breath' giving me full details of the recipe for the tonic and I was very well renumerated for my trouble. I was even made Tobias's godfather, but I don't think Mrs Brackelsham sees me as being in the right social bracket anymore!' said with a cringeworthy attempt at a faux aristocratic accent!

'I had been promised by Archie I would be made a director of the company, but Mrs Bracklesham decided the companies letter head would look much the better, with a touch of nobility. She persuaded Archie to offer a directorship to Lord Sixpenny Handley the spectacularly useless son of the Earl of Pimperne, who she was trying to persuade to marry their second daughter. As a result, Archie paid me off with the capital I needed to set me up here in comfortable retirement. He'd didn't have worried' he cackled again' I'm the loyal sort and I'd not have blabbed.'

Somehow, I was none too convinced as to the voracity of Truscott's self-applied description.

'Given what you have come here to ask me about, you'll doubtless be interested to know' he said archly' that Lord Coggles himself came to see me recently'.

He could see that my interest had been well and truly piqued with that little revelation, which I think he found rather pleasing

'Got you interested now I can see' he cackled.

'I cannot deny it is of interest, so pray tell more'

'His Lordship told me that as the staunchest friend of the Marquis of Hastings, he was determined to stop the Marquis from falling prey to the forces of darkness

'He continued by saying that he was putting together a dossier of evidence about these forces to be passed to the authorities if necessary. To be honest with you, it all sounded like a load of high-minded twaddle, and I asked him if he viewed himself as some sort of guardian of moral rectitude!'

I was just about to question him further, when Truscott stuck a finger in a hair sprouting earhole and waggled it around before saying' 'He did not say as much but he clearly saw Tobias as one of those dark forces, I keep my ear to the ground and Its fair to say that when Lady Amelia Irthlingborough changed her affections to Tobias, my godson had broken every rule in the MCC rule book to achieve his goal'

'Tobias paid me a visit the following week and I told him about the conversation I'd had with Coggles. Tobias made out that he was blithely unconcerned, but I could see he was rattled! Mind Tobias has a few other pressing problems.'

'And what would those be?'

'Tobias and that milksop Bowlhead have managed to tread on a few of the wrong toes in the world of racing, and not ones you'd want standing back on yours!'

'The one shining light in their rag bag empire of indifferent nags is the miler Lurgashall' The horse had trounced allcomers in gallops at home and there was confidence he could land a big touch. The aim was the Headley Handicap on Derby Day. I don't doubt it was Tobais, who came up with the idea that talking up the chances of another horse would help to supress any interest in their own. Heaven knows why, they chose Merry's horse and woe betide anyone who spoils his chances of getting his money down at the right price.'

'Bloody typical the horse should lose anyway' he continued accompanied this time by a cackling laugh' Let's hope Merry and his grim old pair of Merry Men were satisfied with the prize money from winning the race, since from what I know if its Buchanan coming to see you it's a stream of vitriol but a painful experience is on the way if Parker ever comes a calling!' My mind was immediately taken back to Derby Day and the mutual hurling of insults I had witnessed.

Try as I might I could not seem to get Truscott back onto the subject of Tobias Bracklesham and after half an hour or so, mainly discussing Truscott's fancies for Royal Ascot, I thanked him for his time and was 'rewarded' with a final cackle and phlegm filled wheeze but mercifully no more waggling his finger round in his ear!

Chapter 16– A very brief reacquaintance with Sergeant Proudfoot!

Finding myself running late for my meeting at the Fortunes of War, I swiftly hailed a cab, with the promise of a good tip for a speedy journey, usually open season for the cabbie to drive with even more reckless haste than usual! To those not familiar with the Fortunes, it was until the early part of the century, the chief dropping off place for the Resurrectionists, or as they were better known, the London Burker body snatchers, who would sell their wares to surgeons from the nearby Barts Hospital

As we raced along the Lambeth Palace Road and then over Waterloo Bridge, I reflected on what I had learned from my conversation with Truscott. Two things stood out to me, Jimmy was right with his conjecture that there could be more dossiers out there and secondly, there was little love lost between David and Tobias Bracklesham.

I was still pondering when we pulled up at my destination twenty minutes late, just as another cab was pulling away. Sitting in the back was Seargent Proudfoot! By the time I had alighted, his cab was round the corner of the street and away.

I quickly made my way to the Lounge Bar, where Jimmy was sat in a discrete corner.

'I'm sorry Mate...

'I know Jimmy, I've just seen him taking off down the road. The only time I seem to see Proudfoot is in a pony and trap, least ways he was not hiding under a blanket this time!

'Not to worry Mate, he was not trying to avoid you and intended offering you, a fulsome apology for Hackney Wick all those years ago'

'Gratifying as that would have been Jimmy, what did he have to say?

'Knowing and respecting you as he does Mate, Proudfoot's view would be to pursue what you witnessed with the utmost vigour. 'Unfortunately, that view is not shared by Tanner, particularly given a search of Lord Coggles home for clues, revealed no dossiers or any reference to them'

'Confound the man' I expostulated' it's not something I'm going to go around making up!

'Quite so Mate but I fear we are going to need to do a lot more to persuade Tanner as to the wrongness of his view. What I did get from the meeting was an agreement from the Sergeant, that he would do his best to tip us off on important developments.,

'Well Jimmy, it's probably best I was not in attendance, since I am not sure I could have kept my equanimity on being told, by a man whose former line of defence was a blanket, saying the police think I am making things up!'

After a pause Jimmy said' he does believe you Mate, we've just got to have to make sure that belief is shared by others.'

Yes', I conceded with a sigh' I was perhaps a little intemperate there Jimmy. Good thing you are here to take the considered view'

'Many thanks Mate and before we go any further, I took the liberty of ordering you a pint of Godding's Best Porter and for your delectation a large slab of the pubs pork and egg pie, together with as diverse a range of pickles as you could wish to see'!

I had quite forgotten how hungry I was and over the excellent pie, I talked Jimmy through my morning with Lionel Truscott, missing out his disturbing personal habits! Throughout which Jimmy was assiduously writing everything up in his Case Notes.

'An excellent morning's work Mate and I have already taken the liberty of adding Mr Bracklesham's name to our list of persons of interest'

By the time I had finished the pie and dusted off all the assorted pickles over another pint of Godding's, Jimmy I noted having limited himself an egg sandwich, we had agreed our next actions.

Regarding Bracklesham' I began 'I am aware the Frensham Partnership are keen to have a fancied runner at Royal Ascot. Whilst I have nothing in the class of Hermit, they will know that my horse Old Bolingbroke, has an entry at a decent weight for the Royal Hunt Cup. For the purposes of discussion at least, my intention is to offer to lease the horse to them for the Race. I'm going to make an approach through Bowlhead, an altogether more malleable personality than his friend. In between the bumps thundering along the Embankment, I managed to pen a note to Bowlhead asking if he might like to meet to discuss.

'A capital idea Mate and better than approaching Bracklesham directly, albeit I doubt it'll be long before Mr Truscott's admirable sense of loyalty leads him to tell his godson of your visit! For my part Mate, I thought to myself, where is the epicentre of interest for the Danebury Confederates in London, somewhere they can use their business model to best effect? The obvious answer – Limmers Hotel on Conduit Street!'

To that end' Jimmy continued 'I have made an appointment to see your favourite member of the bookmaking fraternity Mr Ouseley Higgins, to ask if he is happy for me to attend one evening very soon as his clerk to see what I can find out'

'Brilliant idea Jimmy, I remember reading old Rees Howell Gronow, a dandy to rival Beau Brummel himself, say that Limmers was a place where men *with not very clean hands used to make up their books whilst in the gloomy, comfortless coffee-room sat many members of the rich squirearchy, eager to place their bets.*'

'Glad you agree Mate' Jimmy answered quickly' doubtless keen to halt another of my little anecdotes going any further!'

We discussed the case for a few minutes more, arranging to meet again the day 1.30pm the next day at the Pillars of Hercules in Greek Street. After posting my letter to Bowlhead's home at the Albany, I elected to avoid another cab journey and walked through Smithfield Market, to catch the train from Farringdon Station.

Chapter 17– A Meeting with the Viscount gets rudely interrupted!

On arriving home, I penned a note to Lewis and Harry updating them on the emergence of Bracklesham as a person of potential interest to our investigations. I thought it prudent not to mention our undercover source at the Yard!

Thereafter I retired to my favourite armchair for what transpired be a rather longer nap than intended, possibly the result of all that rushing about or just perhaps the three pints of Goddings and the slab of pie! By the time I awoke at around 6.00pm, I found what had been hoping for, an envelope marked with the crest of the Albany. Inside was a note from Viscount Bowlhead proposing in small and neat handwriting, that we meet at Boodles Club in Mayfair at 8.00pm that evening.

Assuming we would likely dine there, I resisted asking Mrs Crumpbucket to rustle up something for dinner, all of which left me an hour to kill. Go through the Estate Papers or checking the runners and riders for the next day's meetings at Chester and Newmarket, no marks for guessing Joseth which won on this occasion!

Boodles is located on St James Street and for someone like me coming via Bury Street, there is a quiet cut through to the rear of the building. About halfway along the lane, darker than usual due to heavy clouds, I became aware of a major kerfuffle ahead. I hurried forward and saw a badly battered top hat, and just beyond that its owner, also getting badly battered by two large men!

Instinct took over and I rushed at them with a cry of "Desist you ruffians! Unhand that man!' I lunged at them with my walking stick, waving my hat to try and increase the effect. Whilst the odds were still stacked heavily in the ruffian's favour, the element of surprise seemed to work and, they high tailed it off down the lane. Both were dressed in black coats and hats so I could not get a look at their faces but had no doubts, they had partaken of fisticuffs before.

The unfortunate victim was groaning mightily but was at least conscious. I quickly realised however, that I'd not be discussing the merits of Old Bolingbroke's chances at Ascot, for the victim was Viscount Bowlhead"

'Are you alright my dear chap' perhaps a superfluous question in the circumstances, given he reminded me of my own company after our first assault on Balaclava,

'Frightfully sorry Mr Astley, he mumbled' not sure I'm up to discussing Royal Ascot, it's not been the jolliest of evenings.'

'Have you any idea of who those ruffians were or why they attacked you?

'I'm afraid I can be no help there Mr Astley, I can only think they were after something or a case of mistaken identity' he replied rather unsurely.

From my vantage point I could see no obvious signs of their trying to rob Lord Bowlhead. Of more import, however, was the need to get assistance. Very fortunately, help was at hand, since striding purposely towards me was a most determined looking young lady, who briskly introduced herself as Mademoiselle Dupont, Governess to the children of the Duc de Carcassonne.

Mademoiselle immediately took charge of the situation, ordering me to go and get help whilst she ministered to the Viscount. I swiftly made my way to Boodles where, by a stroke of luck, Sir David Dumbreck the Queens physician, readily agreed to come and help.

By the time we got back to him, Bowlhead had managed to get to his feet and despite Sir David advising him to lie down in the Club for a full examination, he would only agree to a cursory check before asking for help in getting a cab home. Bowlhead also showed no desire to involve the Peelers, albeit I had to admit the likelihood of catching anyone was remote.

I did manage to have a quick word with Mademoiselle Dupont to see if Bowlhead had said anything more about his attackers whilst I was getting help. Seemingly he had merely said 'It's all been a bit of a misunderstanding' but the rest made little sense, and she could only assume this was due to Bowlhead being delirious.

I asked Mademoiselle if she had managed to catch a good look at either of the two men. She had not but did manage to catch one of them a heavy blow to the solar plexus with her bag, which had brought forth a loud obscenity in a flat sounding accent she did not recognise. I gave her my calling card and asked that if she did remember anything to kindly let me know.

After what had happened, I had lost the desire to go back into Boodles and I started my walk home ruminating on recent events, most particularly whether the attack was premeditated, purely a random assault or just possibly something to do with the attack on David Coggles? Albeit I could see no obvious reason why that would be the case.

I broke off from my ruminations when I came to Hanover Square and a food stall run by Peg Leg Joe, late of the 15th Kings Hussars. I decided to both help swell Old Joe's funds and assuage my growing hunger pangs. I have always had a weakness for a street pie washed down with a mug of rice milk, best practiced with my Eleanor safely at home in Lincolnshire and not able to remind me about my ever-expanding waistline.

On arriving home, I had a comforting ginger brandy, and soon found myself starting to nod off for a welcome night's sleep after a most disturbing evening.

Chapter 18 – A trip to the Coast for The Mate with less than merry travelling companions!

I awoke early the following morning, to attend that day's meet at Brighton Racecourse, before making way by train over to Lewes to stay with Drewitt to observe morning gallops, then back to London the following day for my meeting with Jimmy.

By lucky happenchance I had spotted in Bells Life that the Frensham Partnership had a fancied runner, at Brighton, where I was expecting to see Tobias Bracklesham in attendance.

After dashing off a letter to Bowlhead wishing him a speedy recovery, there was just time for a light breakfast of Kedgeree, potted spiced ham and Scottish Woodcock on toast. Thereafter I made my way to Victoria Station, needing to persuade my loquacious cabbie that 9.00am was too early to stop for a drink. On arrival, I found the station horribly dusty and noisy, with work going on to complete the new extension of the District Line from South Kensington to Westminster. I did not doubt the leader of the project Sir John Fowler was enjoying the experience, his £157,000 fee apparently making him the world's best paid engineer!

With Brighton being a very popular course, the train was inevitably packed with eager punters. Spotting a spare seat in a first class compartment I jumped up onto the footplate and dived into the seat. After adjusting my coat, I looked up to find that I was sat opposite to the glowering features of James Merry, together with the granite faced Parker and ever snide Buchanan. Merry looked particularly unhappy being hemmed in against the window, with his wealth I'm quite surprised he'd not availed himself of his own carriage!

Not quite the companions I would have chosen to be penned in with for the journey. Touching the brim of my hat I enquired 'Any runners today Merry?'

'A couple' came the terse response, with Challoner in the saddle, I'm at least confident that, unlike Grimshaw, he can see the horse in front of him!

It was difficult to know what one could say of an amiable nature, to such a comment but before I had a chance to say anything, Buchanan was early into his stride sneering' Coming down to the coast to watch one of your nags'

'Not this time Buchanan but I'm hoping to see my trainer later to assess prospects for the Royal Meeting'

Buchanan's attempt at a follow-up comment was mercifully cut short by a gentleman who looked as if he been eating double portions of chef's latest suet creations at the Turf Club, trying to cram himself into our compartment as the guard blew for the off.

With the trains horn blocking out further conversation until we had left the station, it was Merry himself who restarted things' I had that man Field come to see me yesterday, telling me how he was pleased to be working for that wastrel Hastings! Said he was trying to speak with all leading lights in the world of racing'

'Be a long time before he gets to you Mate' Buchanan sneered.

Even Merry ignored him this time and continued' He also wanted to speak to anyone who like us was staying at The Spreadeagle, the night of the murder.

Whilst very keen to hear what Field had asked, I restricted myself to saying with an attempted nonchalance' Yes, I've heard he has been awfully active'

'I told him that together with my associates Mr Buchanan and Mr Parker we had dined early elsewhere, particularly emphasising our desire to be out of the way of his raucous client and his followers!'' He seemed particularly interested in your friend Chaplin he added archly.

I declined to rise to the bait and merely decided to enquire 'Did you know Coggles yourself Merry'

'No, we never even spoke' was the blunt answer. I looked momentarily to my left and felt sure I saw the briefest flicker of Parker's normally immobile features but in an instant, it was gone.

At that moment all conversation ceased as the train charged into a long tunnel. Once out of the tunnel I excused myself and stood in the corridor to smoke my largest cigars, which would hopefully last the rest of the journey. One thought dominated as I puffed away. Within the gossip ridden world of racing, people were seriously beginning to see Harry as a live suspect for the murder.

On arriving at Brighton, I quickly detached myself from the Merry Men and espying my old friends Lord and Lady Baumber, joined them in taking a cab up to Whitehawk Hill where the course was located. Always a lively atmosphere, I'd best describe Brighton as a reverse Epsom, with the starting gate at the lowest point of the course, followed by an undulating climb up hill to the winning post and the grandstand. There must have been at least 15,000 people in attendance on what was a fine day and unlike the Derby, no snow or sleet to be seen!

On getting to the course, I had a quick scout around to see if I could spot Bracklesham but no luck. I did however spot his trainer Gus Balchin, who informed me that his patron had not made the trip down to Brighton, which surprised him since he felt their runner in the one mile Rottingdean Stakes had a good chance of victory.

'To be honest Mr Astley, without wishing to seem disloyal, Mr Bracklesham is not the easiest of young men with whom to deal, increasingly erratic he has no problems creating new enemies for himself. As for the Viscount a nice young man but would only say 'boo to a goose', if he was sure the goose would not hear!'

I bid Balchin farewell and good luck with his runner but as things transpired, Bracklesham had saved himself a trip. Despite being backed down to second favourite, the horse failed to see out the mile trip and faded into third place coming up the hill.

For a change, I managed to make it a profitable visit to Brighton. I had concluded that friend Merry had not forced himself into the 'indignity' of a cramped journey down to the coast without good reason. That being the case, I availed myself of a Pony at 5/1 on his sprinter Troon Gold in the third race, winning myself £125 when the horse romped home by five lengths!

Despite being a financially successful afternoon, I did not feel I had achieved much on my trip to the South Coast. I have however always tried to look on the positive side of life and one never knew what might be round the next corner!

Chapter 19 – Another train journey for The Mate with another unexpected travelling companion!

Arriving back at the Station and with plenty of time to kill before the 7.00pm train to Lewes, I decided to avail myself of something to eat at the Station Café. Aside from the large hotels at the major termini, Station food was notoriously dreadful. I remember reading a newspaper article describing railway tea as "liquid nausea" and the coffee as being "made with a slight suspicion of coffee, as if a coffee berry had bathed in it earlier in the day"

Mercifully my mutton stew was edible, keeping it on the hob for several days had at least ensured it could be masticated in less than twenty chomps per lump of gristle!

The train, unlike my morning journey, was not busy and I soon found myself an empty first-class compartment. On the opposite side of the compartment was a small hole through to the next compartment, commonly known as a Muller Light. So named in dubious honour of one Franz Muller; the first railway murderer!

The intention of the light being that passengers from adjoining compartments, could spot what was happening next door and hopefully ensure, that no one was being bludgeoned to death by a latter-day Muller. They were later filled in following complaints from courting couples unhappy at having their mutual expressions of love for one another watched by prurient passengers in adjacent compartments!

In a slightly worrying parallel with Harry Chaplin's current spot of bother with the boys in blue, the lead detective who brought Muller to justice, following a chase across the Atlantic Ocean to New York City, was Inspector Richard Tanner!

With the train just about to leave the station, a slight figure, his face hidden under a large hat dived into my compartment carrying a travelling bag almost as large as himself.

'Good evening and welcome to the 7.00pm to Lewes' I said in a welcoming fashion.

The figure placed his seat on the bag, removed his hat and replied. 'Good evening, Mate, long time no see'

To my great surprise, my companion for the journey, was the well-known jockey Ephriam Dalrymple, noted as much for his riding ability as his dapper sense of fashion, something evident tonight from his brightly patterned waistcoat.

Dalrymple had only just returned to England after riding in Austria. Prior to leaving, he had enjoyed the benefit of a very large retainer from the Marquis of Hastings. There had been intense speculation as to why he had suddenly upped and left, much of it less than flattering to Dalrymple. For my part I had found him an engaging fellow and rather soberer than many jockeys I could name!

'Good to see you Dalrymple, I'd noticed you were back from your sojourn in delightful Vienna' a city Eleanor and I visited on our long-extended honeymoon.

'A delightful city indeed Mate but it is good to be back'

'I saw you had a ride today on one of the Duke of Alderney's horses and I'm guessing, that is the reason you are on your way to Lewes this evening to ride work in the morning for his trainer Mr William Winchelsea.

'Completely right on both scores Mate, His Grace and Mr Winchelsea have both been very kind since my return'

'Something I don't doubt you get asked often but why the sudden departure?

'I'll happily tell you Mate and it's not what certain scurrilous rumour mongers amongst the racing community have suggested'.

'I don't doubt that! I make it my business to never listen to what such people say about me, I doubt I'd leave Elsham Hall again if I did'

'You needn't worry Mate; I know few men better liked across the world of racing than you. One man I know who held you in the highest esteem was Lord Coggles. It's my saddest regret since coming back to England, that I did not get a chance to see him and thank him for the kindness he showed me at the time of my departure. A totally trustworthy gentleman, which is more than I can say for certain of the Marquises friends!

I was just about to ask him to tell me more about The Marquises friends, when the train juddered loudly to a halt as we pulled into Falmer Station, sadly best remember for the 1851 Falmer Rail Disaster. The accident inquiry I recall, came up with the startling conclusion that having the engine pointing backwards whilst the train went forward reduced driver visibility!

Any hopes of restarting the conversation were dashed when, into our compartment jumped a group of rather inebriated racegoers. They had apparently hoped off an earlier train for a top-up libation, en route home to Lewes. On spotting a famous jockey in the compartment, they proceeded to spend the rest of the journey quizzing him for tips.

It was not long before I could see the lights of Lewes Station in the distance. Rather a peculiar place where they had retained the old classical style booking hall, demolished the rest and built what appeared to be a Swiss Chalet in its place!

With it being impossible to separate Dalrymple from his new band of admirers we said a rather hurried goodbye and agreed it would be good to speak again soon. I was certainly keen to know more about Dalrymple's views on both David Coggles and the Marquises untrustworthy friend, no doubts in my mind Tobias Bracklesham!'

Outside the station was a pony and trap with a young man who identified himself as having been sent by Drewitt to take me to his employer's stables. As we trotted into town, I asked the lad which of Mr Drewitt's horses he particularly fancied, noting that none were in my ownership!

On arrival at the stables, and after an inspection of my horses, Drewitt opened a 40-year-old Fettercairn single malt, a welcome antidote to the mutton stew and to end what had been a slightly frustrating day. A day where I felt I might have been close to discovering something of value but not sure what that might have been!!'

Chapter 20 – Back to London, Dickens hove's into view again and Jimmy recounts an informative visit to Epsom!

Aided by the Fettercairn I'd no doubt, I enjoyed a sound night's sleep and was up early the next morning to join Drewitt up on the gallops by the racecourse. As ever the world seemed a better place watching beautiful thoroughbreds being put through their paces, set against a backdrop of the rolling South Downs.

With morning work over, it was a quick sprint in the horse and trap to catch the 9.30am London, Brighton and South Coast Railway train to London. During a quiet journey, with not a tipsy racegoer in sight, I resolved to make a further attempt to speak with Viscount Bowlhead. On getting back to Victoria, I posted him a note, asking if I could come and see him that evening in the Albany, before hailing myself a cab to Soho to meet Jimmy at the Pillars of Hercules.

The Pillars featured in Dickens 'A Tale of Two Cities' and as I entered the pub, who should be standing at the bar, surrounded as ever by eager devotees, than Dickens himself. How on earth did that man find the time to write such weighty tomes!

I made my way to the back of the pub, as far as possible from the noise surrounding Dickens, found myself a table and ordered a glass of Gonzalez Byass Sherry. A drink which always reminds me of the only bit of Shakespeare I can recall, where Sir John Falstaff, a figure to whom I am said to bear a less than flattering resemblance, utters '"*If I had a thousand sons, the first humane principle I would teach them should be, to forswear thin potations and to addict themselves to sherry*'!

For once I had arrived before Jimmy, a rare occurrence indeed. The only person near to my table was a most peculiar chap with thick glasses, wearing an exceptionally colourful waistcoat and atop his head, a heavily checked deerstalker since popularised by Mr Conan Doyle's creation Sherlock Homes!

Every so often the chap would peer at me myopically as if I should know him! For my part I could not think of any friend or acquaintance of mine who would dress so terribly. I looked away and hoped that Jimmy would hurry up and arrive soon. Eventually, the gentleman came over and in a bucolic accent asked' Are you not the famous racehorse owner Mr John Astley also known to all as 'The Mate"?

I could only nod my agreement before adding' I don't think we have had the pleasure sir?'

'I think we have Mr Astley' he said with a confidence I frankly found rather presumptuous. Before pulling from the pocket of frock coat a small book titled 'Case Notes'

' Jimmy?' I asked with incredulity.

'Yes, indeed Mate' and with a swift movement he whipped off the glasses and the ridiculous hat revealing a very large grin.

'Whilst I lack your significant level of fame Mate, I do know plenty of people in the racing game, so I decided to take a leaf out of Inspector Field's book and get into disguise for my evening at Limmers.'

Joining me at my table Jimmy continued' I duly met with Mr Higgins and explained that we were trying to help Mr Chaplin. Unlike many of his counterparts, Mr Higgins is an honourable man and knowing Mr Chaplin to be the same, readily agreed to help. He has given his normal clerk the night off and I am to be at his office for 8.00pm this evening. On leaving Mr Higgins, I made my way to the Alhambra Music Hall in Leicester Square'

'Ah yes' I interjected' I remember visiting it in 1854 when it opened as the Royal Panopticon showcase for the arts and sciences, a far cry from the very interesting version of the Can Can performed there of a night now I am told!'

'I went there' Jimmy patiently continued after my latest irrelevant anecdote' to see my friend Mr John Hollingshead the Stage Manager. Often described as a 'licensed dealer in legs, short skirts, French adaptations and Shakespeare, I had become acquainted with Mr Hollingshead when he came to be fitted for a new suit at Mr Hill's shop. He readily agreed to my request to have free rein of the theatres wardrobe. My aim was to leave the theatre unrecognisable from my arrival. Mission accomplished I believe, albeit I will check in the mirror next time before leaving the dressing room!'

'I'll agree Jimmy its maybe not the most understated of disguises but had me completely foxed and will, I suspect, have a similar effect on others too, even if they may not be seeking out the name of your tailor!'

After ordering a fresh sherry for me and a first for Jimmy, I quickly ran through my day in Brighton - my unfortunately foreshortened chat with Dalrymple and the delights of spending a journey with the Merry Men!

At this point, Jimmy handed me an envelope embossed with the name of Lewis & Lewis

'I think Mate that you will find a copy of this letter waiting for your when you get home'

'Good news?' I intoned optimistically.

'If I'm honest Mate, not the most welcome of reads and bears out your concerns about ex-Inspector Field snooping around. Jimmy handed me the letter which read:

Dear Gentlemen,

I trust that this letter finds you both well. My sincere apologies for not being able to see you in person but as ever my thanks for all the investigations you are kindly undertaking.

Without prevaricating further, Mr Chaplin has been visited again by Inspector Tanner, and this time the discussions were of a specific nature.

As a part of his own investigation, Ex-Inspector Field revisited The Spreadeagle and asked if he could see Mr Chaplin's room. Given Mr Chaplin's room had been let several times since the murder it was not at all obvious what Fields was expecting to find. However, whilst the sheets

and towels had been changed, as a matter of course, the same regime did not apply to the rooms writing desk, upon which sat a blotter.

By applying the schoolboy trick of shading across the top page of the blotter, Field found etched into the blotter, an indent left by a high-quality dip pen. The indent was incomplete but read 'Following our recent discussion I need to see you as soon as possible, can we meet, and there it unfortunately ended. Field 'borrowed' the blotting sheet and took it to Tanner at the Yard. Tanner in turn, showed the etching to Mr Chaplin and asked if it was his writing.

Being an upright English Gentleman, my client confirmed that it was indeed his writing. When invited to confirm if he sent the completed note to Lord Coggles on that fateful night, Mr Chaplin issued a forthright denial. When asked, to whom the note had been written, to my surprise he refused to say, merely stating it had no connection with the case and as a matter of honour, he would not be divulging the name.

Whilst even the most optimistic of detectives cannot base their case on two lines on a blotter with no names and dates, I am bound to admit Mr Chaplin's refusal, however nobly intentioned, to confirm the name will, lead to his remaining at the forefront of police thinking.

I have of course advised Mr Chaplin of my concerns, but he was completely adamant that the name of the recipient would not be revealed. As a close friend of his, may I ask that you try and use your powers of persuasion upon him.

I would like to propose a meeting between the four of us tomorrow at 2.00pm at the Euston Hotel to the front of the new station, Reception will be able to direct you to where we will be sitting.

I remain yours sincerely.

Edward Lewis

I paused a moment before responding 'Well Jimmy, there is a lot to take in. As ever I can only admire Harry for his decency and sense of honour.

'But maybe not quite the time to be so honourable'.

'I could not have put that better myself. I will do my best tomorrow to persuade Harry that telling the police in confidence, would not be ignoble'.

'Let's hope Mate he is more amenable to that from a close friend than from a trusted legal advisor!

'Quite so Jimmy, quite so.'

We soon drew things to a close and feeling rather peckish I popped into a nearby branch of Slaters Restaurants. Knowing they provided the food for the Turf Club, I was able to indulge in beef suet pudding, with boiled potatoes, Jerusalem Artichokes and turnips to keep me going!

Chapter 21 – A visit to the Albany with a most unexpected outcome!

On arriving home, I found a note from Bowlhead thanking me for my concern and asking if I would care to pop round for a light supper at 8.00pm. Unlike his earlier note, which had been neatly written, this latest one was a scrawl, no doubt I concluded, his recent coshing having impacted on his penmanship!

Having had precious little sleep over the last day or I so, I opted to put my feet up for what transpired to be a longer nap than I had intended, possibly assisted by the lunchtime suet intake! Meaning once again, I had failed to tackle the bundle of estate papers on my desk, I needed to tackle them very soon but just for the moment, I moved the envelopes to a less prominent position, rather than their sitting there in the middle of my desk!

With just over an hour to my appointment, I set off for The Albany at a brief trot and was there with five minutes to spare. For those not familiar with the Albany, it is accessed to the front from Piccadilly and to the rear via Burlington Gardens, adjacent to Shudall's, London's oldest tailor, where I first met young Jimmy, when he was an apprentice there.

The Albany was originally built in the 1770's for the highly extravagant Viscount Melbourne, before being sold to George III's son the Duke of York & Albany. To give you an idea as to the size of the place its now split into 69 apartments, only available to bachelors, including at one time the dreaded Lord Gladstone. Known to his supporters as The Grand Old Man or as we on the other side of the political chasm were wont to call him, 'Gods Only Mistake'!

On reaching Bowlhead's rooms, I found pinned to the door, a scrawled note saying 'Apologies Mr Astley valets' night off, do make yourself comfortable in the salon and I will join you there, Best Wishes, Bowlhead'

I made my way as instructed to the salon, where neatly arranged on the Chippendale sideboard was a fine selection of drinks from which I poured myself a generous glass of Taylor Fladgate & Yeatman vintage port.

To the side of the room was a Sheraton Dinning Table covered with a cloth but nothing else. I had rather assumed that the valet would have left something out, but no doubt things would become clearer when my host made his appearance.

No sooner had I sat down and started on the excellent Port than things did become much clearer but not in the way I had expected! Firstly, the person who had just come into the room was nor suffering from any injury and secondly it was not Viscount Bowlhead who stood in front of me but Tobias Bracklesham!

I fair jumped out of my seat in surprise and could only blurt out the rather obvious' You're not Bowlhead!

'A brilliant deduction Mr Astley, or should I call you Mate' Bracklesham sneered' the Viscount is not here. In view of what happened to him the other night, I persuaded my friend that this would be much less injurious to his health than risking meeting you again

'You what' I exclaimed 'I was the one who, aided by the gallant Mademoiselle Dupont, chased off those ruffians!'

'You were also the one who set up the meeting in the first place, so you knew where he would be at that time'

'This is complete poppycock if not to say total balderdash'! I responded struggling to keep my temper

'I'm fully aware' he continued' that you are playing detective on behalf of your friend Chaplin'

'I am proud to confirm that I am doing all I can, to lift current unfounded suspicions against my good and noble friend Harry Chaplin.'

'Bravo' Brackelsham responded with an ironic clap of his hands' Its time you took off your blinkers, evidence is mounting against Chaplin and whatever nonsense my delusional old godfather may have told you about dossiers and the like, David Coggles and I remained the best of friends!

Before I had a chance to respond with something a damn sight stronger than balderdash, Bracklesham was off again'

'You can now do me the courtesy of leaving my friends home……oh and by the way there is no dinner either! I'd suggest stopping off at one of the street vendors on Piccadilly for a nice bowl of tripe!

'I've no idea what your game is Bracklesham but it's not going to stop us from finding the truth' and with that I picked up my hat, downed the remainder of my port and left with a very loud slam of the door.

As I angrily made my way back home, it was all too clear to me that Bracklesham was issuing us with a warning to desist investigating him. The suggestion that David and he were good friends was clearly ludicrous and, whilst Mr Truscott had some rather disturbing personal habits, he was a long way from being delusional. To my mind Bracklesahm clearly had something to hide and had earned his place already alongside Padwick & Co on our list of suspects!

I decided to ignore Bracklesham's 'kind' suggestion of a bowl of tripe, tempting as it might have been at another time, in favour of asking Mrs Crumpbucket to prepare a tray of pickles, sandwiches and the last slice of one of Enoch Evans delicious pork pies.

At which point Sir John announced he was going to have to call a halt, since Lady Eleanor was insisting, he join her for a dinner that evening in support of the Lincoln Home for Penitent Women and would not be back until later Sunday.

Seeing that I was more than a little disappointed to be stopping at this point, Sir John pulled out from under his chair, a small book entitled 'Case Notes 1867 – Lord Coggles'

'Is that what I think it is Sir John?

'The very same, I thought I had lost it but as my wife will testify, throwing things out is well beyond me! Dear Jimmy kindly prepared for me a facsimile copy of his original notes and thoughts on the whole affair as a keepsake. Only thing I would ask Joseph is, that you give me your word that you will not skip ahead to the end!'

'Tempting as it would be Sir John, I do of course give you my word'

I knew you would my boy, in which case, I would suggest going as far as Page 28 and when I am back on Monday, we will resume from that point.'

Chapter 22– Jimmy spends the evening at Limmers Hotel

I managed to hold back my eagerness back until the Saturday morning when, with Sir John's kind permission, I settled myself in a most comfortable armchair in his study and began.

'After saying goodbye to the Mate and extracting a promise from him that he would not simply walk across the road to Slaters for another gigantic slab of suet, I made my way home in Lloyd Barker Street, just off the Kings Cross Road. The estate was built in the 1820's, the small pairs of pedimented villas intended to resemble the Parthenon in Rome, The Mate's home city as he often reminds me!

I rested until late afternoon, then set off to the West End and was at Mr Higgins office for the agreed time. The effectiveness of my disguise was further vindicated, by the look of complete bemusement on his face on my arrival!

Once my identity had been established (!), Mr Higgins set about explaining what was expected of me as his clerk. My primary duty as replacement clerk, was to record the bets he took and to calculate whether he was remaining over-round rather than over-broke on each race, the former meaning a guaranteed profit the later a guaranteed loss!

With the briefing over, we set out to walk the fifteen minutes, to Limmers, or to give its full name, The Prince of Wales Coffee House and Limmer's Hotel. It was built in the 1790's for one Stephen Limmer, a later day Dick Whittington, who had left his home village of Tuddenham in Suffolk to seek fame and fortune in London. Much of that fortune came from his client Prince of Wales, later King George IV, a man noted for his massive and constant unplanned over expenditure!

As we walked along, Mr Higgins told me a few tales of characters of old, one such being the 3rd Marquis of Waterford. A resident of the hotel, the Marquis delighted in taking pot shots at the hotels clocks and employing a Scottish bagpiper to play to the fullest extent his lungs would allow, whilst dexterously stripping himself naked!

On arriving at the hotel, a grand looking five storey affair, we set up stall in Mr Higgins usual corner of the Coffee Room, an odd name given that no one appeared to be drinking coffee. Virtually all the room's occupants were imbibing from large glasses called brimmers, filled to the top with a cocktail, based on Hodges Old Tom Gin, known as a John Collins, named after the former manager of the room.

As I had expected, the coffee room was both gloomy and smoky. Seldom had I seen so many members of the British Aristocracy crowded into such a dismal space. Aristocratic voices were braying loudly about the Sport of Kings, together with bawdy discussions about those not in attendance. In particular two characters named Bufty and Tufty who were the subject of a high degree of speculation about their libidos, and peccadillos relating to said libidos!

I was surprised to learn from Mr Higgins, who had been attending Limmers for over thirty years, that the atmosphere was more restrained than in former times, when fights and duels, with each other or those simply passing the hotel, were all the rage!

We were soon being visited by a steady stream of well-spoken punters, all with brimmers to hand. When confronted with a client with a particularly unwise idea of how to invest his money, Mr Higgins might suggest they a look again at the form book and consider a lower level of wager. This honest approach had served Mr Higgins well, with assorted young lords believing they were less likely to be thrown to the dogs than by bookies with less scruples.

And about bookies for whom scruples were never the order of the day, with neither Padwick or Hill in attendance, the Danebury crowd were represented by Tom Pedley, difficult to miss due to his equally loud voice and waistcoat. Pedley's clients, looked rather younger and indeed drunker than Mr Higgins.

In between writing down the various wagers, I listened out for the conversation going on around. Much of the discussion concerned Hermits unexpected win in the snow at Epsom. Doubtless many of the participants were talking through their badly battered wallets but Mr Machel was patently not a popular man and to my surprise neither was Harry Chaplin, who I had always assumed to be a highly popular figure in the world of racing'

There seemed however to be a high degree of support and sympathy for the Marquis of Hastings, albeit maybe not such a surprise, when most of the attendees, the bookie being an 'honourable' exception, had doubtless also lost thousands between them!

It was also clear that Mr Lewis's was right to be concerned at the level of unhelpful gossip. Whilst I heard no one outright accuse Mr Chaplin of being responsible for Lord Coggles death, he was certainly featuring in the speculation. Of Lord Coggles there was little comment, perhaps not a surprise given he was not an habitue of Limmers.

After a couple of hours, Mr Higgins decided that it was time to take a break for something to eat. Having eaten already I opted to wander the room and see if I could strike up conversation with other clerks. I did not have to wait long, before I was approached by another clerk, a burly fellow, with the seemingly standard colourful waistcoat, albeit even he seemed a little overwhelmed by the loudness of the waistcoat I had chosen to wear!

'Not seen you hear before' he commented in a jocular South London accent.

'My first time, standing in for Mr Higgins regular clerk. I've always been good with figures and been keen to get into the racing game'

'Well,' my new friend said' with a waistcoat like that I don't think many people will miss you!'

'You think I'm perhaps a touch too colourfully attired' I asked.

'Nothing wrong with being colourful my old mucker but you don't want to upstage the later day dandies floating around this room'

'I'm taking it you have been involved in racing for some years' I enquired.

'Yes indeed! I started out as an apprentice jockey to the trainer Porteus de Villiers but like so many lads, I quickly became too heavy, but I was always good with numbers. Mr de Villiers often placed his own wagers with my now employer Mr Edgar Billingborough, bookmaker to the nobility – or at least a fair smattering of those who frequent this dark and dingy room'

I decided it was time to introduce myself, or at least to introduce this evening's alias 'Joshua Pecksmith, trainee clerk to the nobility'

'Pleased to meet you Joshua, I am Benjamin Twelvetrees, Benny to my friends both old and new'

'On the subject of friends, he continued' a good way for you to meet people in the know is to pay a lunch time visit to 'The Only Running Footman' in Charles Street, just to the west of Berkeley Square. Quite a few of the Danebury Confederacies lads drink there and they're always well in the know, even if it takes a few pints to get them sufficiently loquacious to tell you what's in the know. All being well I'll be there the next couple of lunchtimes '

This was manna from heaven, first conversation and an invite to mix with the Danebury mob!

'That is most generous Benny, and I will look forward to seeing you there very soon'

After saying goodbye to my new friend, I made my way back to join Mr Higgins, who had returned to his position, replete from his repast and armed with a John Collins brimmer.

We had been taking bets and altering prices to keep Mr Higgins betting book over-round for an hour, when the room broke into a warm round of spontaneous applause from both gentry and bookies. I wondered if it might be Bertie, Prince of Wales but instead, placing himself down on a Chesterfield in the middle of the room was Harry, Marquis of Hastings, fresh back from Paris.

I was pleased that my temporary employer Mr Higgins was not one of those to join in the applause, unlike Pedley, who bellowed the loudest of huzzahs!

I had expected to see with Hastings another doyen of the over-loud waistcoat, the chortling mound of blubber Viscount Zeals. Instead, it was a quite a different figure sitting, or more accurately gently sliding down the Chesterfield, Lord Woldingham, son of the Earl of Remenham. Not a regular member of Hastings inner circle, more an occasional emissary.

An altogether slighter figure than Zeals, or Hastings for that matter, Lord Woldingham was known to be a doyen of the opium dens of the East End and regular partaker of, a new one on me, Heroin. All apparently stemming from a childhood addiction to Ayers Cherry Pectoral!

As for Hastings, he waved a lazy hand acknowledging the applause and with a wide sweep of his arm ordered brimmers all round. He was soon joined by a steady stream of equally louche young men welcoming him back into the fold.

It was not long before Tom Pedley himself came over to express his own barely concealed delight at having Lord Hastings back in the fold. For his part, Lord Hastings looked far from delighted to see Pedley. It was obvious that he had no desire at all to be the Confederacies next tasty target!

By 2.00pm, Mr Higgins declared it time to pack up for the night and get some sleep. I had apparently passed muster in the clerking stakes and if ever I fancied a change in career to let him know. I thanked him profusely and said I would make sure that another time, I would abandon my hideous waistcoat in favour of something a little more dapper.

On leaving, I could see the Marquis was now in full swing, carousing with all around him. As for Lord Woldingham, he had slumped to a point of being almost horizontal, the result no doubt of a large injection of opium or heroin.

With it being so late and the omnibuses having ceased to run I hailed myself a cab and reflected that our key objective, an introduction to the underbelly of the Danebury organisation, had been achieved far quicker than I could have hoped.

When I finally reached home, as my head hit the pillow, my last thought was that one clearly needed a lot of stamina to be a bookie!

Chapter 23 – The morning after Limmers and with no suet in sight, the Mate settles for a recap over coffee and a nice bun!

I was due to meet The Mate at 10.30am in The Strand, and rather unusually The Mate had requested that instead of a pub, we should meet in a coffee shop. The Mate's general view on such institutions being, that they were the work of the temperance movement and those devils 'The Chartists' currently melded together in a movement known as 'Temperance Chartism'!

In this instance however the lure was not just the fact that Café Divan on The Strand, served possibly the best coffee in London but for a one shilling entrance fee, one received not just a cup of excellent coffee but also one of their equally fine cigars and, when time allowed all the papers to read and a game of chess. We had never played chess together, The Mate claiming I had far too strategic a brain for him and if we'd been in the Crimea, I would have had the good sense to find an Intelligence post, miles behind the front line rather than rushing up a hill dodging canon fire!

It was, therefore, no great surprise to find The Mate already ensconced in a high-backed leather armchair, devouring both that mornings copy of the Thunderer and his first cigar, which would soon be two since as a non-smoker he knew I would feel obliged to pass over my cigar - but not my coffee!

'Good day Jimmy and how did you find Limmers? A touch too dark and smoky for my tastes' the Mate remarked, through a large plume of his own cigar smoke!

'A very interesting evening Mate and fully convinced me that gentleman's tailoring is an altogether healthier occupation than bookies clerk!

I quickly talked The Mate through all I had seen and heard, eliciting the occasional harrumph and an even larger harrumph when I mentioned the speculation about Mr Chaplin. As well as a well meant 'bravo' at news of my breakthrough concerning the Danebury crew.

The Mate then talked me through his extraordinary meeting with Tobias Bracklesham, albeit The Mate still seemed quite put out at having to gulp down his glass of Fladgate's excellent port.

With the recap complete, I suggested that in view of our forthcoming meeting with Mr Chaplin and Mr Lewis, we should review what we had found out and next steps

'Quite so Jimmy, just what I was going to suggest but you've beaten me to it again!

'Good to know Mate that as ever, we are on the same page!

After half an hour of further discussion, by which time The Mate had finished my cigar as well, we had agreed that the dossiers offered the prime motive for the murder, and we now had two live suspects in the Danebury Confederates and Tobias Bracklesham. We could not however, rule out there being dossiers and therefore more potential suspects.

As for next steps The Mate advised that he intended having a further word with young Mavis, to see if the passing of a few more days may have recalled something else that might aid our cause!

For my part, I was going to find a quiet spot to put all our notes into a detailed form ready for handing over to Mr Lewis and Mr Chaplin this afternoon'

And with that The Mate was up and out of his seat' No time like the present Jimmy I will make haste to Pimlico with alacrity!

'See you at Euston this afternoon Mate!

I was out of Café Divan just after the motivated Mate and as I had half-expected, he had opted to take a slight deviation and was heading back up The Strand, towards Caldwell's, purveyors of fine baked delights. I concluded that The Mate's powers of detection would doubtless be enhanced by a high-quality bun!

And it was at that point, I put down Jimmys notes, a cracking read as they were, but I had promised Sir John I would go no further.

Chapter 24 - Back to Pimlico, a catch up with Ernest Enderby!

It was not until late afternoon Monday, after Sir John's return from London and a session on his memoirs that we returned to the murder of Lord Coggles, albeit without reference to his visit to Caldwell & Co!

After leaving Jimmy, with no cabs in sight, I spotted an omnibus with the word Times painted on the side. This told me it was a Tilling's Bus the only one of the otherwise motley collection of bus operators I and many others trusted.

Rather than advertising a route and then simply stopping wherever they pleased, Tillings followed the radical policy of having a fixed timetable and then sticking to it, hence the nickname on the buses. Once inside the bus, I was greeted as old friend by the conductor, one Joseph Edge, who proudly informed me he was Thomas Tilling's first employee in 1846 and is I'm told still conducting to this day!

We soon reached the southern end of St George's Gardens on the South Embankment, just past Vauxhall Bridge, from whence it was but a few minutes' walk to the Enderby abode. On arrival, I knocked on the door and was met by the friendly young maid, who informed me that Mavis was not in but would let Mr Enderby know I was here.

I was shown into a small drawing room, where hung on the wall was a Lincolnshire landscape, by the celebrated artist Peter de Wint. I had bought one for Mrs Astley from the winnings of Aceta in the Cambridgeshire Handicap. Whilst delighted to have made my Eleanor happy, keeping more of the £5000 in winnings may have helped me to avoid borrowing money from that infernal man Padwick!

Within a couple of minutes Ernest came bustling into the room. Whilst a little stout, he nonetheless possessed a rapid gait and a general air of good health, doubtless aided by long walks across the Wolds with his beloved dogs. He was closely followed by the young housemaid with a pot of coffee and a plate of Huntley & Palmers excellent Garibaldi and Osbourne biscuits.

'To what do I owe the pleasure John? He asked.

'I am not sure if Mavis may have mentioned but together with my friend Jimmy 'The Flying Tailor' Patterson, we are assisting Harry Chaplin in a few enquiries about David's murder. The police and the Marquis of Hastings private detective Field are taking an unwarranted amount of interest in Harry, as opposed to trying to find poor David's killers'

'Sorry John but I do not recall Mavis having mentioned that. I have however, at both Whites and The Travellers Club, overheard unpleasant title tattle, of which I heartily disapprove, linking Harry to the crime.'

'I had been hoping that Mavis might just have been able to bring something to mind from that dreadful day that might be of help. I appreciate she must have been very upset, but I was very impressed by the fortitude she is showing'

'The Enderby's may not be one of the great families of England, but we've shown admirable fortitude in hanging onto our small part of Lincolnshire for over seven hundred years. And now, that small part of the county is providing Mavis, together with her mother, an escape from being a focus of public curiosity'

'A very good idea Ernest and I doubt many of the denizens of our national newspapers will find their way to Bag Enderby in a hurry' I joked.

After a slight pause Ernest asked' Can I be candid with you John, given how many years we have been friends?'

'Of course you can Ernest'

'Despite his inexplicable devotion to the Marquis of Hastings, Lord Coggles seemed to me a young man with a strong sense of duty who had it come to pass, would have proved to be a most honourable husband for my daughter. What I am not sure about is whether he and Mavis were a present-day Abelard & Heloise.'

I nodded my head in agreement, together with a note to self to see if these two might give any clues to the current case!

'Whilst I am sure that there was a level of devotion, I am not sure either my daughter or David's hearts were truly in the betrothal. My wife Jane, I know believed it to be a matter of true devotion, for my part all I want is for my daughter to be happy.'

I had wondered' he continued' if there might have been someone else for whom Mavis held a candle, I know she admired Harry Chaplin very much and she mentioned to me that one of the Marquis's friends was keen to be her suitor, but I was sure that was not reciprocated'

I was about to ask Ernest who, when there was a knock at the door and the maid reappeared, begging our pardons, but reminding her employer that he had to be in Temple Bar for a meeting at Child & Co.

'My apologies John, since the Countess of Jersey passed away in January it's been all change at the Bank'

'Fully understood Ernest, albeit I try hard not seeing anyone from my bank Holts, even though they remain keen to see me!'

When the Maid had left, Ernest promised to mention my visit to Mavis and with that, we wished each other goodbye. With it now being noon, I decided that I would walk the hour and a bit to Euston, the exercise would do me good and allow me the luxury of stopping at The Porcupine in Charing Cross Road for one of the excellent pork pies (definitely my last for the week) and quick pint of Whitbread's Pale Ale to quench my likely thirst. Dating from the 18th Century the Porcupine had once been the home of the Freemasons from the Lodge of Confidence, whose centenary I attended three years ago and a jolly fine evening was had by all, but like many of my little stories probably best saved for another day!'

I dwelt rather longer than I had intended over my pie and consequently had to trot on at a vigorous pace but contended myself, that I had hopefully walked off the effects of lunch!

Chapter 25 – A visit to Lewis becomes a mad dash to the Chaplin residence with a most unwelcome outcome!

Huffing and puffing rather more than I would have done in my running days, when the army food I was fed seldom promoted any form of over-indulgence, I arrived at Euston on the stoke of 2.00pm.

Even by today's standards of colossal railway termini, Euston Station was an essay in opulence, no doubt something Mr George Stephenson was trying to achieve. To the front of the station sits the 72 feet high Arch, intended to represent a magnificent gateway to the North!

To the left of the Arch sits the Victoria Hotel, intended for passengers on a reduced budget, and to the right my destination, the Euston Hotel, designed to cater for First Class passengers, willing it was believed to pay more for an extra dash of luxury.

Despite my best efforts, both Jimmy and Lewis had arrived already. Tea and some rather delicate looking cakes awaited and from my first sip, the tea was far from the dark brown liquid served up at many a station rest stop!

'My apologies' Lewis commenced' but Mr Chaplin' seems to have been unexpectedly delayed but I am sure will be with us very shortly,'

In the meantime, we started to debrief Lewis with all our news. By a quarter past the hour, I was just about to relate my mornings discussion with Ernest, when Lewis called out' Over here Oswald?'

I turned my head to see rapidly making his way across the room young Osmotherly. It was immediately clear that his appearance was not expected by Lewis.

'My most sincere apologies for disturbing your meeting gentlemen but soon after you left this morning Mr Lewis for your meeting with Lord Pucklechurch, a young police constable arrived at the office, sent by Sergeant Proudfoot.'

Please explain young man' I exclaimed.

'The Sergeant wished us to know, that Inspector Tanner would be making his way shortly to see Mr Chaplin, with the aim of bringing him in for further questioning, given further evidence that has just come to light!

'What evidence' I exclaimed' there is no evidence'!

To which Lewis added' Whilst sharing your strong doubts as to the voracity of any such evidence, I would suggest gentlemen there is not a moment to lose. We must put our discussion aside and make haste to the Chaplin residence!'

Fortunately, our location made the hiring of a cab the work of a moment and we were soon heading out of the station forecourt, with maximum haste, our driver heavily incentivised by Lewis to get to Harry's London home as rapidly as possible.

I doubt I had ever travelled quite so fast in a cab but despite our record-breaking journey, as we pulled up outside Harry's home, coming out of the large front door down the steps was Harry followed by Inspector Tanner. To either side of Harry were, two of the largest be-whiskered policemen I had ever seen, their foot high top hats perched most precariously upon their heads.

Belying his sedentary job but not his youthful years, Lewis was out of the hansom in a trice.

'What is the meaning of this he shouted over to Inspector Tanner' albeit the meaning was all too clear!

Tanner politely but firmly explained to Lewis that he now had sufficient evidence to arrest Harry and to take him into custody, a witness having come forward who had positively identified seeing him on the Burgh Heath Road on the night in question.

'Aside from the fact that your so-called witness can only be profoundly mistaken' Lewis responded' I hardly consider it necessary to have my client publicly escorted from his house by what appear to be the two largest policeman this side of the Euphrates!

'I can assure you I treat all suspects the same. It is not something that brings me any pleasure, but justice needs to be the same for all. I have sadly found that otherwise law-abiding citizens may find themselves pushed to commit the most heinous crime, even when they would never dream of committing the pettiest of felonies'

'Whilst I've no doubt Inspector that from your long firsthand experience, you may well be correct' Lewis responded' I can assure this is not the case with my client and I will be needing to 'examine' this so-called evidence as soon as possible'

To which I felt compelled to add 'Here, here, never heard so much bunkum and indeed piffle in all my life!'

Attention however moved quickly from my righteous chuntering to the shocking sight of the burly officers bundling Harry unceremoniously into the back of a Black Mariah.

'Don't worry Harry' I called out' we'll have you out in no time' I am not sure if he heard what I had said but if he had, I could not have blamed him if he reflected that despite our best efforts, he was heading towards a currently very uncertain future.

Everything had happened so fast that the carriage in which we arrived was still there, the driving looking as shocked as us as to what had just happened. Lewis quickly commandeered the carriage so that he and Osmotherly could follow on to Scotland Yard to try and persuade the police as to the folly of their actions. As he climbed back into the cab, Lewis asked if we could be at his office for 3.00pm the following afternoon.

Finding ourselves alone, we decided to repair to the nearest cafe and over a desultory pot of tea, Jimmy and I reflected on the events we had just witnessed. Whilst we had the utmost faith in Lewis, we had to accept the dismal likelihood that the case could well proceed to court.

All of which left us, as men of action, needing to act! For my part I was still mightily annoyed about events on my last visit to The Albany and intended to return, with the aim of seeing Bowlhead, without the odious presence of Bracklesham.

For Jimmy's part he would be making his first visit to the 'Only Running Footman', to make the acquaintance of the Danebury Confederacy underlings in their natural habitat. The afternoon would see us meeting with Lewis and for the next day, a return visit to Epsom and The Spreadeagle would be the order of the day!

Having said goodbye to Jimmy, I opted for another quiet walk home rather than a visit to the Club. I generally enjoyed nothing more than the good company of likeminded men of the world, but this was not one of those evenings. My walk certainly ensured I spoke to no one, whether it helped to clear my mind of its current jumble of conflicting thoughts I was less then sure!

On my way home, I picked up a copy of the final edition of the Evening Standard and as I had feared, it carried the headline 'Derby Winning Owner taken into custody for murder of peer'. I paused to sit on a bench to read the article. Much as to be expected, it was long on speculation and limited on facts, the only real 'fact' being that a witness had come forward claiming to have seen Harry that night which, together with other apparently compelling 'evidence', had persuaded our brave 'boys in blue' to arrest this dangerous fugitive.

The article seemed to describe a completely different person to the honourable man I knew Harry to be, leaving me to wonder if the entire staff of the paper had backed Vauban or Marksman in the Derby and were talking through their collective wallets. Also getting his own special mention was ex-Inspector Field, for the role he had been appointed to by the mendacious Marquis!

On arriving home, I had little appetite, so merely asked Mrs C to kindly cut me four rounds of beef, gammon, chicken and cheese sandwiches, with the usual assorted pickles to stave off any pangs of hunger.

I retired to bed in a depressed state unable to banish from my mind the peril that Harry found himself in and a determination to put things right!

Chapter 26 – Another visit for The Mate to The Albany but with a different result than the last one!

Fortunately, I managed a better night's sleep than I had expected. The large tumbler of brandy I had mixed in with the mug of warm milk Mrs Crumpbucket brought me doubtless aided my rest, as well diluting the terrible taste of milk!

Come the next morning, my intention was to be at The Albany at around 11.00am, meaning I had time to deal with some of the increasingly high pile of unopened letters on my desk. Prominent amongst them were the large Estate related envelopes. I decided that time was too short to do them justice, but I would see to them very soon! Instead, I answered a few simple Estate letters, enough to 'convince' myself I was doing everything I could for Eleanor and the nine mouths at home that needed constant feeding!

I left home at 10.30am and quickly hailed a cab to take me to the Albany. The cabbie seemed unusually focused, with no suggestion of a stop for early morning drinks. I soon discovered why, for on my seat was a pamphlet produced by one of my mortal enemies, The Temperance Movement, extolling the alleged virtues of a life of sobriety! Even the almost complete absence of jolts along the journey, was not enough to persuade me to sign any pledges renouncing the demon drink!

I alighted from my cab outside of Burlington House on Piccadilly, acquired earlier that year by the Royal Academy who were undertaking some substantial works. Rather less substantial than the Government, who had intended to knock the building down and replace it with the new University of London, a potentially sad end for such an impressive structure.

Quickly putting aside my architectural musings, I made my way up Sackville Street past the Metropolitan Ear Institute. where I had some years before gone to see the founder Dr James Yearsley, having come back from the Crimea half deaf from standing beside too many canons. The one and only time I have ever met an Otologist!

Dragging myself away again from yet more extraneous recollections, I spotted, no more than thirty yards ahead, a young man limping along with some difficulty. As I drew closer, I realised I had struck lucky, it was clearly Viscount Bowlhead, this time with Bracklesham nowhere in sight!

After a few more yards, I called out in my heartiest of tones 'My dear fellow, just who I had been hoping to see'

Bowlhead turned round in surprise and some degree of apparent alarm not I think realising from whom the cheery greeting had come 'Why Mr Astley, what a surprise'

'A welcome one I hope?'

'Oh quite, quite and at least no ruffians in wait' he replied with a wan attempt at a smile.

'It was that I came to see you about last night'

At this point, Bowlhead looked rather confused.' It may be due to taking a bump on the old noggin' but I do not recall our arranging to meet'

'Well, that's very interesting my dear fellow' I replied.

By this time, we had reached the Sunderland Arms, almost empty at that time of the morning, and I gently guided Bowlhead through the door to a discrete spot at the back of the bar, calling out to the landlord John Hawes, with whom I was familiar from my running days, to bring us two pints of Gordon's Imperial Double Stout.

Bowlhead seemed a little surprised but did not put up any objection, albeit from what I had observed, fate had dealt him a supremely acquiescent personality!

'Sit down my good man, a pint of Gordon's never fails to perk one up. I hope you are feeling a little improved from the other nights misfortune?'

'Some way below topping Mr Astley but a little less pained'

'Good man, good man! Any idea as to who the ruffians might have been?'

'It all happened so fast; I remember very little' he answered quietly' hence my not wishing to involve the police.

I was beginning to wonder if this was because he might have some inkling as to the identity of his attackers, or because he was never very certain. Rather difficult to say either way!

'Thank you for your help that night Mr Astley' he added his voicing almost tailing off completely. Needing to keep the conversation going, I shouted across to the bar, two more pints of your finest Imperial Stout please Mr Hawes. Another glass of Gordon's my dear fellow and you'll start feeling considerably better!'

Bowlhead looked very unsure as to whether another pint was really what he wanted but to my no great surprise acquiesced again!

'I am not sure if you are aware' I began' that together with my friend Jimmy 'The Flying Tailor' Patterson we are doing some independent investigating into the terrible murder of David Coggles. As I am sure you cannot fail to have heard, the police have got a damned fool notion into their heads that Harry Chaplin was involved'

'No er smoke without ahem fire perhaps Mr Astley?'

Making sure to keep my temper I replied, 'in all seriousness do you really see Harry Chaplin as the kind of man who would lure an old friend out into the darkness of the night and then murder him?'

'Well, er no' he mumbled gulping down some more beer,' he'd not be someone that would come to mind in that respect. To be honest Mr Astley, if you don't mind my saying, I find Chaplin a touch arrogant, but an unlikely murderer'

'Good man! Get the rest of that pint of Dr Gordon's medicine down you and we'll have another'

'Oh well er perhaps not this time'

More beer bar keep I called to Hawes'

'I can assure you' hoping to goodness I was correct' it will not be long before all suspicion is cleared away and Harry will be there to lead Hermit into the winners enclosure at Royal Ascot Getting to the muttons of the matter' I continued' I wanted to speak with you about that ill-fated night in Epsom, given you were in the room when David unknowingly left for his final destination'.

Bowlhead hesitated a moment, still looking rather vexed 'Before we get to, as you put it, the muttons of the matter, can you tell me why you thought we were meeting the other night because I issued no such invitation'

At this point I thrust my hand into my pocket and brought forth the badly scrawled letter inviting me round for supper and handed it over with a flourish. 'Exhibit A! As the headed paper confirms, straight from your rooms in The Albany'

'But that is not my handwriting' he stammered. From the look on his face, I was confident he knew full well whose handwriting it was but preferred to keep up the pretence of not knowing. 'I am very sorry, if you had a wasted evening since neither I nor my man Davenport were there, I was with friends out in Barnes for the evening '

'I am indeed fully aware that you were not there since I did indeed make my way over for what I thought to be a kind invite to supper. It was not however a wasted evening since I did find someone waiting for me'

'There was?' his voice becoming quiet again.

'Someone you know very well indeed'

'Charles Dickens perhaps? I'm told he's awfully ubiquitous' which I assumed to be a feeble attempt at humour.

'Little less ubiquitous and rather less loved by the public at large. It was your good friend and confederate Tobias Bracklesham.

'But that cannot be possible' Tobias was at an evening soirée at the Mayfair home of Lord & Lady Quantock'

'I think not my dear chap, he was at your home, and I must compliment you on the excellent Fladgate's Reserve in the crystal decanter on your Chippendale sideboard

'Oh, I see you really were there' he conceded almost inaudible now.

'Indeed, I was there. Would Bracklesham happen to have a key to your set of rooms?

'He did ask for one the other day, Tobias was concerned that the bump to my noggin' may have increased my forgetfulness'

'Are you forgetful?

'Not that I'm especially aware, albeit I guess I wouldn't know if I was so forgetful' he replied with yet another weak attempt at humour.

'Bracklesham invited me' I persevered' posing as your good self, on the pretext of discussing the events of the other night outside of Boodles. Instead, I was treated to a rapacious diatribe, accusing me of being behind the attack on you and warning me against blackening his fine name! Something which, from my observation he needs no help in achieving himself!

"Oh dear....

'I knew little more about Bracklesham than his family's confounded tonic. What I have now learnt, has led me to view him as a most unpleasant and reckless young man. I can well understand why David had serious concerns about him, on behalf of the Merry Marquis, and even more reason to hold a hearty dislike himself'

This was inevitably followed by a double' Oh dear oh dear'

Resisting the urge to tell Bowlhead to pull himself together I decided a gentler approach was needed. It was difficult to see any malice in Bowlhead, or I'm afraid any obvious sign of a backbone being present beneath his frock coat!

'Would I be right in thinking that it was Brackelsham's suggestion for a night's convalescence in Barnes?

'Er that would be correct; I agreed it would probably be for the best, though in truth lying in my bath for a very long period would probably have been my preference'

'I think we both know that this was not the reason for getting you out of the way. Can you think of any reason why, aside from warning me off, your ever so caring friend, might not wish us to continue our little investigation, could it have been to do with David Coggles?

'I am sure that Tobias was acting with the best of intentions'

'You cannot really believe that Bowlhead?' I asked trying to mask my incredulity.

After what seemed a rather interminable pause and with the deepest of breaths taken, Bowlhead finally restarted

'I will admit Mr Astley that Tobias was no great admirer of David Coggles but pretended to like him to placate Lord Hastings. In private however he mockingly referred to David as 'Little Lord Morality', a man lacking the good humour of even the driest subsidiary character in a Trollope novel!'

I was about to intercede, but Bowlhead seemed to have finally got into this stride, the beer no doubt proving to be a useful stimulant'

'I always liked David, unlike most of the Marquises friends, he seemed to care what happened to Lord Hastings and was not there just for the merriment, which could be quite wearing at times'

'I can see that may not have made him popular; I replied

'It certainly did not with Tobias, who seemed to have got it into his head that David was keeping some sort of dossier on him, and I am none too sure as to the efficacy of Tobias's behaviour in relation to Lady Amelia'

Perhaps it was the beer or more the fact that deep down, Bowlhead felt able to say what he really felt, without Bracklesham around. It was certainly proving to be a most interesting conversation.

'And of the fateful evening in question' I gently asked again.

'From what I can recall, the evening started around noon and the group were in high spirits by the time we reached the dinner table. All except David, who seemed very preoccupied. I recall, the Marquis was gleefully anticipating the money he expected to be winning when Hermit lost and the hoped for ruination of Harry Chaplin. It was generally very difficult to tell which gave him the most potential satisfaction

At that point the rapid intake of beer seemed to have got to Bowlhead, who now appeared close to nodding off. I doubted I would get any more from Bowlhead, but he had provided further grist for the mill when it came to our view that Bracklesham was a live suspect'

'You know Bowlhead, you are allowing yourself to be led by a bully, in fact I would go as far as to describe Bracklesham as a perfect bounder. You should get yourself as far away from him as you can!'

After another significant pause...' I will try Mr Astley, since I know you to be right'

'And if you remember anything else that might just help to find David's killer let me know'

'I will indeed sir'

'Good fellow and now I must be off' I rather doubted he would come up with anything but one never knew and I was also far from sure if he would take my advice! Really not a bad young man but far too easily put upon.

At which point Sir John' leapt from his chair declaring 'All good things must come to an end and sadly this is one of them! I must ready myself for the annual dinner of the Federation of Trades and Industries of Brigg. An organisation of which I have the privilege of being Chairman, presumably due to my equal lack of knowledge of either subject.

'I don't suppose' he continued with a twinkle in his eye' I would be able to stop you reading on to say around the end of Chapter 12 of Jimmy's notes whilst I am out this evening!

Chapter 27 – Another visit to a well-known hostelry for Jimmy in the line of duty!

I had intended to try and hold out until late in the evening, but it was at little more than eight o'clock when I had curled up in an armchair in the library and began to read the next instalment of Jimmy's notes.

'On returning home still shocked by the dramatic events of the afternoon, my first action was to pen a letter to Belvedere, the Duty Manager at the Spreadeagle saying I would be in Epsom the following day and would be grateful for an hour of his valuable time.

Given I had met Belvedere in the guise of crusading undercover journalist Tommy Cornelius, I could not easily send the letter with any form of return address, so would have to trust to luck that he would be there. Based on the readiness with which he had accepted a 'reward' for the information obtained last time, I had few doubts he would be keen to make my acquaintance again. I suggested that we reconvene at The Amato.

Moving to another of my alter egos, I had decided to make my appearance as Joshua Pecksmith, trainee bookie to the nobility at around 1.00pm at the Only Running Footman. As with Belvedere I would have to trust to luck, that my new acquaintance Benny Twelvetrees would be there.

First stop on my way was The Alhambra. I had decided that I needed to don something a little less sartorially vivid, most especially replacing the deerstalker with a little less noticeable headgear!

Suitably attired, I continued my way to Charles Street to the pub, I had read that, its full name 'I am the Only Running Footman' was, at 24 characters the longest pub name in London and on arrival, the pub sign was noticeably wider than normal!

Once inside it was clear that the Footman was a very a popular lunchtime watering hole, the air thick with smoke from a combination of cigars, imported American cigarettes and a few of the old gents, with spectacularly bad dental work, puffing away on their clay pipes!

After purchasing a pint of Bass, I made my way around the Saloon bar, squeezing my way between one group and another but no sign of Benny. Alighting upon an empty single table and chair, conveniently half-hidden behind a column, I quickly sat down.

I had been sitting for no more than ten minutes, quietly reading my copy of Bell's Life, when the group to my right opted, as one, to give up their seats for a burly group of 'gents' who were, it would seem the regular habitues of that spot. They did not look the type with whom to debate the point.

From the first minute of their loud conversation, it was clear that, by happenchance, I was sitting right next to a group of Danebury operatives. Ones who I suspected, dealt on occasion, with some of the more physical aspects of relieving the aristocracy of their inheritances!

For the most part the discussion, liberally littered with the most popular profanities of the day, centred around horse racing tips and their assorted ribald views on the members of the establishment, with whom the Confederacy had dealings.

Almost inevitably, conversation turned to the news of Mr Chaplin arrest. I'd hardly say sentiment was positive towards Mr Chaplin, nor for that matter Lord Coggles. The seeming leader of the group, a large man with a giant dome of a head, bent nose, florid complexion and non-aligned ears, probably the result of a stint of prize fighting, declared Lord Coggles to have been a 'Dratted nuisance and a moralising flapdoodle!

In response, the smallest of their number, a rat faced man with a highly furtive air, declared 'nothing turns up soon and we'll be paying our first visit to Lincolnshire enquiring after Little Lord Coggles moralising masterpiece' which was met with a rasping cackle from Cauliflower ears.

This certainly made my own ears prick up, since these could well be the two Belvedere had referenced as having visited the Spreadeagle. After this, conversation returned to more ribaldry about assorted 'toffs' and much speculation about an appearance in the office of someone referred to as The Cat, something that seemed to cause amusement and curiosity in equal measure. The consensus being that something must be afoot if he was about, albeit I did not doubt, something was 'always afoot' in the offices of The Confederacy!

By this point time had moved on and with the meeting with Mr Lewis being at 3.00pm, I concluded that I should bid goodbye to the 'The Footman' but would be back.

It had indeed been a most enlightening visit, proof positive that the Confederacy remained very keen to lay their hands on the dossier but nothing yet, to link them to the murder of Lord Coggles. They were however, still fully justifying their status as our favourites to be behind the murder.

I will admit the temptation to read the next chapter of Jimmy's notes was strong but once again I decided to fall in line with Sir John's request. Somehow, I was convinced he would know if I hadn't!

Chapter 28 – A meeting with the legal bods and The Mate sends a message!

Sir John's evening with the Federation of Trades & industries of Brigg proved to be a rather more restrained affair than expected, meaning we could start work earlier than expected and as Sir John put it, 'We can have a quick canter through the Hermit Affair, prior to a full-scale gallop through 'My Sporting Life. Hopefully bringing closer the flurry of nonesies, that will once again be bulging out of my trouser and waistcoat pockets!'

After leaving friend Bowlhead to sleep off his unexpected visit to the Sunderland Arms' Sir John commenced' I popped into The Ship & Shovell at Charing Cross, for a slice of their rather excellent Lark pudding, washed down with a small bottle of Adey & White's Champagne Nectar. Odd name for a pub, apparently denominated after Admiral Sir Cloudsley Shovell who together with 2000 of his men, sadly lost their lives in the Isles of Scilly Naval Disaster of 1707, but there I go digressing again.'

From Charing Cross I hailed a cab to Lewis's office. In between bumps I was able to find time to read The Sporting Times, or The Pink'un as it was more normally known on account of the salmon covered paper on which it was printed. Whilst ostensibly a sporting paper it was equally well known for the vituperative nuggets of gossip it contained, mercifully nothing about Harry Chaplin but sadly only likely to be a matter of time.

I was soon ensconced with Jimmy, Lewis and the ever-present Osmotherly in the now all too familiar library, with its row upon row of heavy legal tomes. Still to my mind of rather less interest or value than good old Bradshaw's!

We quickly gave our legal friends updates on our respective activities since last, we had met and advised that we would be making our way back down to Epsom to follow up on some leads, making ourselves sound every bit leading lights of the noble fraternity of detectives!

Lewis listened and after a pause for consideration, chin cupped in his hands, gave us his thoughts.

'As ever gentleman your efforts have been of great value, and I think we can safely conclude that both Mr Bracklesham and Mr Padwick's Danebury Confederacy are both very keen to locate their respective dossiers. In the meantime, I have been informed that Mr Chaplin's case is due to go before Middlesex Magistrates next Wednesday morning at 11.00am. Suffice to say we will be doing our very best; to get the charges struck out at this juncture but unfortunately not even Demosthenes himself could write a speech that would guarantee success.' I was tempted to ask if we could perhaps hire this chap to help but did not want to impugn Lewis's own abilities!

Lewis went onto explain the mechanics of what would occur on the day. Whilst I'd had a few scrapes as a young man, with a strong attraction for removing Peelers hats from their heads without getting caught, neither Jimmy nor I had any experience of the workings of a court.

We departed Lewis's office, confirming that we would see them on Wednesday and in the meantime, leave no stone unturned to help get Harry out of this dreadful situation.

After saying goodbye to Jimmy, as so often when I needed to think, I decided that rather than get the Metropolitan Railway back, I would walk at least a part of the way, my aim being to pick up a cab in The Strand.

I had been mulling over in my mind from my conversation with jockey Dalrymple, his throwaway remark about one of Hastings acolytes, not being what they seemed. I had no doubts this was Tobias Bracklesham and I needed to find out more.

At that precise moment, perambulating the short distance that forms the historic street of Lothbury, I found myself, by good fortune, outside of the Central Station of the Electric Telegraph Company in Founder Court.

The building was narrow but nonetheless rather grand with Ionic pilasters, stone wreaths of flower and a sunken panel into which was engraved the words 'Central Telegraph Station. I walked up the steps, into a most capacious hall, easily seventy foot in length. I made my way to the Counter and gave the Clerk my message 'Hope well, ref our last conversation need to speak with you about Harry H's friends. Many thanks, Astley'. I handed over my shilling but received in response, a quizzical look from the Clerk' It would help sir if you could tell me where I might find the recipient Mr Dalrymple?'

That was a good point, since I was none too sure where Dalrymple lived! I opted to send it care of trainer Winchelsea in Lewes, hoping it would get to him swiftly. With that, and much to the relief of the queue already forming behind me, the Clerk placed the message onto a tiny 'lift', pressed a bell to alert the clerk in the office above and turned a winch elevating the tray on its merry way to be sent out by a Cooke & Wheatstone Electrical Telegraph machine!

Job done; I made my way down Old Jewry to Cheapside to pick up a cab. By the time I reached home I felt rather weary, no doubt due to the realisation that our mission to help Harry was no longer simply asking a few questions but instead, potentially a matter of life and death!

I had Mrs Crumpbucket prepare me a light supper of oysters, soup, venison with vegetables and potatoes, a small salad (mainly there so I could tell Eleanor hand on heart that I wasn't eating wall to wall suet) and a steamed carrot pudding with vanilla sauce to finish.

I made my way to bed early and was soon asleep with no need of a sleeping draught or nightcap.

Chapter 29 – A train trip to Epsom for Jimmy and his sidekick!

Come the next morning I awoke invigorated and set off in good time for the station. For Waterloo, as well as being London's largest rail terminus, is also, without doubt, the most confusing! Opened in 1848 by the London & Southwestern Railway, with only four platforms, it has grown haphazardly, with Platform One, still in its original position, now marooned in the middle of the station!

The Epsom train was due to depart from a platform adjacent to the private line of the London Necropolis & National Mausoleum Company, which had been built to take the bodies of recently departed Londoners to the companies 200 acre cemetery at Brookwood in Surrey! Not a subject upon which I was keen to dwell at the best of times, particularly given the ghastly predicament facing Harry Chaplin.

I was joined by Jimmy at the ticket office, and we were soon on our way.

On alighting from our train at Epsom, given we were not due to meet Thaddaeus Belvedere until 1.00pm earliest, we decided to stop for a reviving cup of coffee at the Railway Hotel. A better option than risking whatever local ditchwater might be masquerading as the aforementioned beverage at the station café!

Before setting off to meet Belvedere I asked jimmy what role I should I play in this most impressive fabrication?

'I think Mate, Tommy Cornelius's ever reliable Number Two! At which we both laughed, albeit I was left with a strong inkling that despite the comment being made in jest, there may well have been more than the odd grain of truth there too! No matter we worked as team and getting Harry out of jail remained the only aim rather than my ridiculous pride!

On arrival I found The Amato, to be an altogether less pre-possessing place than the Spreadeagle, with not even a cheese roll on the menu, let alone a decent pudding. Albeit well suited for a discrete chat.

We made our way to the lounge bar and fortunately, our luck was in, as a smartly dressed figure from the corner of the empty bar called out 'over here Cornelius'. It took me a moment to realise it was Jimmy he meant!

The bar was gloomy and heavy with cigarette smoke, despite the absence of any other patrons and none of us partaking. Belvedere was a tall man of about fifty with what I had no doubt to be dyed black hair.

He had no drink to hand, clearly awaiting the generous largess of Jimmy's alter ego. I was duly introduced as Jimmy's assistant, Fredie Fotheringham and as pre-agreed, for the greater good, dispatched to the bar to purchase two pints of J.D. Mantell's Mitcham Brewery Best Bitter for us and a large glass of whiskey for Belvedere.

On returning to the table, the others were already deep in conversation.

'So, Mr Belevedere, have there been any more visits from the gentlemen from 48 Berkeley Square? Jimmy enquired.

'Gentlemen' he sorted' I'll be raised to the Earldom of Essex before those two make it into the pages of Burkes Peerage?

'Are you able to describe them? Jimmy asked solicitously.

'The larger one, a Mr Dalston, if that was his real name, looked like he'd gone twenty rounds with the Redditch Needlepointer and the smaller, a Mr Hoxton, a devious rat faced looking fellow.'

After a pause he added 'not the kind I'd necessarily want to meet of a dark evening if you get my drift'

We did indeed and from looking at Jimmy, I could see he was certain they were the two he had sat beside in The Footman.

'Has anyone else come by seeking to recover something left at the hotel that fateful night' Jimmy enquired, with a look that suggested there 'could be more in this for you?' A bait taken up immediately by Belvedere!

'Well, It could mean nothing at all but a couple of days ago, I had a rather odd visit from one of the late Lord's friends Mr Bracklesham, a far less agreeable gent than Mr Chaplin.'

'And to what did you owe the pleasure of this visit?'

'He too was very interested to find out if any form of dossier or notebook had been handed in, since it would undoubtedly be his property. I asked for a description, but he assured me that he would definitely recognise it if he saw the thing! Different tack from the other two with no offers to make it worth my while. Sufficed to say he went home empty handed as well, I wasn't sure if he seemed disappointed or even pleased that nothing had turned up! Odd bunch Coggles friends, the only one of the Marquis's friends who does not seem to have been drunk or coshed was Lord Zeals!'

How come? Jimmy enquired?

'He didn't arrive until late' his train was delayed and with his valet apparently unwell, he probably got confused trying to carry his own luggage to the hotel'

Jimmy continued to ask further questions, but it was clear that we had got all we could from Belvedere, and Jimmy discretely passed him something for his trouble saying we needed to get back to London, which unlike our little subterfuge was at least true!

Just before we left Belvedere remarked to Jimmy that' Your 'young' sidekick doesn't seem to say a lot then peered at me and said' Don't I know you from somewhere, you remind me of one of those fancy caricatures you see in the magazines of our so-called betters!'

I was rather nonplussed by the question but hastily denied being anyone he would know and that even my dear wife, would not want to spend the cover price of Punch Magazine on a caricature of yours truly!

Belvedere seemed satisfied with my answer, which was just as well, since I didn't fancy too many questions on my role of sidekick!

After leaving the Amato we trotted back into town, managing to get the train back to London by the proverbial skin of our teeth. Once ensconced in our seats and my long awaited first Partagas Cuban cigar of the day lit, we sat back to review our trip to Epsom.

For my part, I was still convinced, the Confederates were behind the murder. They may not necessarily have meant to kill David Coggles, merely rough him up in pursuit of the dossier but the net result was David was dead and the evidence he had built up against them was still at large.

Jimmy however urged that given his appearance at the hotel with such an improbable story, together with what we had learned about him in recent days, Bracklesham must be considered a live suspect. Albeit given he was eight hours into a major drinking session with the Marquis and friends, he did not appear well placed to have committed the foul deed himself.

We further agreed that in conclusion, we needed to be able to actually link either party to the crime and it would be awfully helpful if we knew where to locate the dossiers ourselves!

Upon arriving back at Waterloo late afternoon, with neither of us having had a feed since breakfast we agreed that some sustenance was needed. Albeit on expressing my concern, Jimmy did wryly suggest that I should remain confident that I would not simply fade away!

Rather than take the more leisurely option of leaving the station to find somewhere of higher repute, we took the convenient option of using the Station Refreshment Room. My hunger filling pork pie did little to enhance my view on railway catering. Jimmy, with more good sense opted for the pot of tepid tea and a slice of chocolate cake, before setting off for his promised once a week visit to his grandmother in Poplar.

One thing I had decided whilst musing over my cigar on the train, the time had come to go and see Harry, Marquis of Hastings. I could not shake the feeling that he might know something that would help. Whatever his dislike of Harry Chaplin, he surely owed it to David to help!

Chapter 30 – The Mate makes straight to see a Marquis!

With there being no time like the present, I made my way to The Boltons in Kensington, to a large four storey house, London home to the Marquis of Hastings.

I pulled on the doorbell and was answered by a footman, ostentatiously grand but to my mind ever so slightly tipsy. Given his employer, maybe not a total surprise.

'Can I help you sir?'

'I hope you can my good fellow. I would like to see your employer as a matter of the utmost urgency. I passed over my calling card and was shown into the morning room. Quite some minutes passed before finally, the footman reappeared but instead of announcing the Marquis, it was the Marchioness, the famed Pocket Venus who appeared!

My concerns that a small army of tipsy footmen would arrive to send me away with the proverbial flea in my ear, were quickly assuaged by the charming reception I received. I confess my views on the Marchioness, her delightful visage aside, were heavily weighed down by the way in which Harry had been treated.

After thanking the Marchioness for seeing me I continued 'I feel I should offer you an explanation as to why I am here'

'I believe I have a very good idea Mr Astley why you wish to see my husband and the subject would be Mr Chaplin. I am not certain how palatable or otherwise you would have found his answers. For my part I will never believe Harry could possibly be guilty of the heinous murder of poor David'.

'I am fully aware' she continued' of all the detective work you and your friend are doing to help Harry, particularly given my husband's own detective ex-Inspector Field helped place Harry in his current state of incarceration' As the Marchioness spoke, I could see a small tear gently venturing its way down her fine features.

'I am both gratified to find that you in accord with our view, that a man as noble as Harry Chaplin could not possibly be guilty of such a crime. I am also gratified to be accorded the title of detective' which I am pleased to say produced the smallest of smiles, albeit it could not stop a second tear from gently following the course of its predecessor.

The Marchioness paused to dab away her tears before continuing. 'I know there is nothing I can do to reverse the terrible wrong my husband and I perpetrated on Harry. I had concluded that I admired rather than loved Harry Chaplin and I was indeed taken by my husband's raffish charms. Without wishing to sound disloyal, I am not without my regrets, but I have made my choice and must live with the consequences'

I found it difficult not to be touched by her obvious distress at the situation in which Harry found himself.

'If you would be willing to answer a few questions, even unknowingly they might further our amateur investigations'

'Of course I will Mr Astley'

All I had to do now was to think of some pertinent questions! I decided to start by giving the Marchioness some general background about our suspicions of the Danebury Confederacy, the dossier and see where that might take us.

After listening carefully, the Marchioness responded 'I too admired David he was a devoted friend to my husband, a devotion never truly appreciated. I know he was very worried that the Marquis would fall into the hands of the Danebury Confederacy, or unholy mob as he called them.'

'I cannot pretend to admire many of your husbands' actions, but I do not wish to see anyone fall into their web, it will not end well.'

'My husband is equally anxious not to fall into their clutches, but I am fearful that David may have been the last person left able to save him and indeed us from that fate. Sadly, of the dossier I know nothing, but its emergence would be very welcome'

I decided to try a different tack 'Maybe' I enquired' you might know of someone within your husband's inner circle who might have wished David harm?

I was sure I saw a flicker across her fine features' Oh I cannot imagine that to have been the case, if poor Bowlhead were forced into mortal combat with a common house fly there could only be one winner'

'It was not Bowlhead' I advised. 'It is Mr Tobias Bracklesham of whom I am speaking'

'Oh, I'm sure it could not be Tobias, but her eyes seemed to me to tell a different story'

I was just about to try and press further on this point when there was a knock at the door and a young maid entered the room, to remind the Marchioness that she needed to complete preparations for a dinner engagement.

The Marchioness offered her profuse apologies and promised that if she could think of anything that would be of assistance she would be in touch. She also added rather tellingly' 'As for the Marquis he is otherwise engaged, by which I really mean I have no idea where he is aside from the fact that it will doubtless involving drinking or gambling but most likely both'

Whilst my visit had unfortunately not moved our investigations forward one single jot, I was left with a feeling of sadness. I could only imagine that the bed of roses in which The Marchioness had chosen very publicly to go and lie in was extremely thorny! I doubted however, that I would hear from the Marchioness again.

On arriving home, I opted to dine on Mrs Crumpbuckets lamb stew, accompanied by a burgundy and a large slab of St Clements Steam Pudding, I needed something to set me up for what was going to be a big and indeed very unwelcome day come the morrow.

Chapter 31 – A most unwelcome visit to court for The Mate and Jimmy!

Next morning, Jimmy joined me at 8.00am for a light breakfast of eggs on toast, fish, porridge, bacon, sausage, pork chops, and cold-smoked herring or in Jimmy's case, toast! Once fully sated, we set off at 9.30am for the pre-trail at the Middlesex Sessions House on Clerkenwell Green, requiring yet another trip along the Metropolitan Line from Baker Street to Farringdon Street Station. With it being peak time, a train soon arrived, packed to the gunnels as usual. I found myself pressed much nearer than I wanted to one of the gas lamps lighting the compact wooden carriages. I was sure that with this being the world's first underground railway, lessons would be learned and in centuries to come overcrowding would be a thing of the past!

On alighting from train, it was just a few minutes to the Court, which was just as well, since the trial had attracted a large crowd, all keen to watch one of the landed gentry standing where, more normally stood those of humbler origins. Fortunately, Lewis had been able to reserve us a couple of seats. There would undoubtedly be many disappointed people unable to gain entry, doubtless retreating to the nearby Crown public house to continue their speculations, over an early pint of Whitbread's from its nearby Chiswell Street Brewery.

The Middlesex Sessions House, despite the grim nature of its purpose, is a rather grand edifice, dating from the 1780's and built in the Classical style with rusticated blockwork and four Ionic columns to the front. I am no great student of architecture but have received plenty of lectures on the subject from my erudite father-in-law, so clearly something must have stuck in my brain!

The most impressive feature is the dome which covers its entrance hall, the staircase a copy of the Parthenon in Rome, birthplace of yours truly! We were not however there to admire the architecture and on arrival we were greeted by young Osmotherley.

'Good to see you both, I will take you directly to your seats. Mr Lewis is making final preparations, and I am pleased to say, that Mr Chaplin is in good spirits.' Harry had been brought from the nearby Middlesex House of Detention, or as it was also known the Newgate Prison, where later that year a group of Irish Nationalists blew a sixty feet hole in the prison wall in an unsuccessful attempt to rescue several of their compatriots!

The seats we had been allotted provided us with an excellent view over an already packed Courtroom, looking towards the presiding magistrate. I took the opportunity to look around and see who might be there. No surprise at all the Marquis of Hastings was there and to my mind, appeared to be revelling in his rival's predicament.

Zeals was, as to be expected, chortling away and seemed to be treating the hearing as more akin to a day at the races. As for Bracklesham, I'd best describe him as having a look of grim satisfaction upon his face. Bowlhead was there too, looking decidedly uncomfortable, tightly hemmed in by Bracklesham to one side and the bulky figure of Zeals to the other. Next to Zeals was Lord Woldingham, who already appeared to be sliding down his seat.

There was no sign of Padwick, Hill or Pedley, albeit I had few doubts that emissaries of the Confederacy would be somewhere in the Court, possibly given the setting one of the less shifty looking of their associates!

In a prominent spot near to the prosecution team was ex-Inspector Field, sitting in front of Inspector Tanner and Sergeant Proudfoot. Close by was the more reassuring presence of Jem Machell.

Come 11.00am the Usher, not without some difficulty, brought the noisy Courtroom to order and the five Justices of the Peace entered the room. They were led in by the septuagenarian Sir John Scott Lillie. A former Lieutenant Colonel in the British Army, whilst simultaneously a Major General in the Portuguese Army, in his spare time Lillie had invented both an early form of machine-gun, as well as a mechanism for kneading bread!

Next to enter the Court, flanked by two more of the Met's largest Rozzers, was Harry Chaplin. It felt like the start of Adelphi Screamer melodrama in the theatre of that name but unfortunately this was real life.

In a booming voice, reminiscent of one accustomed to addressing a large regiment, Sir John asked Harry to confirm his name and address. Harry answered Sir John in a most assured manner, a man confident in his own innocence. This was the first time we had seen Harry since the arrest and I whispered to Jimmy, that he seemed in remarkably good fettle considering the frightful situation in which he found himself.

With the formalities over, Sir John invited Hardinge Giffard QC, later to become famous for representing Thomas Castro, a butcher from Wagga Wagga in his claim for the Tichborne estate and baronetcy, to outline the case for the Crown Prosecutors.

After some initial scene setting, Giffard began by Harry asking about the disagreement between him and Lord Coggles the afternoon before the latter's murder. Harry responded confidently 'As explained to the police, the argument merely concerned the merits of my horse Hermit and whether he should run in the following days Epsom Derby.'

With a feigned air of quizzical surprise, Giffard asked whether Harry would like to elucidate further. To which Harry replied that he felt no need to elucidate further but as an English Gentleman, could assure the Court that it had no bearing at all on the terrible murder of Lord Coggles.

Harry's response drew an audible reaction of surprise from the gathered throng who were clearly enjoying the 'show'. Giffard merely observed he was sure that Members of the Bench would draw their own conclusions from this answer!

'Moving on from the disagreement with Lord Coggles' Giffard continued' perhaps you would feel able to be more forthcoming about the note found indented in your hotel blotter.

To this Harry responded' I did indeed write a note that evening, but it was not directed to David Coggles and given it has no bearing on the case, I see no reason to discuss further in this courthouse.' Clearly Lewis had not been able to persuade Harry to confirm the recipient.

After another gasp of surprise from the public gallery, Giffard moved on to the main plank of the Crown's case' Were you not on the Downs the evening of Lord Coggles tragic murder, with no alibi and bruising to your face, having left a dinner engagement unexpectedly early?

Still with the same assured confidence Harry replied' I was indeed on the Downs that night but headed directly back to the Spreadeagle Hotel, which is in completely the opposite direction to where poor David was murdered, my journey only interrupted by a stumble in the dark which resulted in the bruising to which you have referred.'

'As you will be fully aware Mr Chaplin' Giffard continued with equal confidence' we have a witness who confirmed that he had seen you strike Lord Coggles on the Burgh Heath Road that night'

'He may well be willing to swear that he witnessed such a fight, but he is clearly completely mistaken as to who was involved, since I was not there!'

Giffard asked, with what seemed to be almost a tone of feigned amusement, if Harry was absolutely sure he had nothing to add to what he had said?

To which, Harry confirmed he did indeed have nothing to add and was perfectly content with the answers he had given. Thereafter, Giffard lost little time in recommending the Bench to commit the case forthwith to the Old Bailey!

Speech over, Jimmy turned to me and whispered' I'd not want to speak out of turn Mate, but I am not certain as to whether the answers Mr Chaplin has given are going to help his case?'

'Quite so Jimmy' I have few doubts that Harry's decision not to comment further was done for the most honourable of reasons, but a more pragmatic approach may well have yielded better results' I replied.

Lewis quickly rose to speak on behalf of Harry, asserting calmly but authoritatively his client's complete innocence and proceeded to do all he could to undermine the Crown's case, ending with a firm recommendation to the Bench that they should dismiss this case forthwith!

With Lewis finished, Sir John announced that the Justices of the Peace would be retiring to consider their decision. Barely fifteen minutes had elapsed before they reappeared and in booming tones, Sir John confirmed what we had been fearing, the case was to be committed to trial at the Old Bailey on a date to be decided. Upon which, the Court inevitably broke into a cacophony of excited chatter and shouting.

Rendered almost inaudible by the din, Sir John ordered the burly policemen remove Harry from the Court. With Harry having been committed to trail, he would be taken immediately on a half-mile subterranean walk through a dank, dark and foul-smelling tunnel under the streets back to Newgate Gaol!

Of Newgate, nothing good could be said. The gaol had been in operation since the 12th Century and although the original building had been lost in the Great Fire of London, conditions in the Sir Christopher Wren designed replacement were apparently dreadful and would I have no doubt come as an awful shock, even to someone as stoic as Harry Chaplin.

With the Court moving on to new business, practically the whole of the public gallery rose as one still chattering excitedly, with many doubtless moving straight to the nearest public houses, to continue their lurid speculations and inform those already imbibing there awaiting news.

With the honourable exception of Bowlhead who looked shocked, the result did not seem to be causing his friends any great distress. The Marquis himself looked very satisfied, from Zeals the inevitable chortle, Woldingham did not appear to know quite where he was and as for Bracklesham he looked almost triumphant. What a loathsome young man and one with plenty to hide!

By the time we had extricated ourselves from the gallery, we found Osmotherley waiting patiently for us in the huge hall, with a request to kindly join Mr Lewis at his office for a meeting, before scurrying off in pursuit of his employer.

On leaving the Sessions House we passed William Calcraft, the official Newgate executioner. A man who had worked his way up from merely flogging the prisoners to hanging them! Since the advent of the train, he had been able to take his macabre profession around the country to other gaols. No offence to the man but probably not the person I wanted to see at this moment!

A rather more welcome sight than Calcraft, Jem Machell came across to speak with us, looking the angry side of livid.

'Good to see you Gents and doubtless like you both, unable to contemplate what is happening in front of our very eyes'

'Sadly, all too true Jem but we're still doing all we can to help'

'I know that Mate but detections not the easiest game, any more than betting (albeit he spoke from the vantage point of someone who had made a huge success of that difficult area of life)' Must be off back to Newmarket but make sure to let me know if I can be of assistance'

After saying goodbye to Jem, we hot footed it to Lewis's offices, where it was straight into the now all too familiar legal library, where Lewis immediately took up the running.

'Good of you to join us today gentlemen and much as we would have liked it to be otherwise, we had anticipated that the case would be referred to the Old Bailey. To this end, I would like to introduce to you Mr Montagu Williams QC who has been appointed to lead Mr Chaplin's defence.

A young man in his early thirties, Williams was tall, debonair of good bearing with dark hair, a monocle and like me an Old Etonian former army officer. There however, the similarities ended, for as well as being called to the Bar in 1862, Williams enjoyed a parallel career as an actor and playwright working with F C Burnand, who according to Jimmy, wrote amusingly for Punch Magazine's younger rival Fun!

Beneath the wit and charm, it was clear that Williams was a man of intellect and doubtless a highly persuasive speaker, I didn't doubt his thespian experience would come in handy in court.

After introductions and the acceptance of a Russian cigarette, offered round by Williams, it was down to business. Our lawyer declared himself confident that he could demolish large parts of the Crown's case, particularly the lack of a compelling motive on Harry's part. His request of us was to continue our efforts on finding out everything we could about Bracklesham, the Danebury Confederates and preferably lay our hands on the Dossiers! Of Padwick he admitted that on his sole introduction to the man, he had found him to be an oleaginous hanger on to the great and the good!

For our part he confirmed' We will continue with all matters legal and like my friend Lewis, I will be doing my very best to persuade Mr Chaplin that, he might wish to take a pragmatic view on matters of honour and explain to whom his note was addressed!'

The meeting soon came to an end and finding ourselves in need of sustenance, we alighted upon that relic of the 14th Century, the Ship & Turtle in Leadenhall Street. A place so keen to ensure that its patrons knew they were eating turtle and not any kind of substitute, Mock Turtle soup I am told coming from calves' brains, that the walls were lined with aquariums filled with the blighters!

With the unspoken concern we both felt if justice did not prevail in Harry's case, neither of us felt inclined towards ending the life of one of the turtles at this moment and opted for stewed rabbit and savoury vegetables. As one who favoured a slightly healthier approach than I to food and drink, Jimmy persuaded me to try something called Perrier Water, which he assured me was becoming quite the thing and known as the 'Champagne of Mineral Water's! Frankly, I'd still rather wash my rabbit down with a pint of Jenner's Empress Pale Ale, but at least it wasn't a bottle of Bracklesham's Tonic!

By the time I returned home, having spent the rest of the day with my father's estate lawyers I felt very tired, and decided that a good night's sleep was the order of the day. To that end, on going to bed I mixed a glass of Mother Batley's Sedative Solution with a drop of wine, I've seen the effects of too much laudanum, but a judicious tincture can work wonders as proved to be the case!

Chapter 32 – A letter from Bowlhead and The Mate takes the train west to Windsor!

The following morning feeling refreshed I read the morning papers over my breakfast, Inevitably Harry's hearing was the main headline, pushing aside further debate on the recent rejection by parliament of votes for women.

I had half an hour to spare, before Jimmy was due to come round, time enough to quickly go through my mounting correspondence, so much of which I had been putting to one aside. There were the usual begging letters from well-known bookies, albeit I tended to put them aside anyway, one from Drewitt about entries for Ascot and another from Mrs Astley telling me that, I really needed to deal with the estate's business including the three bulky envelopes sent down several days previous.

At the bottom of the pile was a letter with the now very familiar crest of The Albany, this time it was in the neat hand of Viscount Bowlhead himself, rather than that of 'friend' Bracklesham.

I quickly tore the letter open and read the letters surprising contents.

Dear Mr Astley,

Having seen you and your associate Mr Patterson at today's hearing, I felt compelled to write.

Like any law-abiding man I wish to see David's killer brought to justice, I do not however think for one moment that Harry Chaplin is guilty. I can also say, without fear or favour, that I was dismayed by the reactions of my associates. However much Lord Hastings might be trying to recover from the loss of his Scottish Estate, he seemed to gain a high degree of balm from watching Chaplin in the witness box and the reactions of Zeals and Tobias were no more edifying.

All of which led me to reflect again on the events of the fateful night when David met his demise. I am ashamed to say that due to my being too easily led and my needlessly imbibing far too much alcohol, my memory of the evening is not what it should be, I have however been trying as hard as I can to recall what I can.

By the evening, given we had been drinking since noon, things had become very raucous, to the obvious discomfort of the ladies and any other guests with the bad luck to be present. At around 9.00pm, Tobias declared himself to be feeling a little under the weather and made for his room. Given that Tobias was normally one of the leaders in the charge towards exuberant over excess, this was quite a surprise, and I recall the Marquis calling after him, that it was a good thing his room was on the ground floor, and he did not have to tackle any stairs!

I also recall being slightly surprised at this turn of event since Tobias did not seem unwell or, by his own heroic standards had he over imbibed to any great extent.

It was not long after this that David Coggles made his own abrupt and sadly final departure. The evening continued on its raucous way and best as I can recall, Tobias returned to the table about an hour later. Shortly after which Lord Zeals arrived, chortling away as ever declaring that the journey down had left him with a roaring thirst, with no time like the present to start the quenching process!

Of the rest of the evening, I can recall very little, as you will have seen for yourself, I am something of an alcoholic lightweight!

I will be returning to the family estate, from where I will seek to untangle myself from my confederacy with Tobias Bracklesham.

I hope my ramblings may be of help with your vital endeavours and if I have been of help, I will be pleased, if the fog of the evening lifts further I will be back in touch again.

With all good wishes,

Quinten Bowlhead

I had just finished reading, when there was a knock on the front door and Jimmy was ushered into my study by Mrs Crumpbucket, who also handed me a telegram from Dalrymple advising that he would be at Windsor races today and would be happy to meet between races.

After the usual felicitations, I handed Bowlhead's letter to Jimmy, who after perusing, responded.

'First thing that comes to mind Mate is that contrary to what we had thought, friend Bracklesham had the opportunity to both lure Lord Coggles up to the Burgh Heath Road and, by slipping out of the window of his bedroom, the chance to race up to the meeting place and commit the foul deed.

'Agreed! I replied' and a very positive start to the day thanks to the Viscount!'

Jimmy confirmed that he would be going back to The Footman to see what else he could find out and would, later in the day, drop off the latest case notes with the lawyers and see what may have occurred on the legal front.

For my part, I would be beetling off to Windsor, where I hoped that Dalrymple would be able to provide me with even more ammunition regarding Tobias Bracklesham, particularly now his odds had shortened!

Having said goodbye to Jimmy, I reached once again for Mr Bradshaw's trusty Railway Companion, its 946 pages for just one shilling being my best annual investment and most avidly read tome! I recall reading an article in Punch which said of Bradshaw's "seldom has the gigantic intellect of man been employed upon a work of greater utility!"

With Bradshaw's duly consulted, I was soon on my way to Paddington to catch a 10.27am train to Windsor and arranged to meet Jimmy at 6.30pm that evening, at the Station Bar back at Paddington.

As a child I had made my first visit to Central London into the original Paddington station on Bishop Bridge Road. The old station was, however, nothing like grand enough for Mr Isambard Kingdom Brunel's Great Western Railway, and he had a big hand in designing the much larger station we see now. The whole edifice was inspired by the Crystal Palace with a near seven hundred feet long glazed roof!

I found the terminal as busy as ever with a good few, bowler hatted gentlemen carrying copies of Bells Life and the Sporting Life, also making their way to the Windsor train for the races.

Unlike Paddington, the station that we pulled into at Windsor, was at that time little more than a glorified train shed. Once outside the station, I had no trouble hailing a cab and was soon on my way. The course, which had only opened in 1866, was picturesquely located to the west of the town on an island between the River Thames and the Clewer Mill Stream.

Once there, I quickly made my way to the Members Enclosure, where I espied Mr John Frail, the developer of the course, with whom I had enjoyed a splendid lunch on my last visit. A most enterprising chap, he had risen from humble beginnings to become political campaign manager for soon to become Prime Minister Benjamin Disraeli, . Frail was just the man, to help me get a message to Dalrymple in The Weighing Room, an area to which non-jockeys could not gain entry. With my girth, I was not going to persuade anyone that I would be riding the favourite in the first race of the afternoon!

Frail readily agreed to my request and quickly returned with a message from Dalrymple saying he would be riding in the first two races but had a gap before riding in the fourth. The message also came with a suggestion that Dalrymple was feeling very confident about his mount in the second race. Given my view that jockeys were the worst tipsters, I decided it was prudent not to take up this well-meaning recommendation, it duly cantered home by five lengths!

After the second race, Dalrymple emerged from the Weighing Room, and we made our way to a small office beneath the main stand that Frail had kindly made available for our use. Once sat down Dalrymple was keen to know how much I had made on his tip and looked a little disappointed, albeit not totally surprised that I had failed to follow his good advice!

I decided to provide Dalrymple with some background on how Jimmy and I came to be helping Harry Chaplin. Hence my interest in following up on his remark about one of the Marquis's acolytes not being what he seemed, to see if it tallied with our strong suspicions as to his identity.

'More than happy to assist Mate' Dalrymple responded eagerly.

'I know' he continued' there was a lot of surprise and doubtless talk when I upped and left the Marquis of Hastings' employ. His all-consuming dislike of Mr Chaplin, someone for whom I had also ridden and greatly admired, made me uncomfortable but he was, unlike many owners, highly generous, so overall I could have few complaints. It was not however the Marquis himself that was the problem but what was going on around him'

'I imagine that this is where one of our prime suspects Mr Tobias Bracklesham comes into the picture?

Dalrymple paused and looked at me with genuine curiosity' Frankly Mate, I consider Mr Bracklesham to be a lying braggard, but it is not him to whom I am referring.'

'But it must be' I responded urgently.

 No, I am talking about Viscount Zeals'

'Zeals', I exclaimed with incredulity' that chuckling clown'

'The world's foremost chortler he may be but behind the façade, resides an altogether more devious person'

'Zeals' I pointlessly repeated' but the man is a buffoon!

'Buffoon or not race fixing is not what one would expect from one of England noblest families, with the moto 'Fidelity to the Fore'!

'I see' I said with an involuntary expulsion of my cheeks.

'Like most jockeys' Dalrymple continued' I've followed the instructions of even the straightest of trainers to give a promising young horse a gentle introduction to racing, I don't however fix races' he added with force. 'Albeit I am, unlike many jockeys, good at tipping winners to those who listen; he added with an amused grin.

'Can I enquire if the Marquis was involved in these shenanigans?'

'For all his failings, the Marquis is no race fixer. Lord Zeals' he continued; asked me to go easy on one of the Marquises horses, at Newmarket, a horse in whom the Marquis had great confidence and intended backing accordingly. Whatever way one dressed things up, the meaning was clear he wanted to ensure that the Marquises horse did not win.'

'I had no intention of going along with what was proposed. I was, however, doubtful the Marquis would believe me, if I told him what had been said. Knowing Lord Coggles spent a considerable amount of his time protecting Lord Hastings interests, I decided to confide in him instead.'

'Lord Coggles had no doubts as to the voracity of my tale and said that he was already building up quite a case against Zeals, in what he jokingly called one of his 'Dossiers of Moral Rectitude. He was aware that the Viscount was particularly pally with that most unlovable of bookies Thomas Pedley, and already harboured strong concerns that he was working in league with him'

In the meantime, Lord Coggles kindly arranged for me to ride for the wonderful Prince Batthany's Austrian stable. Not quite the same as riding at Royal Ascot, but a diverting experience and took me out of the clutches of Zeals and his pals in the Danebury Confederacy.' My head was in a whirl as Dalrymple continued.

'Whether Lord Coggles told the Marquis about Zeals actions I do not know but before leaving for Vienna, I had the distinct impression that Viscount Zeals was aware of what Lord Coggles was doing. Since I've been back, I've tried to stay out of Lord Zeals way, at least his foghorn laugh gives me ample warning as to when he is about!

Before I knew it, we had been talking for half an hour and Dalrymple had to go back to weigh out for the next race, riding for Viscount Ventnor in his familiar lurid purple and green racing colours! I thanked him once again for his help and he promised to let me know should he learn anything more to our advantage.

For my part, much as watching just another race was always a big temptation, in this instance returning to London was the preferred option. As I left, I passed Lord Woldingham, who seemed to be in his usual supine stupor, making it difficult to tell if he was aware of my presence as I walked past, or even the young lady accompanying him.

I hailed a cab and was soon on the train back to London. Leaving Windsor Station one can see, to the right, the extensive grounds of Eton College, which inevitably left me reminiscing about my own school days, specifically the time spent on the playing fields and not the lessons! Perhaps no surprise that my alma mater has yet to invite me back to give a speech to inspire the present crop in their studies!

By the time the train pulled into Paddington it was 6.00pm and I made my way to the bar and ordered a reviving glass of Ben Nevis Single Malt. I was reminded of how some years back, after a successful day at Royal Ascot, I had bought a drink for a dishevelled but noble looking figure sitting alone in the bar. I soon established that I was speaking to Richard Plantagenet Temple-Nugent-Brydges-Chandos-Grenville, 2nd Duke of Buckingham and Chandos, who had managed to squander an income of £70000 per year and sink into bankruptcy with debts of over £1m in 1847, no wonder he had seemed so dispirited!

I was jolted out of my reverie by the sight of Jimmy bustling over to join me, holding in his hand as ever his notebook. And there Joseph, I am afraid we must stop to resume the sporting memoirs'!

Sir John's sudden fit of guilt did not come as a total surprise, given I had been told by Lady Astley that her husband has received a letter from Mr Thorold pleading with him to finally finish his magnum opus, without which, the ponies and monkeys would remain highly reticent about taking up their previously rightful place in his trouser pocket!

Chapter 33 – A quick recap with the Flying Tailor!

It was the following afternoon before we were able to restart the tale. Sir John admitted to having forgotten exactly where we were, aside from the fact it was yet another bloomin' railway terminus somewhere in Central London. Once reminded the words rolled off his tongue in their usual fashion!

'After the all-important task of ordering Jimmy a drink, in his case a dram of Old Pulteney from the Scottish distillery of the same name, we were quickly into our stride, informing each other of our respective doings of the day. Sensing that I clearly had a report I wished to get off my chest, Jimmy kindly suggested I open the batting. With which, I quickly ran through my eventful trip to Windsor and Dalrymple's explosive revelation about Viscount Zeals.

'Excellent work Mate, once again excelling in your role of lead detective' Jimmy exulted.

Whilst I had some doubts as to my role as 'lead detective', it was nice to have earned Jimmy's praise! I did however need to caveat that, unlike Bracklesham, Zeals had not arrived in Epsom until after the murder.

'Nonetheless Mate' Jimmy added' the ignoble Viscount needs to join our list of those, all equally keen to get a hold of their dossier and therefore a personage of interest'

'Agreed Jimmy and all we need to do now, is to establish which of them or their agents may have delivered the fatal blow to poor David! After my little revelation, pray tell Jimmy what of your day?

'A little frustrating Mate. I was setting off for the Alhambra to select another overly loud suit for my next visit to the Footman, when I received an urgent message from Mr Henry Hill, for which he offers you his profoundest apologies, asking if I could please help out on an urgent matter relating to his busiest customer Lord Whaplode. A man whose patience is more limited than his purse and who always insists on being measured up by yours truly!'

Whilst a little disappointed with this turn of events I knew Jimmy would simply redouble his efforts the next day. 'Understood Jimmy and I have met Lord Whaplode, a rather foppish and petulant young man in my view, who would doubtless have fitted in admirably with Beau Brummel and his fellow dandies of days gone by!

Once finished with Lord Whaplode' Jimmy continued' I hot footed it over to Lewis & Lewis, where I was able to obtain an update from young Osmotherley who confirmed, that the judge for Harry's trial will be Sir Maitland Mattingham, best known for his regret at no longer being able to send minor felons, union members and papists to the colonies. Not the trial judge the legal team would have chosen but one with whom our lawyer has dealt with successfully before.'

'Secondly' the name of the alleged witness, is Cuthbert Algernon Troutbridge, an export agent from Hackney specialising in importing from the Far East. Troutbridge was apparently paying his first visit to the Derby and became lost, trying to find his way his way to Epsom Downs Station, having erroneously started walking down the hill to Epsom's main station'

'One would have thought Jimmy that even the most myopic of export traders would have been able to spot a new nine platform station with a concourse on top of a hill. Then again given Mr Troutbridge appears to have been myopic enough to swear to having seen Harry when he was not there, perhaps not a great surprise!'

'Indeed Mate! The statement claims that by the time Troutbridge arrived on the scene, Mr Chaplin was standing over the body before beating a hasty retreat from the scene of the crime. It reads as if Troutbridge has taken advice from a lawyer with a devious turn of mind'

'Which instantly make me think of Old Man Padwick' I conjectured.

'Same here' Jimmy concurred' the lawyers are going to do what they can to find out who Cuthbert Algernon Troutbridge is and any known business associates

'Following on from today's diversion, Jimmy continued' we now have Mr Hill's solemn promise that however much Lord Whaplode or any other customer may demand, I will be free until the trial to do my very best to help unmask the real killer. My first step being to return to the Only Running Footman tomorrow lunch to make deeper inroads into the Confederacy'

With time having marched on we decamped to the nearby Victoria Pub in Strathearn Place where we partook of mutton chops, with greens and boiled potatoes. Yet another pub where one might run into that man Dickens, apparently Queen Vicotria had also visited in 1854 but no sign of either of them that night!

On returning home, my mind was a confused melee of all that had happened during the day, but a drop of laudanum soon saw me off to a good night's sleep

Chapter 34 – The Mate meets an old friend in Regents Park and Jimmy makes a new friend in The Footman!

I awoke the next morning with renewed determination to firmly link one of our suspects to that fateful night in Epsom!

I would be seeing Jimmy later in the afternoon for an update on his latest visit to the Running Footman, for my part, as so often, a good walk would hopefully provide the necessary stimulus to the old thinking juices. It was a bright sun filled morning just right for enjoying the delights of a walk-through Regents Park. Like many I stopped at the Boating Lake to reflect upon the sad demise of the forty people who had drowned there in January, when the ice broke, depositing over 500 people into twelve feet of icy water. It was my understanding that moves were afoot to reduce the depth of the water to something like four feet to stop this happening again.

I had just passed by the zoo and stopped to look in the cage of then the UK's only example of the Quagga, a rather odd-looking animal, like a zebra to the front and a horse to the rear, when I heard a French voice call my name'

I turned round to find that it was Mademoiselle Dupont, who I had met when we both went to the aid of Viscount Bowlhead.

'Good day Mademoiselle' I answered with a doff of my hat' and very nice to see you under more agreeable circumstances'

'And you too Monsieur Astley. I hope that your friend has fully recovered from his unfortunate meeting with those awful men last Wednesday night.'

'Still a bit of a limp but on the road to recovery!'

'It is, as you would say opportune that I should see you today'. This Tuesday one of my employer's dinner guests was the Earl of Birmingham, down in London from his Warwickshire Estate. Whilst his Lordship has a most refined voice, his valet had the same flat accent of one of the men I heard the night the poor Viscount was assaulted.'

I am not sure' she continued' if this would be of assistance' but I promised that I would let you know if anything further occurred to me of that night.

I thanked the Mademoiselle most effusively for what she had told me and said I was sure it would be of help. I could not immediately see how this was pertinent to our current investigations but made a mental note to ask Jimmy what he thought.

On leaving the Park, I found myself outside an office of the Magnetic Cable Company and took the opportunity to telegram Dalrymple to thank him again for his help. I added that I would be very pleased if he would consent to ride one of my horses sometime soon. I doubted if he would regard it as a career highlight but hopefully, he would appreciate the gesture.

By the time I had reached home, it was approaching lunch, and I asked Mrs Crumpbucket to kindly make a few rounds of sandwiches to accompany a large slab of her excellent homemade venison pie, together with a bowl of nuts and dates, to tide me over until afternoon tea.

I had resolved that I needed to get through some more of the estate paperwork whilst waiting for young Jimmy to return from his latest trip to the Only Running Footman. I decided to give myself a gentle reintroduction and concentrated on the thinnest of the envelopes, avoiding those that looked like bills and any that I clearly recognised as being from 'friends' in the bookmaking fraternity!

After a steady couple of hours work, interrupted by the odd quick glance at today's Bells Life, I had cleared all my paperwork save for the large packages of estate papers, which I vowed I would definitely deal with as soon as possible!

Jimmy duly arrived at Chez Astley for 5.30pm in time for a pot of tea and a light snack, of Mrs Crumpbucket's splendid langues de chat, chocolate sponge, wafers, petits fours, rice cakes and a plate of Macfarlane Lang's excellent Granola Digestive Biscuits.

'Once again' Jimmy began' the pub was as busy as it was smoky. I was able to find a stool beside a column, conveniently located near to the Danebury Stooges. As before conversation was dominated by the large gent with the florid complexion with regular comment from rat face.'

After a little while, a tall rather solemn looking gentleman, somewhat reminiscent of a country rector in appearance, came and sat the other side of my column, like me clutching a copy of the Sporting Life. We soon struck up a conversation on prospects for the forthcoming Salisbury races. My new acquaintance introduced himself as Cobblestone Coward commissioning agent to various noble clients. I duly introduced myself as my alter-ego from Limmers, Joshua Pecksmith, freelance bookmakers' clerk and one who carried out commissions of a diverse nature for well-connected individuals, which I hoped made me sound a man suitably in the know.

'Shrewd as ever Jimmy' I added.

'After another pint of Bass, generously purchased by the 'rector', our conversation moved onto the subject of Mr Chaplin, his current incarceration and his chances at the forthcoming trial. I advised Cobblestone that I had some serious doubts about his guilt.'

'Interesting you should say that' he replied' adding that he too had reason for doubt, not something he believed to be shared by others, looking directly at Ratface, who was at that moment making some egregious comments about Mr Chaplin.

Encouraged by his response, I decided to test the waters and suggested that clients of mine, sympathetic to Mr Chaplin's plight, could be interested in finding out anything that might assist in clearing Mr Chaplin. He looked at me in a slightly quizzical way, so I added that my clients realised that there could also be a need to cover a helpful parties normal expenses' added with a very slight nod of the head.

Coward took a few moments it seemed to turn things over in his mind before suggesting, that we get together tomorrow afternoon for a quiet perambulate around Kensington Gardens.

Where, the 'rector' suggested, we would be out of ear shot, of those more likely to prefer a few more hours in the One and Only Footman

'Well Jimmy, as ever you have excelled yourself! Given you have not met this gent before, do you wish me to act as your trusty flag bearer Freddie Fotheringham?'

'Tempting offer thought that is Mate, I think the presence of another party, at this stage might spook him. From what I observed today, I am hopeful that Mr Coward might have something very interesting to tell us about the Danebury Confederates'

I could see the point, albeit I was left with the feeling Jimmy might not rate my abilities to stay inconspicuous too highly and in the event of things not going as planned, I retained upmost faith in Jimmy's ability to sprint to safety!

By this time the Thomas Tompion grandfather clock in the corner of my study had ticked round to around 7.00pm. Jimmy readily accepted my offer of a glass of Egan's Fine Golden British Sherry but when I confirmed, that Mrs Crumpbucket had prepared one of her finest beef suet puddings I observed, not for the first time, Jimmy suddenly remembered an urgent reason why he needed to get home, which at least left more pudding for me, with a large helping of Nesselrode to finish.

Chapter 35 – No sign of Mr Payne at the Club but a very interesting lunch instead with Sir Carlton!

Come the next morning, I awoke a little later than I had meant, possibly consuming all Jimmy's portion of suet pudding had not been such a good idea after all! In the circumstances I settled for a light breakfast of porridge, eggs, bacon and fish.

I had not formulated an exact plan as to how I was going to match Jimmy's progress yesterday but had concluded, that we could benefit from speaking with someone impeccably trustworthy and in possession of a large intellect, with whom I could talk through how I might further my own investigations and I decided I knew just the person!

I had been absenting myself from the Old Turf Club for fear of having to discuss this very subject but now it was an imperative, since the person to whom I wished to speak was my dear friend Mr George Payne, who could usually be found there mid-morning, partaking of coffee and a gentle game of cards.

I set off for the Club at a brisk trot and was there within half an hour. On arrival I made my way to the morning room but no sign of George, only the rather less welcome sight of James Merry. Why did I always seem to keep running into him at the most inopportune of moments!

I tried to leave the room without his noticing me, but I'm none too well equipped at looking inconspicuous! He duly looked up from his paper and fixed me with his usual glower. I had never managed to tell which was a friendly glower and which a hostile one!

'Morning Merry' I called in my most jocular way, something I knew he detested.

'Oh, it's you Astley, how are you finding the world of detection. Last time we spoke your 'client' was enjoying fresh air rather than the foul stench of Newgate, not exactly going to plan!' I had no idea how we had allowed the man into our Club!

'I remain confident Merry that the truth will out, and justice will prevail!

'Oh, I am sure it will' he responded dryly.

Whilst keen to end our conversation very quickly I was even keener to find out if George was in the building'

Have you seen my esteemed friend Mr George Payne, Merry? I asked.

'Payne. On his way to Salisbury to watch another of his nags run, doubtless losing him more money' with which he resumed reading his paper.

Not the answer I had wanted but I decided that, before leaving I would just have a look in the Reading Room to see who else was around. I received a much pleasanter surprise there when, on entering the room, I spotted Sir Carlton Scroop. It would be good to know how David's family were bearing up under the terrible strain of what had happened'.

'Carlton, wonderful to see you my dear fellow' I called across to him, Ignoring I'm afraid the quiet rules of the Reading Room.

'Good to see you too John, perhaps we should' he replied in a sotto voce tone' make our way to the Lounge' to which I nodded my assent, speaking in understated tones not being one of my great skills.

Once sat down in a quiet corner of the Lounge and a pot of coffee ordered I commenced 'It must have been no more than a week since we last spoke and so much has happened in that brief period'

'Indeed, it has John, indeed it has. I really cannot believe that the Crown and the police are still proceeding with this nonsense in relation to poor Harry!

'Too true Carlton, but that nonsense will be overturned' I responded with vehemence. 'How are Bunky Utterby and the Countess?

'Still, I'm afraid in a state of shock but it is good that they have all of their children back at home with them.'

'How is dear Mavis doing' I asked next' when last I saw her, she was holding up remarkably well.'

'She came over to Scroop Hall for tea whilst I was up in Lincolnshire, and you are right, holding up remarkably well'

'The family' Carlton continued' were able to hold a small and private funeral for David on Tuesday, helped no doubt by the church being on the estate and David's uncle being the local vicar'

After a slight pause whilst the Steward placed our coffee and biscuits on the table, we recommenced.

.'Changing tack Carlton, I am curious to know which of David's friends may have attended the funeral'

'From the Marquis' Sir Carlton responded' Just a letter expressing regret for what had happened but no explanation, as to why he would not be able to able to attend the funeral of the man who had done so much to protect his interests!'

'Sadly, not a great surprise to me' I sighed' and what of the others?'

'From Tobias Bracklesham not a word but a most touching letter from Viscount Bowlhead who had some very fine things to say about David. One who did attend was Lord Zeals! Mercifully less boisterous than usual, most solicitous to Mavis and the model of profound grief for the Earl and Countess'

Wherever I turned, Zeals seemed to come into the conversation. I could not help wondering if his attendance was motivated by a keenness to acquire a certain dossier.

'And what John of your own investigations? Carlton enquired.

Whilst conscious of a request from Lewis not to discuss the case our investigations with anyone else, in George's absence and with Carlton being a trusted friend and already aware of my involvement, I was sure he would prove a welcome substitute and possibly one who could come up with some new ideas.

That being the case, and emphasising everything needed to be in the strictest confidence, I explained all we had found out so far: our view that the dossiers played a key role in finding who murdered David Coggles; the three parties we had identified as suspects; where they were on the night of the murder and the mysterious Cuthbert Algernon Troutbridge, of whom Carlton declared himself unaware.

At the end of my summary Carlton finally had a chance to speak! 'My goodness John you and Young Jimmy have been busy, I am most impressed

'As you know from our previous conversations, we had already passed on our suspicions regarding the Danebury Mob, but frustratingly the police proved unwilling to take any notice of what I overheard that night in Stockbridge.

'I fully understand your frustration John, the Danebury Confederates are an unsavoury bunch and whilst I could not see Padwick, Hill or Pedley dirtying their hands they have access to people who will'

'And Tobias Bracklesham? I enquired.

'A rather boorish young man, who I can best describe as a less drunk but considerably ruder version of the Marquis of Hastings. Someone who strikes me as not unwilling to do what was needed to further his own ends'

'From my recent experiences, I'd say you were spot on there.'

'As for Zeals, a real surprise, he has never struck me as over bright, but you always know he if he is present!'

'Too right Carlton, never did a man chortle so much without any obvious reason'

After a slight pause Carlton added' Last time I saw Zeals was on Epsom Station the night before the Derby not even the 7.00pm train from London could drown out the chortle!

Our laughter at Carltons comment was interrupted by the Steward coming over to ask if we would be partaking of luncheon today, which was to be Hachis Parmentier, the Clubs attempt at trying to make Cottage Pie sound haute cuisine, to which we readily consented.

Once the Steward had left, Carlton picked up the conversation again.

'Concerning the missing dossiers John, could you not look to turn them to your advantage?'

'Not quite sure I follow your drift Carlton' I responded a little puzzled.

'What is to stop you telling all three parties you suspect that you have their dossier and use it as a way to smoke out the killer'

'But' I replied still a trifle confused' I don't have even one of the damned dossiers or know where to find them'

'But they don't know that, and my bet is that the one responsible for David's demise will be the one willing to take the biggest chance to acquire their dossier. You'd need to take sensible precautions, but you survived the Crimea, even with a cannon ball through your neck, and Jimmy seems to be a master of disguise'

I found myself involuntarily scratching my beard whilst replying' It certainly is an intriguing idea Carlton'

'Well John, its clearly up to you but from a dispassionate standpoint, with time running out before the trial, the moment may have come to throw a joker into the pack.'

'It's a very tempting thought all ways round' I admitted.

But before we had a chance to debate further, the steward reappeared to lead us to our table for our aristocratic Cottage Pie, paired with an agreeable Merlot, followed by a large slice of Charlotte Russe cake with cream.

We parted company at around 2.30pm, Carlton off to see his lawyers in Holborn. For my part, I had been intending to counterbalance the effects of lunch by a rapid route march home. However, with it looking like the heavens were about to open, I opted to jump onto a passing London General Omnibus Company knifeboard instead.

On the way home, between being simultaneously jolted by the bus and crushed by the masses within the buses, I found myself reflecting on the grim time that Harry would be going through in Newgate. I understood it was almost impossible to know if it was day or night dark with even the brightest of chronometers. And an even grimmer truth that, without a breakthrough, Harry would soon be standing trail at the Old Bailey!

Chapter 36 – A surprise visitor for The Mate with a very interesting tale to tell!

On arriving home, vowing once again never to set foot on a knifeboard, I was met at the door by Mrs Crumpbucket, who informed me that there was a young lady waiting in the salon very keen to speak with me, something of an unusual occurrence.

'Did she say who she was please Mrs C?'

'No, but unlike most of your four-legged filly's the lady seems very well bred'

Mrs C had a strong interest in racing and an equally strong, if not to say withering view on the merits of my own string of racehorses!

'I'll tell her you'll be through when you have had a chance to take off your wet coat' Mrs C announced as left the room'

With Mrs C's instructions duly followed I made my way to the salon, having decided that my visitor must be Miss Enderby. However, on entering the room, I found it was not Mavis but a raven-haired young lady with bright eyes and a clear complexion, a little taller than the average, wearing a fashionable tight pointed bodice and long skirt with the minimum amount of ankle on display

The young lady sprang from her seat and, I found myself gently shaking the hand of Lady Amelia Irthlingborough.

Before I had a chance to say anything more than 'hello my dear', Lady Amelia had urged me to join her on our rather cosy tete a tete couch'. Good thing Mrs Astley was not in residence, but I sensed that whatever the young lady had to say it was important.

'I hope that you do not mind my unexpected appearance' she began urgently' but I need to speak with you about the terrible charges levelled against Harry Chaplin'

'As you will no doubt have guessed' I clearly hadn't but did not like to say' I have been speaking with my friend Florence Marchioness of Hastings' who told me about your conversation with her and urged me to come and see you'

'I had in fact gone to Lady Hastings home to see her husband the Marquis.' I advised' Together with my friend Mr Patterson, we have found ourselves thrust into the role of detectives in what is now a race against time, to help Harry by finding evidence, that will show the charges levelled by the police against him to be arrant nonsense'

On drawing breath, I turned to a slightly started Lady Ameila and said' 'Do please tell me Lady Amelia in what way I can help'

'I think it might be more about what I can do for you'

Somewhat surprised by the response but highly intrigued I asked her to pray continue.

'Little more than a year ago I was betrothed to David Coggles, and everything seemed right in the world. Whilst on occasion a little too serious, I knew David to be a good man with an incredible sense of loyalty. Albeit I seldom saw that loyalty appreciated by the Marquis. I tried hard not to let this become an irritant but, it did become a little wearing, particularly in relation to the Danebury Confederates.'

'I see' noting my reaction' that you must be aware of the dossier of evidence David was collecting against those awful men'

'I can confirm my dear that we are only too aware of the dossier and the brave and principled stand David had taken against the Confederates. I too, am not sure as to whether David's loyalty was fully appreciated.

As Davids betrothed' Lady Amelia continued' I found myself spending a large amount of time with the Marquis and his acolytes. Of his closest friends, I found Viscount Bowlhead to be a very nice young man, in appearance not unlike David, but far too easily put upon; Viscount Zeals, a chortling mound of blubber and Lord Woldingham, there in body but in all other ways completely absent!

'All of which left Tobias, who I know comes across as an arrogant young man' looking at me she added with a gentle laugh' a sentiment with which I can see you agree!

I could not really demur on that point but decided best not to add my views on Bracklesham!

'With David so distracted trying to protect the Marquis, mainly from his own folly, I found myself spending more time with Tobias who, underneath the surface arrogance, can be very amusing company. This did not go unnoticed by Mrs Bracklesham. a very forceful character with, I would say almost unlimited social ambition.'

'Fully in accordance with my own understanding on all counts my dear'

'I have few doubts that Mrs Bracklesham saw my friendship with her son, and that is all it was at that time, as a potentially major step when it came to social advancement. '

'The Coggles are a noble family' Lady Amelia continued' and in Coggles Hall, have a very manageable house and a 5000-acre estate with no mortgages to pay or debts. Quite unlike my own family which, is weighed down by generations of debts'

'What we do have to offer, at the risk of sounding immodest is a Pan-European aristocratic ancestry, from the Plantagenets to the Hohenzollern's via the Hapsburg's None of which' she laughed again' helps to pay for heating the 65 bedrooms left at Irthlingborough Hall after my father demolished the other half!

'I hate to see how my father battles on indomitably to keep the family seat afloat. He is a very caring landowner, which reflects well on him personally, but that kindness unfortunately cuts even further into the limited income the family estate produces.'

'To cut a long story short, whilst my parents would never have expected me to give up the man I loved to save the family seat, with Mrs Bracklesham effectively offering the funds to restore the Hall to its former glories, were for instance, Tobias and I to become engaged, started to play on my mind. The result of my quandy lead to my giving off I believe an air of uncertainty, which sad to say became apparent to David and without wishing to discuss painful personal details, we had a terrible disagreement and called off our engagement.'

'From then on, I *fell into* an increasingly close friendship with Tobias, to the point, that almost inexorably led to our current betrothal. I found my swain amusing company and had I think, persuaded myself, that even though not in love with him, he would make a good husband,

'I am aware here of the obvious parallel with my friend the Marchioness. I do not think a day goes past when Florence does not regret the very public humiliation, she put Harry Chaplin through. merely for what appeared a more exciting life. A life that has transpired to be anything but, with money disappearing with a frightening alacrity'

Of late' Lady Amelia continued' Tobias's character has changed, and he had developed an almost irrational hatred towards David. Not content with having usurped him in love, or what might pass for love, he was convinced David was also writing a dossier on him and his actions.' From the obviously feigned laughter earlier in the conversation, Lady Amelias countenance had changed, and I could see a small tear starting to trickle down her cheek. Even an old Clodhopper in affairs of the heart such as I could not fail to be moved by Lady Amelia's obvious distress.

'I do not think you need to punish yourself unduly my dear, few things in life run quite as smoothly for any of us as we might wish'

'Thank you for being so understanding Mr Astley' she replied gently dabbing away the tear

After pausing a moment whilst Lady Amelia completed the dabbing process I decided to press on gently' I hope that you do not mind my mentioning. Like you, I was at the first meeting of the season at Stockbridge Races. I happened to look across and notice you congratulating David on the victory of his horse. I remember thinking at the time that you both looked very happy and that, despite your engagement having ended you were still happy in each other's company'.

'You are indeed right Mr Astley whilst neither of us said so in words, we were both I am sure still very much in love and both very much regretting what had happened. At the risk of sounding pompous, we were both afflicted by a sense of duty, unwilling to hurt the people to whom we were now betrothed'

'If I may say my dear a sad tale, particularly in the light of the subsequent tragic events. The course of true love does not always run true, but I think you have both acted honourably and time will heal I am sure'

Lady Amelia gave me a gentle smile and paused to dab another small tear from her eyes before continuing.

'Do not worry Mr Astley, I have not come merely seeking a shoulder to cry on,' I have come to tell you something I hope may be of assistance in your very kind efforts to help Harry Chaplin'

'Even now' she continued' I do not have the permission to tell you this, but I cannot hold my piece any longer'

'Permission my dear, whose permission?' I asked in puzzlement,

'Harry Chaplin. For you see the note he wrote that evening in The Spreadeagle was to me and not to David!'

Had I been holding a pin at the time; I don't doubt I would have heard it drop with a shattering crash!

' I am sorry to have to ask you to repeat that my dear, but did you say that you received the note?'

'I am Mr Astley. Whilst Harry let it be known that he had left David's room in high dudgeon and it was indeed true that they had disagreed, neither really wanted to be at the proverbial daggers drawn.'

When things had calmed down, David admitted to Harry that he harboured serious concerns about Tobias, who he believed had sought to undermine our engagement and whose wider dealings were bordering on the nefarious, albeit he gave no specific details'

'He also admitted that whilst fond of Mavis, like me with Tobias, he had rather drifted into his current betrothed state. He had however given his word to Mavis and would keep to his word, despite the love we still felt for each other.'

After returning to his room, Harry pondered upon what had been said. Whilst still unhappy with David's attempts to get him to scratch Hermit, merely to help the Marquis, he still respected David as a man of principle. He was also forcibly struck by the parallels with what happened to him so publicly, with Florence being seduced by the false glamour of another. Harry believed that the same had happened with me and Tobias and he did not wish to see that happen again, he also felt that it was better and ultimately fairer on Mavis to be someone's first choice in love.'

'To that end, Harry wrote the note before leaving for the Durdans asking if we could have a private word as soon as possible. It is I think a mark of Harry as a man that, despite the following morning being Derby Day and with a fortune riding on its result, he still found time to find me to explain in confidence all I have told you now.'

'After David's death and Inspector Field's discovery of the indent in the blotter, I spoke with Harry again, but he was insistent that I should make no mention of my being the recipient of his note. He was confident his innocence would be shown without my becoming embroiled in the case.'

'I am grateful to you for explaining my dear, quite a revelation to be sure!

'I had few doubts that would be the case Mr Astley' with which Lady Amelia handed me a small envelope, bearing the name of The Spreadeagle Hotel and inside the shortest of notes.

'Please Mr Astley' Lady Amelia urged' keep the letter and do with it what you feel to be necessary. Even at the risk of Harry not speaking to me again I cannot simply hold onto it any longer.'

'Thank you so much Lady Amelia and yes, I will do all in my power to ensure that this letter is used to its very best effect'

Once my visitor had bade her leave, I returned to my study and slumped back into my favourite armchair. I had not expected this afternoon to be the day when we could finally say that we had made a breakthrough!

All we had to do now, was to persuade Harry that whilst his principled refusal to drag Lady Amelia into the public eye was admirable, revealing the note to the police had to be the right course of action.

At that moment came a knock on the door and in came Mrs Crumpbucket. 'It's like Piccadilly Circus here this afternoon! No young ladies this time, just a letter'

I thanked Mrs C and could see from the excellent handwriting that it was from Jimmy. I quickly opened the envelope and read'

Dear Mate,

Just to let you know, I had a most productive afternoon with friend Cobblestone Coward, who proved to be most illuminating and only too willing to speak to the 'press'. To which end, he wishes to introduce me to a contact he believes will be a great help in destroying the case against Mr Chaplin.

Said contact has requested that we meet early tomorrow afternoon in the Surrey market town of Dorking. To ensure that he recognises me, Coward has suggested I wear the 'distinctive garb' I had from our first meeting in the Running Footman. This will necessitate another urgent visit to the Alhambra, after which I intend returning home for some shuteye

My good friend Mr Hollingshead has confirmed that he will be able to oblige but not until after tonight's final performance.

I don't doubt that Cobblestone will be looking for some form of 'reward' but at this stage of proceedings it will hopefully be money well spent.

Trusting you have had a similarly productive day and if you could do the honours in terms of updating the case notes for the legal eagles that would be much appreciated.

May I suggest a rendezvous at the Albert in Victoria Street at 7.30pm tomorrow evening

Your faithful friend

Jimmy 'The Flying Tailor' Patterson

Whilst delighted that Jimmy was making progress, I felt a slight pang of disappointment that I would not get the chance yet to share my news with my comrade in arms. However, as I was always fond of reminding others it was the cause that counted not personal vanity!

Having poured myself a large pre-prandial glass of sherry, I sat back to contemplate further Carlton's bold suggestion and the potential impact of taking such an action. By the time dinner came round, I was still considering, which gave me an excellent excuse not to start work on those bulky parcels of estate papers.

I retired to bed at 11.30pm, still unsure as to what action to take but concluded that, with the benefit of a good night's sleep, I would know what to do!

Chapter 37 - The Mate makes his decision!

Come the morrow and I was up with the proverbial lark and had made my decision! As someone who prides themselves on being a man of action, that is exactly what I would take!

I hastened downstairs to my study, well in advance of breakfast, to start work. My intent was clear – to warn the three recipients that I had in my possession a dossier, the contents of which would be very damaging to them, if they were to come into the public domain. The letter would therefore make it clear, that the dossier would remain out of public view if the statement from Mr Cuthbert Algernon Troutbridge was withdrawn immediately.

My expectation was that this would almost certainly be Padwick and Co and by later today, Jimmy would hopefully have returned from Dorking with more news about the Confederates!

Exactly how things were going to work, particularly in the absence of any of the Dossiers, I was not entirely certain but 'faint heart never won fair maiden'. First uttered, Jimmy once told me, by that Don Quixote chap. Fortunate there are none too many windmills at which to tilt in Hyde Park!

Keeping things as simple as possible I set too writing the letters to Padwick, Bracklesham and Zeals. My final decision was, how to sign the letters? I was rather struck by 'Your Nemesis' but this was not the time to reveal my woeful lack of knowledge of Greek Mythology! Possibly 'a friend' would be better but a trifle inaccurate.

Eventually I decided that in for a penny in for a pound, I would continue my policy of boldness and simply signed the letter Astley. Letters signed, I sought out the Crumpbuckets young son Percival who, having negotiated from me an excessive one shilling fee, was soon off to deliver the letters.

I had few doubts, the guilty party would be making contact very soon and I needed to be very much on my guard as to what form that contact might take!

In the meantime, with a light four course breakfast out of the way, it was back to the Metropolitan Line and off to the offices of Lewis & Lewis, Lady Amelia's letter safely ensconced within my waistcoat pocket.

All was going well until midway between Great Portland Street and Euston Square, when the train came to a juddering halt. As ever the carriage was hot on speculation as to what might have happened, low on knowledge of what had happened. Still none the wiser, we eventually started our journey again twenty minutes later.

I had taken something of a chance that either of Lewis or Osmotherly would be in the office. Probably not helped by the impromptu stop, I found I had missed them by a few minutes and learned they had left for a hearing at the Surrey Sessions, on the other side of the Thames in Newington. The soonest they might return would be early afternoon and that could not be fully guaranteed.

I therefore wrote the legal chaps a synopsis of all that had happened over the last day or so, from the progress Jimmy was making with the Confederates to my conversation with Lady

Ameila. Once complete, I handed the synopsis together with Lady Amelia's note, in its envelope to Lewis's secretary to give to the lawyers immediately upon their return.

I decided to hold back from mentioning the letters I had sent out. Whilst I remained convinced my bold approach would pay dividends, it was probably something best explained face to face!

By the time I left Lewis's office, it was one o'clock, so I stopped for a swift pint of Barclays Russian Stout and a beef sandwich at the Hand & Sheers in Cloth Fair, one time home to the Piepowder Court (apparently not for passing judgement on over seasoned suet pies as I had thought) but a means for sorting out disputes relating to local fairs!

I walked back to Farringdon Station through Smithfield Market, like so much of London at this time, a building site, work having started the previous year on the new Central Market. Like many I was delighted to see the back of the old market. Until just twenty years ago, it was home to open air slaughtering of the poor animals, with the associated cruelty, filth, effluvia and pestilence that came with such activities.

On arriving back at Baker Street Station, I walked home past the Baker Street Bazaar, now home to Madame Tussauds, but formerly occupied by the Glaciarium, the country's first artificial ice rink. I had visited as a young officer in 1842 and remember the building smelling strongly of cheese on a hot day!

It was the middle of the afternoon when I finally arrived home. To my disappointment, responses to my letters there were none. I was probably, I reflected, being a little over optimistic, given the recipients would want to plan their next move. I would need to exercise patience, never my strongest suit!

With a few hours to kill before I was due to meet Jimmy, I busied myself with more of the correspondence that had continued to pile up, usual combination of estate papers both from Lincolnshire and my father's estate in Wiltshire. I decided to concentrate on the later, trying hard to avoid catching sight of those especially large envelopes relating to the Elsham Estate!

After a simple afternoon tea of Victoria Sponge, Gypsy Tart, Battenburg Cake, sweet biscuits and Plum Duff, I opted for a quick snooze to complete the revitalisation process. My snooze was soon ended however, by a sharp rap at the door, which heralded the arrival of a letter from Mr Lewis:-

My Dear Mr Astley,

I was delighted.to receive your briefing and with it the note from Lady Ameilia. I have arranged to visit Newgate first thing tomorrow morning. Whilst Mr Chaplin was quite adamant that he wanted to make no comment on the note, I will do all in my power to persuade him of the need to make this known to the Prosecutors.

Sufficed to say, Mr Montagu Williams our esteemed barrister is also extremely pleased by this discovery and his confidence in defeating this gravely erroneous charge has increased.

However, with the trial date fast approaching, anything we can do to either remove, or at the very least, substantially discredit Mr Troutbridge's 'evidence' would be highly welcome.

We look forward to a further update on Mr Patterson's meeting with his new contact and will likewise, inform you as to our further progress.

I remain Sir......

Hopefully Jimmy's trip to Dorking or my own stirring of the pot would soon bring results on the Troutbridge front!

After a quick change I was soon on my way Victoria Street for my rendezvous with Jimmy and was at the Albert a good ten minutes early. Compared to many a public house the newly opened Albert is a grand affair, one of a plethora of buildings erected since 1861 named after the sadly deceased Prince Consort.

I made my way to the busy bar and bought two pints of Artillery Brewery's finest IPA, together with a pork pie and pickles for us to share, before finding myself a small table with a perfect view of the entrance. It was rare for me to arrive before Jimmy, but I had no doubts he would be along very soon

After half an hour waiting and with still no sign of Jimmy, I decided to pass the time by drinking his pint of IPA. I would buy him another as soon as he arrived. Another half an hour passed, by which time I had sunk another pint of IPA and polished off the whole of the pie and all the pickles.

Aside from a mild level of guilt for eating all the pie, I was beginning to get a little concerned. It was so unlike Jimmy to ever be late. After checking with my increasingly tattered copy of Bradshaw's, I could see that the last train from Dorking was due in at 9.00pm at the nearby Victoria Terminal. Deciding that there was little to be gained from staying in the Albert, aside from more pie, I made my way briskly down Victoria Street to the station.

With rush hour well and truly over and work on the new underground paused for the evening, there were few people about and mercifully no clouds of dust with which to contend. I made my way quickly to Platform Five where Jimmy's train was due to arrive in a few minutes.

I had been quite expecting the train, given it was a new route, to arrive late but instead it arrived bang on time, which was a positive. Far less positive, Jimmy was not amongst the fifty or so passengers to emerge from the steam enveloping the platform.

I had been certain that Jimmy would be on the train but knowing him to be the most resourceful of chaps, my assumption was that he had needed to stay over in Dorking and would be back in London early in the morning.

Given I had, with want of much else to do, rather overindulged on the pickle and pie front, I opted to walk up to Hyde Park Corner and catch a cab home from there.

As ever, a solitary walk was what I needed to collect my thoughts. I was aware that I had gone out on something of a limb by sending the letters, hence my reluctance to tell the lawyers just yet. Big question now - when I would receive any form of response?

I did notjk have to wait long for an answer to my question! I had been vaguely aware, between cogitations, that a Brougham Carriage was proceeding very slowly along the other side of Grosvenor Place.

As I approached the junction with Chapel Street, my cogitating was interrupted by a loud clattering as the Brougham suddenly sprang forward. I looked across and heard the driver, whose face was completely obscured by a particularly wide brimmed bowler hat, yell 'Look lively fatty!'

This vulgar comment was accompanied by a hand stretched out of the coach hurling a large rectangular object in my direction. Whilst by my own admission I was well over my prime running weight, I had not lost my quick reactions. With a decisive wave of my cane, I was able to deflect the brick away and save myself from the kind of painful bump on the noggin recently suffered by Bowlhead.

I shouted at the carriage to stop and for the occupants to show themselves. Inevitably my words were lost to the noise of the carriage, as it accelerated towards Hyde Park Corner and after that heaven knows which direction.

Given I was not aware of any new fad for throwing random bricks from carriage windows I could only assume the brick had been deliberately aimed in my direction. I bent down to pick up the brick, to which there was tied an envelope. Inside was a short note in block capitals 'Hand over the dossier! We will be in touch to arrange collection and don't try to be clever, it's not your strong suit! You have been warned'.

I stuffed the letter within the pages of Bradshaws and made my way up to Hyde Park Corner. My luck was in, and I was quickly able to hail a most polite cabbie and sat back in my hansom, I was able to reflect on what had just happened.

I felt a degree of shock but mainly anger at not being able to do more. On the positive side, if it could be so described, I had most certainly provoked a reaction from someone extremely keen to get their hands on the dossier. Less positively, I had no idea who that person was!

it further occurred to me that whoever it was, would have no idea that I had sent letters to three parties and would assume I knew from whom the message on a brick had been sent. Conversely only I knew that there were still two more parties to react. After another five minutes of balancing one thing against another I was back home.

Chapter 38 – Another letter arrives, and The Mate 'enjoys' a nice stroll to Hyde Park to meet a friend!

'On falling asleep the previous night, my hope was that I would wake in the morning with a clear-eyed vision of all that had happened and a way forward. Instead, I woke increasingly concerned at Jimmy's non-appearance and when I might hear from the other parties to whom I had written. I did not have long to find out the answer to one of those questions!

It was at just after eight when Mrs Crumpbucket brought to the breakfast table, another unmarked envelope that had just arrived. At least this time it was not affixed to a brick but on reading the letter it had much the same effect as being struck by one!

I tore the envelope open and read: -

Dear Mr Astley,

Many thanks for your welcome letter and for very helpfully confirming that you have something of great value to us. We too have something of high value to you and can only thank you, for having sent your colleague Mr Patterson to see us as a part of your crusading investigation into the demise of Lord Coggles.

I am pleased to advise Mr Tailor is in excellent health, albeit showing a rather unwise desire to leave our company sooner than we consider appropriate.

We will be in touch again very soon to affect an exchange. Please do not do anything as silly as speaking with the forces of law and order, your home is under constant observation and any such action could be most injurious to Mr Tailors continued good health.

A Friend

As to the identity of 'friend' there could be no doubt that the letter came from Mr Henry Padwick and his cohorts!

I am seldom lost for words, but this was one of those occasions!

What on earth had I done with my hair brained scheme to flush out the killers! I had expected a reaction, the odd brick hurled in my direction I could almost see as par for the course, but kidnapping I had never seen coming!

After I had cast from my mind the idea of a good stiff Scotch, I went to the front of the house to see if I could spot anyone obviously watching the house. No one caught my eye but given they were probably adept at such work, not a great surprise. I could not however, take a chance on there not being someone out there.

I returned to my study for a rapid decision as to my next step and quickly concluded, that I needed tto recruit some high-grade help in lieu of Jimmy.

It only took a moment for me to come up with the obvious candidate - Jem Machell! Not only was he a good friend of Harry Chaplin's but, just the right mix of physical power and significantly over sized brain! He had pledged to do all he could to help Harry, and I did not see him being someone who would let down a friend in need.

Frist step was to hope to blaze's that Jem was in London rather than Newmarket, preparing Hermit for Royal Ascot. To this end, I quickly scribbled a note, explaining in the briefest terms that I needed urgent help in relation to Harry. I gave the letter to young Percival together with payment of another shilling, with instructions to sprint the ten minutes to Machel's London office and hopefully return with his response.

After an anxious thirty-minute wait Percival was back with, to my relief, the briefest of notes from Machel saying that he would be happy to help and suggested meeting in Hyde Park at noon. Replete with yet another shilling from my pocket, Percival set off back to Jem's office to confirm our rendezvous.

This left the little matter of how to get out of the house. First option, simply leave by the front door and by bold and deft footwork, escape any followers. Twenty years back at my running peak I could have left them behind in a cloud of running track dust but not now.

Alternatively, I could try scaling the ten feet high wall to the back pf the house which, given my current level of personal fitness was clearly not practical. I also did not want to simply ask Jem to come to the house, since this would be noted and doubtless relayed back to Padwick's Berkeley Square HQ.

After a further think, I came up with a new plan, requiring me to do something I would not normally think of doing without approval. I made my way to Mrs C's domain - The Kitchen! Once Mrs C had got over the shock of my presence, I dived in' Ahem, Mrs Crumpbucket, I hope you er won't mind me asking you for some help in a rather delicate matter'

Mrs C was not one for beating about the bush!' I know you have been a little distracted of late Mr Astley with all your kind work on behalf of that nice Mr Chaplin, but I'm going to have to put my foot down on suet for breakfast'!

'Heaven forefend Mrs Crumpbrucket, even my over indulgence in suet based creations knows its limits, no it is a little more delicate than that'

With which I dived into my request, prefacing it with some of the background details including the house being watched and my urgent need to get out to meet someone who could help. I omitted to mention Jimmy had been kidnapped. Nor did I mention that Mrs C and I enjoyed, if that was the right word, a similarly well-padded body shape.

'You know Mr Astley I will always do what I can to help you and your family but what is it you want me to do? 'She asked in an enquiring tone.

'Well, I would er like you to dress up in one of my overcoat's topped off with a large brimmed hat. Then walk as rapidly as possible down the street, giving me time to race off in the other direction whilst the observers are distracted.

'Have I got this right Mr Astley? You wish me to pretend to be you' she asked striking a note of barely restrained incredulity.

Yes', I responded with embarrassment' that is the sum and substance of the matter, and I really would not ask if it was not essential, I get out of the house undetected.'

'I don't think it would be right and proper even in current circumstances for me to dress up as my male employer and how are you going to get back into the house without the observers realising, they have been hood winked?'

I had not expected Mrs C to take to the idea with alacrity and had prepared myself for several rounds of gentle persuasion. She had however, made a very good point, even the dimmest of observers would put two and two together when I returned home later'

Having acknowledged Mrs C was right, there followed a rather pregnant pause finally broken by Mrs C who, in an unusually hesitant voice, opined 'I doubt Mr Astley that you will like my suggestion any more than I took to yours. There is a way in which you could get in and out of the house without your watchers knowing you have left the building'

'And pray tell Mrs Crumpbucket how that might work?' I asked with genuine curiosity.

'You dress up as me Mr Astley!

Not for the first time in recent days I was completely lost for words and if anything, even more lost than the previous time

'I'm sorry but are you suggesting that I dress up as lady' I replied in horror!

'Well Mr Astley' Mrs C responded with some level of affront' I fail to see how that is any different to what you suggested'!

We debated the subject for ten minutes, but with time ticking by and Mrs C showing no sign of changing her mind, I decided I would have to very reluctantly follow the logic of her suggestion.

And so, it came to pass Joseph, that I describe to you the single most embarrassing moment of my life, far more so than any number of faux pas on which artistic johnny painted what and terrible choices on horses to back.

I had to strip down to my flannel vest and knee length pants. Then, with 'guidance' from Mrs C, I was kitted out in the most voluminous of dresses to hide my hairy knees; a blouse in what I was assured was a Romanesque style, a Turkish wrap and an overcoat, apparently known as a pelisse, which rather handily reached down to my ankles. All topped off by the widest hat that Mrs C possessed together with the darkest of veils, borrowed from my Eleanor's wardrobe, for which I passed a silent and humble apology.

Finally, the luxuriant growth of my Mutton Chop whiskers, which have always been a source of some pride, had to go and much worse was to follow.

Before leaving and without giving too much away, I made the Crumpbucket's aware that there may be the odd knock on the door from parties wishing to speak with me, about certain papers pertaining to their personal dealings. Not wanting to cause undue panic I decided not to mention the possibility of any messages arriving tied to a brick!

As good fortune would have things, it was a wet morning in London, meaning I could carry an umbrella, further obscuring my less than feminine visage. Thus, I found myself tottering unsteadily towards the Park, where I was to meet Mr Crumpbucket, following a discrete distance behind, to help affect a swift change into my own clothes!

All seemed to be going passably when, hidden behind my umbrella, I suddenly found myself in direct collision with something large and bouncy!!

Do look where you are going' the owner of the bouncy frame exclaimed with a frustrated chortle'. I did not want to look up to confirm what I already knew, I had run slap bang into the mound of many pounds, Viscount Zeals, no doubt heading towards Chez Astley.

In my best attempt at a feminine voice, I managed a 'frightfully sorry and all that' then moved forward as rapidly as I could nearly running into two large figures, neither of any obvious refinement. Once past, I stopped to venture a look round and it was clear to me, that the two oversized oafs were there to assist the Viscount.

I finally reached my destination and was soon joined by Crumpbcuket, who confirmed that he had not caught sight of anyone following me, which was good news. Albeit with a barely concealed grin, he did advise that, as well as crashing into Viscount Zeals I had apparently narrowly avoided a similar accident with the Duke of Hamilton, something I was always keen to avoid!

As for Lord Zeals, Crumpbucket was able to confirm that, together with his pet oafs, he was heading in the direction of my home. To my expression of concern that his beloved would be alright, he merely laughed declaring that he'd not met a viscount yet who was a match for Mrs Crumpbucket!

I quickly made my way into one of the monkey closets in the nearby new public toilets to change into something a little more to my own taste, clamping one of my largest cigars in my mouth to confirm my return to the male species, if only until the journey home.

With my disguise safely packed away and handed over to Crumpbucket, I made my way to the tea house where I had arranged to meet Jem. Just before entering the building, he appeared from behind a tree, with a wry grin spread across his face.

'Don't worry Mate, your interesting approach to a late Spring Walk around the Park is safe with me! I can only assume from that and the tenor of your note there must be something drastic afoot, even more drastic than the loss of your mutton chop whiskers!

'Thank your Jem' I said with some relief' and you could not be any truer in what you say, drastic is the word and drastic action the order of the day!'

Over tea and cake, I cantered through all that had happened since we last discussed the case. save the name of Lady Amelia, which I had left out for reasons of delicacy. For his part, Jem listened impassively, his ever-active brain doubtless computing all I was elucidating.

When I finally drew to a close, Jem, rocked his large frame back in his chair and stroking his chin, bit like that Thinker chap on the statue, began.

'There is no doubts Mate that you and young Jimmy have made impressive progress, far greater than I'd ever expected and you've certainly ruffled a few feathers! I've no doubts, given its rude tone, that last night's message could just as easily have come attached to a bottle of that awful Brackleshams Tonic as a brick!

'As to which of the three parties is likely to be Lord Coggles murderer, whilst Zeals gives every appearance of being an idiot, behind the mask is a very devious individual with no compunction about throwing his friends to the wolves. As for Bracklesham, an unpleasant emotional hot head who acts long before he thinks. It would be no surprise if the unseen figure in the coach last night was Bracklesham himself. Nearly knocking out the person from whom you are expecting an answer doesn't seem to me to be the brightest of actions!'

'It is however hard to look past the Danebury Mob being behind the murder and for whom producing a false witness to fool the police is likely second nature. Added to which they've kidnapped Jimmy into the bargain!'

'Without the dossiers we are going to have to box very clever if we are to get Jimmy back whilst uncovering the murderer. Let's go along with the next stage of their instructions, which I don't doubt will be with you very shortly.

'A most perceptive analysis Jem' I replied more than enough to convince me that recruiting Captain Machell was my best decision of late!

'As an aside Mate' Jem asked quizzically' who was it that persuaded Jimmy of the merit of a trip to Dorking?

'Odd kind of a name Jem - Cobblestone Coward. Jimmy said he struck him as being more like a man of a cloth than a member of the Confederacies workforce. Something that helped to convince him that Coward was genuine'.

With a simultaneous sigh and raise of his eyebrows Jem replied' I'm afraid the 'gent', who befriended Jimmy was none other than Roderick 'The Rev' Rollwright, a most believable individual who impersonates a now deceased West Country vicar by the name of Cobblestone Coward, as a cover for his nefarious business dealings. Usually carried out on behalf of none other than Mr Henry Padwick,

'My guess' Jem continued' is that despite being heavily disguised, certain denizens of the Footman realised who Jimmy was, and informed Padwick who, in turn, instructed Rollwright to befriend Jimmy, then feed him with erroneous information. Hence, the invite to Jimmy to meet an unnamed contact in Dorking. On receiving word that you had the dossier, they must have concluded that hanging onto Jimmy would be the ideal way to seal its release'

'But why Dorking?

"At a guess, because it is just up the train line from Horsham, whose wealthiest resident is none other than……

'Henry Padwick!' I exclaimed.

'I have few doubts that Jimmy is being entertained somewhere in or around Horsham, without the option of an early return home'

'What do you suggest as next steps then Jem?

'Firstly, Mate its time you got your dress back on and make your way home' he replied with a grin' and secondly wait for the next message to arrive. As soon as it does, get Crumpbucket Jnr round to my office straightaway!

'And how about you Jem?

'For my part, I want to put in place some contingency plans for this evening' the later added with a nod and a large wink. 'Don't worry Mate we'll get Jimmy back alright and from there, clear Harry's name and have him out in time to lead Hermit into the winner's enclosure at Royal Ascot'

And with that I found myself the recipient of a large slap on the back and the iron grip of Jem's handshake before he strode off purposefully towards his office. Despite Jem's reassuring confidence, I was still acutely aware that both Harry and now Jimmy were in danger, and we did not have the damn dossiers! My first dread however, was getting back into my disguise. At which point Joseph, I'm afraid it's time we returned to 'Fifty Years of My Sporting Life for the rest of the afternoon!

Frustrating as I found The Mate having to break off at this juncture it was not a total surprise, since I had received a private letter from Mr Thorold asking if I could please persuade Sir John to finish his recollections pronto. Whilst much of the delay was due to Sir John's charming habit of wandering off the subject down the many interesting byways of his fascinating life, much of the delay was down to my regular requests to discuss matters detective!

Chapter 39 – Confined to barracks The Mate settles down to a long session dealing with his paperwork!

After a solid day and a half of work on 'Fifty Years of My Sporting Life', Sir John declared that as far as the book was concerned, we were into the final furlong and coming with a well-timed late run to the line! All of which meant, that Sir John was willing to break off for one final push to complete his tale of detection that very afternoon!

'Taking up the story once more Joseph, we will I think brush over the indignity of my return home but let's just say, Mrs Crumpbucket was as pleased to see the return of her clothes as I was to never be seen in them again!

Little more than an hour later, Sir John began. Just as Jem had predicted, a further note arrived informing me that I should not leave the house and that at 8.00pm I was to place the dossier on the doorstep, and I would be seeing Mr Patterson soon enough. At least they had not rumbled my visit to the park, but it was only a small victory, the war was far from won.

I duly dispatched Crumpbucket Jnr on his latest errand to Jem's office, yet another shilling to the good, with the note and scribbled on it what I intended to say. I also instructed the youngster to purchase a bunch of flowers, that would hopefully cover the real purpose of his latest trip from the house.

About thirty minutes later, Junior arrived with the flowers, costing I suspected rather less than the two shillings I had provided. I asked him to give those to his mother for 'the suffering' she had been through earlier in the day. He also brought confirmation that Jem agreed with my response.

That being the case, I made my way to the front door and ostentatiously placed a note on the doorstep simply saying.

To whom it may concern, a bargain can only be said to have taken place if both parties exchange the goods at the same time!

I had hoped that if I reached my study quickly enough, I might see who picked up the letter but by the time I got there, all I espied was a young lad scurrying away with the envelope. I had few doubts that it was on its way to 48 Berkley Square!

All I could do now was to sit and wait. By the time it had reached eleven o clock and still no note, I decided to retire to bed. Cognisant that tomorrow would be a very big day, I opted for a judicious glass of Mother Batley's Sedative Solution to aid sleep and avoid a likely fitful night.

Come the morning and no sooner had I sat down to breakfast, having plum forgotten to eat the previous night, than there was a light tap on the front door and Mrs Crumpbucket rushed in with the latest note which I tore open with alacrity.

My Dear Mr Astley,

I consider you to be in no position to make demands but we remain reasonable people (which prompted my usual harrumph at such unutterable tosh) *and are willing to meet you at 10.00pm in Holland Park.*

I quickly dashed off a reply to leave on the front door confirming agreement and making it clear I would only be willing to meet in an open area. Not for instance a small, wooded copse where anything could happen!

Whilst relieved that they had agreed to my 'demand', there remained the question of how we were going to simultaneously rescue Jimmy; unmask the Confederacy as paymasters of Troutbridge and ensure the release of Harry all without their dossier! Once again young Crumpbucket found himself the recipient of another shilling to take my latest missive round to Jem's office.

In my note, I asked Jem to be here for 8.30pm and if he could possibly scale the back wall that would be helpful! Having witnessed him jump onto a mantelpiece from a standing start at Lord Pulborough's Mayfair home, I hoped this might be feasible. I also requested that, if he did not have a cannon to hand, could he come armed with a foolproof idea on how to achieve our aim!

Young Percival was soon back confirming Jem's attendance and not long after, Mrs Crumpbucket brought me the regular post observing

'Looks like your usual mail Mr Astley' which I took to mean more letters from members of the bookmaking fraternity asking if I now felt able to meet various financial obligations. For the moment they would have to wait, there was however, at the bottom of the pile a letter from Mrs Astley, which I felt obliged to read!

Dear John

I do appreciate that your energies are directed to helping our dear friend Harry Chaplin, but could you please find ten minutes in your busy day, to look at the accumulated estate papers sent to you over the last two weeks!

Your loving wife seeking to stay patient but currently finding that to be a very testing challenge!

Eleanor

Oh dear, even Mrs Astley's legendary patience was showing signs of fracture! With my having time to kill, rather than simply pace around nervously cogitating, I would be best trying to occupy my mind on Estate business. As well as being of practical value, it would also hopefully put me back in Eleanor's good books!

I made my way to my study where there were now two fearsome piles of paperwork, normal letters in the one and those damned bulky ones in the other! I decided to ease my way in gently by going through the smaller letters first.

I'd been working a solid two hours when I decided, to take a break with a swift perambulation around the park. Near the entrance to the park was old Cariologies, well known paper seller of this parish from whom I purchased the early edition of The Standard.

The main headline concerned "the King of The Sandwich Islands Laying the Foundation Stone of a Cathedral in Honolulu, alongside an article on a steel boat that had been built for an Expedition In Search of Dr. Livingstone. I only had to turn to page three however, to find a long piece speculating on Harry's forthcoming trial, something that once again sent a shudder through me at the very thought.

After about ten minutes of perambulating, I decided to double back a couple of times to see if I could spot anyone following me but nothing doing. The fleeting thought occurred to me that perhaps no one was watching me at all, but how could I take that chance.

On returning home, Mrs Crumpbucket was happy to advise me that we had gone half an hour without any notes or parcel being left on the front doorstep, which should be regarded as a major triumph.

Perhaps as much the result of my perambulations as the need to fill in the time, I requested Mrs C to kindly prepare some lunch. Once replete I went back to my study and quickly nodded off in my favourite armchair. On awakening I hoped to find that I had been dozing for several hours, the reality being barely more than 45 minutes!

All of which left me with another four hours to fill before Jem's arrival. Nothing to it, I really would have to buckle down and go through the three bulkiest envelopes! On looking at them more closely, they did not appear to be from the estate after all but had been redirected from there to our London home. I did not recognise the original handwriting on the thick envelopes but whoever sent them was clearly keen to fill my waking hours with a considerable amount of reading!

I reached for my trusty paper knife, which had been with me since I was a junior office on my way to the Crimea. A truly hellish journey through the Black Sea, but that is yet another story! I duly slit the top of the largest of the envelopes. Whatever was inside was wedged in tight. I tried turning it upside down and out fell a folded sheet of paper. I opened it out and seldom in my life have I been so astounded!

'Dear Mate,

You may recall that sunny morning a few weeks ago, in Stockbridge High Street, the night after you witnessed my contretemps with Padwick and Co. Whilst I brushed the whole affair off at the time, there have been several instances where I was sure I was being followed, and not by people I would wish to meet anytime soon in a dark alley. That being the case, just to be on the safe side, I would be very grateful if you, as a man I trust implicitly, could please provide safe guardianship of my 'Dosiser of Moral Rectitude' concerning the Danebury Confederacy for the time being.

I wish to see whether my friend Harry Hastings' madcap gamble against Hermit puts him back in good financial health, or merely hastens his slide into Padwick's web, before taking action to strike at the heart of this pernicious organisation

For good measure I have also sent you envelopes concerning that duplicitous mound of blubber Lord Zeals and that cad and bounder Tobias Bracklessham. Apologies Mate for my invective in the case of the later 'gentleman'. My thoughts in his case are not untouched by matters of a very personal nature (which I took to mean Lady Amelia).

If for any reason I am not able to reclaim the dossiers, please take any action you see fit with them.

I remain your friend,

David Coggles

I swiftly pulled the dossier from the envelope, a bound document of some fifty pages with the title 'The Illuminating and Terrible Truth Behind Mr Henry Padwick and the Danebury Confederacy'.

I sat down to read and by the end, I was fully conversant with the sheer breadth of the confederacy's activities. Particularly, their cultivation of easily led young men of wealthy families and how they were able to part these young men from their families' historic holdings, or indeed any holdings that might increase the wealth of the confederates.

There was much on the luckless Edward Tredcroft, a young man whose cricketing prowess was matched only, by his sheer gullibility. After trusting his financial affairs to Padwick, he eventually found himself required to hand over the keys to the family home in Horsham, where **Padwick now resided in splendour.**

If exposed to public scrutiny, I had no doubts the dossier would destroy the Confederates activities. Whether it had been their intention to murder David, or 'merely' rough him up in pursuit of the dossier I could have no idea. I was however sure, that they had seen an opportunity to pin the blame on our upstanding friend Harry Chaplin, hence the sudden appearance of Cuthbert Algernon Troutbridge as a so-called witness.

I skipped my way through the documents on Zeals and Bracklesham. Whilst less explosive than the Danebury one, it was very clear why those 'gentlemen' might also be willing to take whatever actions were necessary to ensure their respective dossiers did not see the light of day.

I had barely noticed Mrs Crumpbucket bringing in a light tea of cold pigeon pie, pickles, four rounds of wholewheat meat and cheese sandwiches together with a fruit turnover, blancmange and some jam puffs. Hopefully enough to fill a small gap and provide substance for what I had no doubts would be a very eventful evening.

At 8.30pm, Mr Crumpbucket showed Jem into my study, looking in no way like a man who had just scaled the ten-foot-high wall to the rear of the house, without the aid of a ladder or crampons. His suit showed not a crease out of place or a scintilla of dirt!

'How goes it Mate' Jem exclaimed accompanied by a typically vigorous handshake which I sought in vain to match shake for shake.

'Revelatory as it transpires'

'The revelation being you've not been able to finish tea by yourself' he commented jocularly whilst helping himself to what remained of the food.

'No' I replied' even more revelatory than that.

'Maybe something to match The Seven Angels with the Trumpets, from The Apocalypse, Latin Edition by Albrecht Durer?'

Having no idea as to the identity of this Mr Durer, possibly a German racehorse trainer, I simply pushed the largest of the envelopes across the table to Jem.

'I see before me Mate an envelope rather than a revelation' perhaps because of his high intelligence Jem could be deliberately obtuse even in moments of high importance.

Trying hard not to sound frustrated I merely said' If you would be kind enough to read the contents of the envelope Jem, I think you might find its contents somewhat more revelatory than anything Mr Durer might have to offer!'

Jem duly took the dossier out of the envelope and with elbows planted firmly on the desk and chin cupped in his hands, started to read. It did not take long for the look on Jem's face to change from mild amusement to intense concentration.

'You may also wish to have a quick peruse of these two?' I said passing over the other two envelopes.

By the time Jem had finished he looked up, un-cupped his hands and said with relish' Well Mate, that puts an entirely different perspective on things. To be completely honest, my strategy for tonight was based on bluff and bludgeoning. Now we have something to bargain with we can take an altogether different approach'

'I have had a thought' Jem continued. 'You mentioned that Jimmy heard the Confederacy crew talking about someone by the name of 'The Cat', the same initials as Cuthbert Algernon Troutbridge?'

'By Jove Jem' I exclaimed excitedly' I'm sure you've got it, bravo!'

'As a matter of obvious interest Mate,' Jem enquired' how in heavens name, did you come across this treasure trove?

I quickly explained the circumstances of my surprise but very welcome discovery of the papers. I do not doubt it crossed his mind, but Jem was kind enough not to ask, why I had simply not have opened the envelopes when they arrived! There would, however, be plenty of time to chide myself, for the moment, action was the clarion call!

We placed the Dossier in an envelope, locking the two remaining dossiers securely in my safe. We could after all, not rule out the possibility of either Zeals or Bracklesham's ruffians appearing at the door demanding their dossiers and simply refusing to take 'no' for an answer.

With it having come round to 9.00am, and Holland Park being some forty-five minutes' walk, it was time to set off. With my lacking Jem's dexterity, we opted to simply exit via the front door, given we were going to see their paymasters, it did not really matter if the Danebury lackies observed us or not.

After walking for twenty minutes or so I whispered to Jem' I have a feeling we may have followers trailing in our wake'

'I have a very strong feeling Mate you are right, and I don't think that remaining unseen is these fellow's strong suit.

'Fully agree Jem. We are coming to the junction with Lexham Gardens, where we turn left there is an alcove. I suggest we hide there before jumping out and surprising them'

'I've no doubt Mate we will surprise them' Jem replied coyly.

We agreed to speed up our pace and as soon as we had turned left, we sprinted on and dived into the alcove. Our followers were slow to react and lumbered past us by before realising the need to retrace their steps.

My intention had been to appear from our alcove and depending how they acted, most likely cuff one of them with my walking cane before chasing them away. I was about to jump forward when a large arm shot across my chest restraining me. Much to my surprise, Jem invited the two oafs to join us in the alcove, an offer they readily accepted. I recognised them immediately as the two ruffians accompanying Viscount Zeals earlier in the day. Like their employer the ruffians were large but rather paunchy and I was not convinced they were as tough as they looked. One thing for sure however, their eyes were firmly fixed on the envelope under my arm.

'I thought it would be nice to formally introduce ourselves' Jem addressed them in a wryly amused tone, which seemed to momentarily confuse them.

Eventually the larger of the oafs spoke' give us the bloody dossier or we'll be forced to remove it from your friend' with a menace suggesting that he would relish such a task.

'I don't think we'll be doing anything like that' responded producing in one swift movement from out of his frock coat, a Beaumont Adams .422 double action service revolver!

The look on the faces of the oafs changed from aggressive self-satisfaction to genuine horror. I don't doubt these fellows had been threatened with plenty of weapons in the past but not a service revolver!

'Your journey through the streets of London' Jem continued' has I'm afraid, come to a premature end and without the desired result!' At which point he produced a further surprise, pulling from his coat pocket, a pair of Towers adjustable handcuffs.

'John I would be very grateful if you could please cuff these two gentlemen to the railing conveniently located to your right'

'With the greatest of pleasure Jem' I responded, proceeding to cuff them one arm to each other and one to the railing. Once completed Jem wished them a breezy good night and we left to much hollering and rude comments, questioning our respective manhood's!

'Well Jem I'll admit, not for the first time, to being most surprised by a recent turn of events!'

'I did tell you Mate that I had put in place a few precautions'

'Would you' I had to ask' have fired the gun?

'I could have tried' he laughed. 'It jammed up years ago, but I thought it would prove a useful theatrical prop. Don't worry, I have no intention of brandishing it at our next meeting, unless things become incredibly sticky!'

'By the way' he continued' I am taking it that you recognised our friends?'

'Yes, indeed Jem, they are none other than Viscount Zeals pet oafs, possessed of a colourful vocabulary but no chortling!'

We kept a watchful silence for the rest of our journey, albeit keeping a weather eye out for any other unwanted followers, of whom there fortunately appeared to be none.

On reaching the gate to Holland Park we stopped to regroup

'I doubt Jem, that Padwick & Co are going to be too pleased at my not coming alone'

'Deeply distrustful they maybe but they are pragmatists and for them acquisition of the dossier is paramount, and we do now have what they want!

It was now just a minute before 10.00pm and with night having arrived, the only illumination came from a distant streetlight. We could, however, make out six figures in the distance. We walked forward until standing ten yards in front of us were Henry Padwick, Harry Hill and Thomas Pedley, a trio fit to set off terror in many an indebted nobleman!

'Good evening, Mr Astley, I am disappointed to see you have chosen to ignore our instruction to come alone' Padwick began, sounding as if he was expressing regret at the behaviour of a wayward child.

'I felt it to be a prudent and proportionate precaution in the circumstances' I responded evenly.

'Never mind, as I said in my little note, we are nothing if not reasonable people' I had to stop myself yet again from loudly harrumphing every time I heard Padwick speak.

'Despite our best assurances to him' Pedley interjected in his typically sneering tone' Coggles persisted with his threats to publish his Dossier, undoubtedly full to the brim with idle speculations. We couldn't care less but we need to protect our esteemed clients and their families.'

Before I could respond, Jem spoke, in his calmest of tones 'If the Dossier has so little merit it is difficult to see why you have chosen to take such extreme actions to bring it into your possession!'

'My dear Mr Machell' back to the unctuous tones of Henry Padwick' our interest was piqued by Mr Patterson absurdly linking our confederacy of likeminded businessmen with the tragic death of Lord Coggles. It was for this reason that we asked Mr Patterson to spend a few days with us to discuss our concerns about such false rumours being made public'.

Looking across at Jimmy, who was pincered between two of the roughest looking ruffians I had seen in many a long year, he seemed very calm, but doubtless keen to escape the clutches of l his new friends!

'Enough talk' this time it was the harsh tones of the jut-jawed Hill' handover the dossier, I've had my fill of this nonsense'

I was beginning to become quite aggravated by this odious bunch but before I could say anything, Jem interceded'.

'Gentlemen, however undesirable the situation is to the sensibilities of any of us' both parties have something the other party desires. For you it is the release of the dossier and for our part, it is firstly the release of our friend Mr Patterson.'

Hill was about to start again but Jem, brooking no interruptions continued' I doubt we will ever know exactly what happened that fateful night before the Derby. We believe Lord Coggles was lured up to the Burgh Heath Road on some pretext or other. When it became apparent, he did not have the dossier with him, or willing to admit where it was, a beating was inflicted on him, a beating that went further than probably ever intended, at the end of which Lord Coggles lay dead, and you had no dossier.'

'With the police taking a wholly incorrect interest in our friend Mr Chaplin, you saw a golden opportunity to implicate a wholly innocent party as the murderer. All of which lead to your sending your associate Cuthbert Algernon Troutbridge, or as he is better known to you the CAT, to the police with some cock and bull story about having seen the killing, with details supplied by your murderous ruffians. Therefore, aside from Mr PAtterson's release, we require you to call off the CAT, at which point I am sure my friend Mr Astley will be willing to hand over the dossier.'

Whilst completely rapt by Jem's bravura speech, I could have sworn that, despite the gloom, several of the bushes around where we were standing, appeared to be moving very slightly!

At the conclusion of Jem's little speech, there was a prolonged silence, not what I had been expecting at all. After about five seconds, there came a laugh from Henry Padwick then the same from Hill and Pedley. 'Mr Machell, if you ever tire of horse racing, I am sure that you will find a ready alternative career writing for the West End stage!'

'I'm afraid to say' he continued' that much as you and your compatriots wish to believe this to be what happened, it is a complete fiction

I'd had enough of this 'Poppycock, complete and utter poppycock, I was there when you threatened poor David!'

'I fear Mr Astley that you are conflagrating a slightly heated discussion with the late lamented Lord Coggles into some bizarre plot to murder him. Just as you overheard our private conversation, one of our most trusted lieutenants observed Lord Coggles handing you an envelope the morning afterwards in Stockbridge High Street. Once we received your letter, it did not take a colossal intellect to deduce you were to be his chosen keeper of the dossier'

The hunting photo of course, I remembered at the time David had given me a rather knowing look when he had handed it over. I had thought nothing of that, nor had I remembered to open the envelope either! Note to self, open all envelopes on receipt in the future!

I was about to inform Padwick that this was completely irrelevant since we'd not be releasing the dossier without Troutbridge retracting his statement, when Padwick was back again' As for the person you refer to as the CAT the only one who our junior associates sometimes refer to by such a sobriquet, is our old friend and associate Thelonious Catchpole! We know nothing about this Cuthbert Algernon Troutbridge to whom you refer.'

'You see' he continued, as if speaking to a none too bright child 'the amusing little play on "Cat" as opposed to the person to whom you refer, who would presumably be referred to as 'The Trout' if you will permit me a small moment of humour'.

Padwick's little 'joke' at my expense, was met by Pedley and Hill with howls of derisive, laughter and by Jem and I in complete silence. I had no doubt Jem, was wondering where on earth this other envelope fitted into things, I would explain when time permitted!

Before we had time to consider what to say next, it became immediately apparent that the Confederates had never intended leaving without the dossier. The aforementioned bushes were now advancing at a rapid rate and becoming ever more human in their form!'

I glanced again at Jimmy who had clearly witnessed the same thing and was trying to mouth something to me but unfortunately, I was far from sure what!

To this day I am not sure as the exact order in which everything happened, but Jem shouted to me' Quick mate throw them the bloody dossier'. After but a moment's thought, I opted to hurl the blessed thing as far away from the Confederates as I could. This seemed, as I had hoped, to confuse everyone including the ruffians holding Jimmy, who momentarily loosened their grip, allowing him to deftly slip out his frock coat and sprint towards us with alacrity! Clearly an advantage of working for Mr Henry Hill was owning a coat whose silk lined sleeves allowed for a frictionless exit!

By now the bushes had, lost all appearance of plant life and were clearly five fully formed oafs, no longer hidden behind pieces of vegetation and now heading towards us with considerable momentum!

At that moment I became aware of the sound of thundering hooves and looking round, saw a four-seater Clarence Carriage (or as it used to be nicknamed a Growler) weaving its way between us and the advancing oafs! Sitting atop the carriage was none other than Hermits trainer William Bloss, clearly as skilled at driving horses as training them.

'Jump aboard!' Jem bellowed, with which we bundled ourselves rapidly onto the carriage and Bloss swiftly set the team running, just as the quickest of the oafs reached where we had been standing.

Once I had got my breath back, I turned to Jem and said ironically,' Rather handy that friend Bloss considered this an apposite moment to trying out his carriage driving skills in Holland Park'

With a big grin Jem responded, 'I had a feeling Padwick and Co were not going to be playing by MCC rules''

'I'm bound to agree there Jem and many thanks to you and to Mr Bloss'

An obviously relieved Jimmy also chimed in with his thanks and added 'I had been assured by Old Man Padwick that there would be no 'funny business' when we met, but that proved to be as worthless as one of his assurances that he has client's best interests at heart!'

I glanced back out of the carriage to a scene of confusion. Even the dimmest of the oafs had finally given up their short-lived blundering attempts to catch the carriage. Meanwhile with the dossier of doom having split apart when it fell to earth, the Confederates were stumbling around in the near dark trying to gather up every last page! Had it not been so sad to see David's magnum opus being gathered up by the very people it was intended to bring down, there was something comical about seeing this 'loveable' bunch in such a state!

As we reached the gates to the park, we rounded a very startled policeman, unaccustomed no doubt, to seeing a carriage tearing around at this time of night. In my carefree youth, I had enjoyed few things as much, as creeping up behind a member of the Metropolitan Police's finest and removing their hats, before making haste in the opposite direction as quickly as possible. I could not therefore resist, for old times' sake, reaching my hand out and flipping off the startled rozzers helmet to much amusement!

Once clear of the now irate rozzer, I turned to Jimmy and said' I cannot tell you my friend how relieved I am to have you back in one piece! When we have a chance, I'll be eating a great slice of humble pie as opposed to my usual preference for the game variety'

'Think nothing of it Mate, it's been an illuminating couple of days and pleased to report none the worse for the experience. How did you come by the Dossier?'

'It's an object lesson' I laughed' in taking notice of someone with far more common sense than I, namely Mrs Astley' Jimmy looked a little confused by my explanation but that would not be a first!

After a further couple of minutes of rapid travel, we entered Albemarle Street and Bloss skilfully brought the Clarence to a halt outside Brown's Hotel. Funny enough I heard the other week that Albemarle was London's first one-way street but that might not be entirely pertinent to the story at hand Joseph' Sir John laughed.

On stopping, Jem announced' I thought that with other parties still interested in acquiring their dossiers, a night away from home would be just the ticket' a sentiment with which we heartily concurred.

After thanking Bloss again for his invaluable help, the three of us made our way into Browns. Founded about thirty years prior by the eponymously named James and Sarah Brown, it is one of London's finest hotels, comprising a row of elegant Georgian Town Houses.

Having found a quiet spot in the hotel's sumptuous lounge, Jem quickly gave orders for a large pot of coffee, brandies all round and a mountainous pile of sandwiches and pickles to devour. All this excitement had built up quite an appetite in me and Jimmy had hardly been overfed by his 'hosts'!

Once sat comfortably with our drinks, I kicked off proceedings' Well gents I think we've achieved the prime objective of the evening in getting young Jimmy back but I'm not sure how much further we have advanced things for Harry?

Looking around however, I could see from the looks on their faces that neither Jem nor Jimmy agreed with my assessment.

'On the contrary Mate,' Jem responded' I think a lot has been achieved' we now know for certain that our prime suspects the Danebury Mob can effectively be ruled out of the murder of David Coggles. Revolting bunch, crooked as they come but there is no evidence of their being involved, nor do I believe they had anything to do with the 'employment' of Cuthbert Algernon Troutbridge. They simply took an opportunity we innocently gave them to get all they wanted i.e. the dossier'

'I'm in agreement with Mr Machell, Mate' Jimmy chimed in' my time with the Confederates gave me plenty of time to think about things and I have some thoughts to share.'

At that point however, Jem rose to his feet announcing 'Apologies gents but with Royal Ascot starting the day after tomorrow, Bloss and I will be off at 5.00am to Newmarket to supervise gallops and then arrange for all our runners to be put on the train to Ascot for the start of the Royal Meeting'

We both profusely thanked Jem for his and Bloss's invaluable help and promised to keep him fully updated with future developments.

With Jem leaving, we settled back down into our extremely comfortable easy chairs, which I had noted to be a Howard & Sons product, funny how even in moments of great moment import, one still found oneself noticing the little things in life.

Up to the moment the Confederates laughed at our having chosen the wrong Cat, I had been certain they had to be behind David's murder. Since then, I had already started turning over in my mind the various other suspects we had identified and was keen to learn Jimmy's thoughts.

In the first instance however, I wanted to know how Jimmy had landed up in the clutches of the Danebury Mob and what had happened to him until now.

'Well Mate, as you are aware, I set off from Waterloo on the **London, Brighton and South Coast Railway's** recently opened line to Dorking. The new station is located to the north of the town in the lee of the chalk escarpment of Box Hill. I had been there once before and remembered if to be a pretty market town, with a fine old coaching inn referenced in our old friend Charles Dicken's 'Pickwick Papers'.

'My instructions' Jimmy continued' were to walk into town and make my way to the Surrey Yeoman public house, where I would be met in the lounge bar by a smartly dressed individual, wearing a green checked waistcoat. He would introduce himself by the name of Mr Peaslake and on payment of a fee, be able to give me some vital information relating to the murder of Lord Coggles'

'The train was on time, and I made my way out onto the station forecourt, where there were several hansom cabs waiting. I was hailed by one of the cabbies asking where I wanted to go. I advised that I was content to walk, but before I knew it, I was lifted off my feet by two burly fellows and dumped unceremoniously into the back of his cab, which proceeded to leave the station lickety-split.

Once on our way, one of the oafs growled at me to shut up and not move, whilst the other proceeded to roughly blind fold me. The instant before I became unsighted to the outside world, I realised that the oafs were two of Padwick's low level helpers from the 'Only Running Footman'. My conjecturing was however, brought to a very sudden stop, by a heavy blow to the noggin!

'I was awoken from my enforced slumber by the cab jolting to a halt. I was quickly hauled out, and led, still blindfolded, across a gravel drive into a clearly large building before being dumped in a small room where the blindfold was removed.

'The room did at least have a window, unfortunately barred, precluding any chance of immediate escape. The window offered a view of some trees wall but little more.'

'Given it was now a couple of hours since I had been nabbed, I concluded that I was likely incarcerated thirteen miles to the south of Dorking, in Mr Henry Padwicks Horsham manor house. I had few doubts the one "acquired" from the luckless Edward Tedcraft'.

'After what seemed an interminable wait, the door opened, and two different oafs informed me that 'my presence was requested' as if I was being invited to a Ducal home in Mayfair!'

I was led through a long drab corridor into a large austere room, quite possibly the staff dining hall where, sat at the end of a long table, were Messer's Padwick, Hill and Pedley – unctuous, uncouth and unconscionable by turn.

Padwick opened proceedings' Thank you so much for joining us and my apologies for the unorthodox manner of your arrival,

I decided it was best to play along with Padwick and responded 'Thank you very much for the welcome Mr Padwick, may I ask what I have done to warrant such an unexpected invitation to, I believe Horsham, rather than the lounge bar of the Surrey Yeoman Public House in Dorking?'

'And you can stop trying to be so bloody clever' Pedley snarled, I could see in that moment Mate, why you find him perhaps the most repulsive of the terrible trio'

Before I had a chance to answer Hill sneered' what my friend Mr Pedley means' is that you and your ace crime reporter alter ego, have been asking a lot of damn fool questions about our operation'

I was racking my brains as to how they could have found out it was me, since I was confident that my disguise was the best my friends at the Alhambra Musci Hall could devise?

'And to save you racking your brains' Padwick responded' our source was your old friend Thadeus Belvedere the ever-helpful Duty Manager of the Spreadeagle Hotel in Epsom. If it's any crumb of comfort, which I doubt, Thadeus was by his own admission totally fooled by your disguise, he did however recognise your bulky "sidekick" and decided, for a small fee, that it was his duty to let us know'

I recalled that he had taken something of an interest in me and shot me an odd, strange glance. I was also sure that Jimmy had kindly downplayed Padwick's description of yours truly'

'Suffice to say, our interest was heightened by Mr Astley kindly sending us a note confirming that had in his possession, Lord Coggles libelous dossier concerning our well-respected activities assisting the sporting interests of the aristocracy'

'I'll admit Mate I was more than a little surprised at this turn of events, since I was certain that you did not have the dossier!'

'To cut a long story short Mr Patterson we decided to invite you here in order to ensure that dear Mr Astley fully understood the need to return the dossier forthwith.'

'I did not feel inclined to push them too far' Jimmy continued 'but decided to respond in similar vein' Dear Mr Padwick, my sole reason for donning a disguise which, in my day job, I would regard as completely lacking in style or elegance, was to assist in efforts to prove Mr Chaplin's innocence'

'An interesting concept innocence, it's such a many-sided thing? Padwick responded almost wistfully 'Can a man who with his friend Mr Machell, deceived the racing public over a horse they knew to be amply fit enough to win the Derby, be described as innocent. Costing our dear friend the Marquis of Hastings so much.'

I'll admit Mate I was more than a mite confused as to what on earth the Marquis of Hastings had to do with this discussion. Before however, I had a chance to speak Padwick continued' Our only interest remains ensuring that half-truths and outright lies are not spread about our organisation'

At this point Pedley butted in' I've had enough of this Henry, send him back to his little room'

'Too right Tom' Hill added with a menacing laugh.

With Padwick concurring, I was escorted back to my little room. My first thought on being left alone - The Mate will be working out a cunning plan for my release, but what on earth was he going to be able to offer the Confederates in lieu of the Dossier?'

'I had been considering an envelope full of begging letters from the bookmaking community' I replied 'but truth be told Jimmy, the explanation is a little more surprising!' I proceeded over the next half an hour, to explain all that had happened – Carlton's suggestion to write to all the suspect parties; having bricks lobbed at me on the Buckingham Palace Road; my own embarrassing foray into the world of disguise; recruiting Jem as my trusted partner and my accidental discovery of the Dossiers'.

At the end of which Jimmy could only say' Well Mate, it's been a veritable blizzard of activity, not only have you knocked for six a major plank in the prosecution's case with the Lady Amelia letter, but you have also proved yourself a master of disguise to rival ex-Inspector Field himself!

It was nice to get a pat on the back from my closest ally, but never again would I be swapping places with Mrs Crumpbucket!.

'Within a few hours' Jimmy continued' of being returned to my room, my charming gaolers blindfolded and bundled me into a carriage. After what seemed an eternity of bumping back and forth, we finally arrived in Holland Park, where I was to reacquaint myself with you and Mr Machell, not forgetting Mr Bloss'

'My enforced stay in Horsham' Jimmy continued' gave me a lot of time to ponder the case……….

At that moment the study door swung open and into the room rushed Lady Astley.

'I am sorry to interrupt John, but I did remind you, that Lady Dymoke is coming for tea and you promised to be present.'

'Yes of course my dear, to the forefront of my mind. Why, I was only describing to young Joseph, an occasion which clearly demonstrated listening to my beloved is always the best course of action.'

'I cannot imagine John when that may have been' Lady Astley responded with a tone of amused resignation 'but I remain hopeful that the occasion when you do listen to me is not far away. In the meantime, do please get ready for my friend's arrival and my apologies Joseph for breaking you away from my husband's colourful sporting life.'

Whilst once again frustrated by the latest break in the story, I saw no reason to let her ladyship know that we had once again strayed from the story of the Mates sporting life!

Chapter 40 – The Mate and Jimmy reveal the truth!

Sir John and I gathered again in his study at 10.00am the following morning, for the denouement of his tale of detection. To be followed, Sir John declared, by a full-on gallop to the winning post through his sporting memoirs!

'So where were we Joseph?'

'I believe Sir John that Mr Patterson was about to reveal the result of his pondering.'

'Yes, indeed he did but only after I recall, I had ordered a further large brandy each and the night porter had found for me a large slice of chefs truly heroic jugged hare and venison pie. For some reason Jimmy, with a look of mild desperation, turned down a slice, declaring that such a treat was best enjoyed after breakfast!

'I think Mate' Jimmy commenced, that the guilty party is still out there and if we put the collective knowledge in our respective noggins together, we might just find we are a good deal closer to solving this mystery and freeing Mr Chaplin from incarceration than we had thought.'

And so it was that for the remainder of the night and through to breakfast the next morning, we debated back and forth all matters pertaining to the case. Come 8.00am and we had concluded which party had both the motive and opportunity to commit the crime. With, a fair wind, we could have Harry out of prison and leading Hermit into the Winners Enclosure on the final day of the Royal Ascot Meeting, rather than standing trial at the Old Bailey!

We had also concluded that Bracklesham, Zeals or even the Confederates might still have my home under watch, so we would remain at Brown's for a further night. Before taking the train from Waterloo early the next morning to Ascot and the first day of the Royal Meeting.

With breakfast partaken, Jimmy and I started on the urgent tasks we had allotted ourselves. First on the agenda for Jimmy, a private word with Sergeant Proudfoot. For my part, I needed to drop a line to the Crumpbuckets telling them I would not be back yet, and for anyone who called, to say I would be at Ascot the following day.

Next action was to drop a line to Lewis & Osmotherly advising them I would be coming over for 3.00pm with very important news and to ask, if they could ascertain the answer to a question regarding C A Troutbridge and obtain urgent agreement from Harry to use his box at Ascot the next day. I then arranged for a note to be delivered to David's cousin James Hydestile with a single question and another note to both Lady Amelia Irthlingborough and Lady Hastings, again with a single question.

Come 3.00pm and I was in Lewis's office and in full flow recounting all that had happened, missing a few details such as how I escaped from my own home without being spotted by those watching the house!

At the end of my recap, Lewis kindly said 'Remarkable progress Mr Astley both you and Mr Patterson, are to be congratulated'.

'Many thanks Mr Lewis' I responded' for the kind words, I believe we have come from the back of the pack to take up the running entering the final furlong!' An amusing description of the current state of play I felt, although from the quizzical look on Lewis's face, I had a feeling he found some of my racing allusions a little baffling at times!

'I think Mr Astley, what you are saying, is that come tomorrow, if everything falls into place, we will have our murderer, and Mr Chaplin can be set free?'

'Absolutely correct' I replied. Upon which Osmotherly, passed me two envelopes. One concerning Troutbeck and the other, details of how to access Harry's box and the services that would be provided for the preparation of drinks.

After saying adieu to our legal friends, I returned to the hotel late afternoon where the replies to all the notes I had sent out, were waiting for me at Reception. I found Jimmy, in the lounge, where he handed me a neatly tied package 'with the compliments of Mr Henry Hill, for tomorrow's trip to Ascot, a morning suit to your latest measurements and one silk plush top hat!'

'Many thanks indeed Jimmy, albeit my measurements tend to be a moving feast but seldom reducing!'

We dined quietly that evening, going through all our plans for the morrow. Whilst in good humour, we were both fully aware of the enormity of what was planned and, as a result we retired early to our respective beds.'

Next morning we were up early and at Waterloo for the first London & South Western Railway train of the day to Ascot, well ahead of the large crowds who would soon be flocking to the course. In those days one was required to change at Staines, the line having been developed by the Staines, Wokingham and Woking Junction Railway Company, albeit they never actually operated the line!

We were in Ascot by 9.00am and made our way to the newly built Station Hotel for a light breakfast, after which it was a short walk to the course. Even at that hour, the crowds were beginning to build, all strands of society equally represented.

Normally I thoroughly enjoyed the build up to a day's racing, affording the chance to say hello to friends across all the aforementioned social strands but on this occasion, I was particularly keen not to run into too many chums or acquaintances. Getting Harry out of jail was all that mattered.

We made our way up to the second floor of the main stand and unlocked the door to Harry's box. The room boasted a splendid view across the heath upon which the racecourse had been laid out in the 18th century, on the instructions of Queen Anne, who had declared it to be an ideal space for 'horses to gallop at full stretch'.

The box was a most generous size with room for twelve chairs, a large table, fine balcony and the obligatory paintings of horses associated with the Royal Meeting. There were double doors through to the next room, if the hosts largesse ran to an even larger party. Already in the room was the steward, who would be on hand to serve drinks. On this occasion however, there would not be one of the lavish spreads for which Harry was renowned and to which my waistline could attest.

We had made sure to establish that Lord Zeals, Tobias Bracklesham and the Danebury Confederates would be in attendance. In the first instance, however, we had arranged to meet Jem, kindly taking a short time out of his very busy schedule for the day. and Sir Carlton, as a member of David's family.

The time had reached noon and the noise from the large crowds on the lawns below had risen markedly, letting us know that the Royal Procession was on its way. From the balcony we could see the train of carriages led by Lord Colville, Master of the Buckhounds, wearing his silver couples' badge of office. He was followed by Mr. King, the Royal Huntsman, then the Whips, the Royal Park Keepers, Footmen and Postilions, resplendent in scarlet and gold uniforms.

The cheering reached a crescendo as the Prince of Wales carriage drew parallel to the enclosure to our right, his highness receiving a particularly raucous cheer from all the bookies present. Unlike his mother the Queen, who regarded gambling as one of life's greatest evils, the Prince was a huge supporter of the turf and indeed any other opportunities for a spot of gaming! As we have seen of late with the Royal Baccarat Affair' Sir John added with a grim laugh'.

Within a couple of minutes of the Royal Parade passed by, there was a knock on the door and into the room stepped Sir Carlton, bang on time as I would have expected, looking as dapper as ever in his morning suit with his gold crested family stick to hand.

'Good to see you Carlton and thank you so much for joining us' I intoned followed by our usual vigorous shake of the hands.

'I am pleased to be here John and very keen indeed to hear what happened regarding those dossiers, I just hope my suggestion was a wise one and did not cause you unforeseen problems?'

'I think Carlton, you can say Jimmy and I have had a very interesting last few days but yes, ultimately a very worthwhile exercise, of which more anon.'

Five minutes later there came another knock on the door and in bowled Jem large as life.

'Sorry I am late chaps but just needed to speak with Bloss about today's runners.'

'With it being just gone noon' I replied' can I suggest a quick snifter to help the juices to the brain.'

Orders taken; our steward duly prepared the drinks. From watching him I concluded a little more practice was needed on the mixing front! Once everyone had their drinks, I began by swiftly recapping the events of the last few days, accompanied by various utterances of surprise from Sir Carlton. I concluded by confirming our confidence that David' murderer was present at Ascot today, before handing over to Jimmy to elucidate further.'

'Many thanks Mate and happy to take up the running. Begging everyone's forbearance, I would just like to start on the terrible night of Lord Coggles murder. With his Lordship having been found with £500 upon his person, the likelihood of his having been seized upon by passing ruffians seems remote. Meaning, he must have been lured to his fate by someone he knew and trusted before venturing up to the Burgh Heath Road, on such a foul night.'

'Through a combination of factors suspicion fell onto Mr Chaplin, who we all know to be innocent. With the Mate having witnessed the Danebury Confederacy threatening Lord Coggles over his dossier, they have formed the prime focus of our investigations. It soon became clear to us that Lord Coggles had also penned unflattering dossiers on two members of the Marquis of Hastings set to wit Viscount Zeals and Tobias Bracklesham.'

'What about the other members of the set' Sir Carlton chimed in' I've often heard it said one should always look close to home for the murderer.'

'A good point' I responded before Jimmy could answer' we did indeed give them all consideration.'

'Whatever I may think about the Marquis and his behaviour' I continued' he simply had no motive for killing his loyalist friend or arranging for others to do so at his behest. David represented perhaps his only chance to avoid becoming the next fly to fall into Padwick's web. As for Lord Bowlhead, when it comes to coshing someone on the head, it's difficult to envision anyone less suited to the job. The six hundred would never have charged into the Valley of Death with Bowlhead in charge!'

'Lord Woldingham' I continued 'seems intent on taking care of the countries entire stock of heroin and would need to wake up to even be semi-comatose!'

'So that leaves us chaps' Jem chipped in 'with the subjects of the dossiers as being either the murderer themselves, or the employers of both the murderer and presumably the mysterious Cuthbert Algernon Troutbridge, to cover their tracks and to ensure Harry, is convicted of their crime?!'

'Indeed Jem, and we have been giving considerable thought to all three parties being our murderer.'

I quickly handed back to Jimmy, having cut across him in my eagerness to share my views on the Marquises friends!

'Thanks again Mate and with the benefit of what we knew already and the recent actions of all three parties, it is quite clear that none of them wished to see their dossiers aired in the public domain.'

'For the Danebury Mob, release of their Dossier would have caused massive embarrassment to a large section of the landed gentry and more critically a hideous loss of profit. For Padwick it would also have meant an end to his political ambitions and a complete loss of face with his 'noble' friends.'

In the case of Tobias Bracklesham, Lord Coggles dossier was of a more personal nature. As well as laying bare his duplicitous behaviour in 'stealing' Lady Amelia Irthlingborough. It also reveals Brackelsham's shady dealings, heavy gambling and use of family money to further personal vendettas. Release of the dossier would undoubtedly have cost him the hand of Lady Irthlingborough, brought huge embarrassment to his family and potential prosecution to boot.'

'Then there is Viscount Zeals, a latecomer to the suspect party., His dossier shows that beneath the appearance of an overbearing buffoon. lies an altogether darker and more devious individual. One who enjoys a close 'business' relationship with the loathsome Thomas Pedley. '

'We know from the dossier, that his initial forays into the world of gambling could only be described as disastrous pushing him, along with many other young aristocrats, into the arms of the Danebury Confederacy. However, when offered the opportunity to recruit other young aristocrats, he took to it like a duck to water soon becoming a trusted lieutenant of Padwick and Co. It did not take Lord Coggles long to realise that he was doing his best to ensure the Marquis of Hastings joined the others in Padwick's web!'

Jimmy was just about to continue when Jem, who had been unusually quiet, spoke. 'My apologies Mate but my first runner of the afternoon will need saddling soon.'

'No fears Jem, we will soon be coming to our conclusions very soon in fact Back to you Jimmy!'

'Thanks Mate and using the same running order our thoughts about the three parties!'

'Whilst the note that Lord Coggles received remains lost, we can be certain that he would not have been willing to accept an invitation from Padwick and Co to join them for an evening meet on the blasted heath. With the Confederates having, despite all our earlier assumptions, no connection with Cuthbert Algernon Troutbridge, there is nothing linking the unholy trinity to the murder.'

'As for Tobias Bracklesham, he was clearly extremely agitated by Lord Coggles and as we have shown, could in theory at least, have made his way up to the Burgh Heath Road, coshed his adversary and returned to the party. Whilst possible, it seems highly unlikely that Lord Coggles would have agreed to walk up to the Burgh Heath Road to speak to someone already in the room with him.'

'In the case of Lord Zeals, he could presumably have arranged for an accomplice to have taken the note to the hotel then, on arriving at Epsom Station, sprinted up to the Burgh Heath Road, committed the foul deed, returned to town for his luggage before sauntering into the hotel as if nothing had happened. We consider the likelihood of the Viscount sprinting up to the Heath as likely as Lord Coggles accepting his invitation'

'Apologies chaps' Carlton interceded with a look of perplexity on his face' but haven't you effectively dismissed all your prime suspects, still leaving poor Harry facing an imminent trial'

'I agree Carlton that is the case' I replied' the note could only have come from someone David trusted implicitly.'

'As far as I can see John 'Carlton replied with a laugh 'that only appears to leave your good self!

'Actually Carlton, we think it is more likely to be a member of his family.'

Still looking perplexed Carlton responded 'Do you mean his cousin and racing confederate the Hon James Hydestile, I hardly seem him as the type to cosh a member of his own family!'

'No Carlton my old friend' I responded' I'm afraid to say we are thinking of another member of his family and it's with a heavy heart, that we believe that person to be you, Sir Carlton Scroop, someone he trusted and would have been willing to make that fateful last journey to meet.'

'Have you taken leave of your senses John! Carlton exclaimed, the look of perplexity replaced by one of shock and anger' I have been doing my very best to help you find David's killer.'

'I will explain our thinking Carlton' I responded patiently.

'Explain! What is there to explain, I'm not staying here listening to any more of this arrant nonsense, what on earth reason would I have for killing David!'

Sir Carlton's attempts to jump up from his seat were however immediately thwarted, as Jem, who had been sitting to his side, reached out and placed a large hand on his arm, doubtless applying far more force than was visible. 'I think Carlton we should all listen to what John and Jimmy have to say first'.

Very reluctantly Sir Carlton appeared to accept the situation as any attempt at throwing off Jem, would be doomed to failure.

Calm as ever, Jimmy recommenced 'On the night of the murder you were staying at The Spreadeagle and chose to dine in your room. Given the raucous nature of the Hastings party, a fully understandable choice but it did leave you free for the evening and unlike Mr Bracklesham, you would have needed no excuse to leave the dinner table and exit through a ground floor window, before running up to the Burgh Heath Road.'

'Whilst we subsequently found him to be a most duplicitous figure, Mr Belvedere the Duty Manager at the Spreadeagle showed me the guest book, from which I noticed that you signed into the hotel at around 6.00pm that night. I thought nothing of that until, last night, the Mate mentioned that you had apparently seen Viscount Zeals on the station four hours before he actually signed into the hotel.'

'This is complete balderdash' a now very agitated Sir Carlton shouted to which Jem forcefully responded, 'Shut up Carlton I want to hear what they have to say', which seemed to do the trick, at least for the moment.

'When meeting Mavis on Derby Day' I continued 'I enquired about David's whereabouts and was informed that he had not appeared that evening. It seems you had advised Mavis, that you recalled David simply wandering off without warning several times at family events and then turning up again safe and sound.'

'I had taken this assurance without question given it came from an old friend, I have however sought comment from the aforementioned James Hydestyle who' I said, pulling a letter from my pocket' assured me that he could remember no such occasions where this had happened and was sure that this unusual habit would have at least been remarked upon.'

'I repeat what I have already said' Carlton shouted, clearly no longer willing to take no notice of Jem's orders 'this is all nonsense, a cockeyed joining up of random unrelated hearsay, put together to fit your ridiculous hypothesis!'

'What is not ridiculous is Mr Cuthbert Algernon Troutbridge! Whoever put this gentleman up to his untrue claims of being a witness, clearly wanted to ensure that the forces of justice remained convinced they had the right man in Harry Chaplin.'

'Whilst I would seldom if ever believe anything I am told by Mr Henry Padwick' I have no doubts that he was also blithely unaware of this gentleman when put to him the other night'

'Both Jimmy and I had been separately pondering what an unknown export agent with no obvious connection to horse racing have to do with any of our suspected parties. Possibly an employee of Bracklesham's Tonics or maybe an old family retainer of the Zeals family. I also had a small bell ringing in the back of my mind that his residing in Hackney must be relevant.'

'To which end, I asked Lewis & Lewis, to kindly confirm Troutbecks address, which they advised as being Honington Villas, Scroop Street, Hackney, London. I should stress here and now, that I had never mentioned to the lawyers Carlton, about how we had discussed the case. Given I was under instruction not to discuss with anyone, a request I singularly failed to observe!'

'They would also not have known that the land around the small Lincolnshire village of Honnignton falls within the Scroop Estate of which you are the sole owner, as well as a fair chunk of Hackney'

'This is just all some of form of fantastic coincidence' Sir Carlton responded, albeit he sounded considerably less assured than before.

'Indeed, it might be Carlton, albeit Mr Troutbeck's sole area of importing is Jade and whilst I'm no expert on the stuff, I do know that Scroop Hall has one of the very finest collections in the whole of England. Another surprising coincidence perhaps Carlton?'

'It could still all be coincidence' Carlton responded, in an even weaker tone.

'There is I am afraid Carlton more to tell' which, as I said starting to reach one again into my case roused Carlton to utter 'Oh not another bloody letter' before slumping back into his seat'.

'From speaking with Mavis, we had been under the impression that the note to Lord Coggles was brought into the room by a member of staff. We have however had it confirmed to us by two of the ladies present that fateful night that it was Mavis, on returning from a brief visit to the lady's room who handed the note to David, apparently Mavis had found this on the temporarily empty reception desk.'

'With the police convinced that Harry was the author of the note, we have it on unimpeachable authority that how it was delivered to David was not a major consideration in their thinking.'

'It is our belief' I continued 'you handed Mavis the note and she duly gave it to David, who consequently rushed to get his coat and head off one final time into the dark and unforgiving night.'

'Only you and Mavis will know if Miss Enderby was aware of the contents of the note she was asked to handover. What I do know is that when this is all presented to the police, Mr Troutbeck will be found to have seriously perjured himself and Mavis will be inexorably dragged into this whole sad affair. You may not I suspect be too worried about the consequences awaiting Troutbeck, but I cannot' I added as gently as I could' really believe that you wish Mavis to be brought into public view in this way?'

There followed a long silence that no one seemed willing to break. For my part, I could think of few things that had given me less pleasure than to confront an old friend and accuse him of murder.

At long last the silence was broken.

'Alright John you win, I did write the note, but Mavis had no part in any of this. She is a young lady for whom I have strong feelings' I found myself taken back several months when I had asked Carlton if there was to ever be another Lady Scroop and he had responded, somewhat wistfully, that he could see someone on the horizon. Never in my wildest of imaginings, most of which revolved around making horse racing pay(!), did I imagine that it was Miss Enderby to whom he was referring.

'To be frank, David did not cherish Mavis for the fine young woman she is. I found it difficult to stomach, seeing him devote more time to his terminally ungrateful friend Hastings than trying to make Mavis happy. Added to which he was patently still in love with Lady Amelia Irthlingborough! And don't get me started on all the high-minded moralising!'

'By the night in question, I had come to the end of my tether and wanted to have things out with him, hence the invite to meet on the Burgh Heath Road. I fortified myself with perhaps more brandy than I should have before leaving the hotel which, together with the poor weather, meant I arrived slight after the allotted time. David had obviously arrived early and was in the process of being set upon by a couple of ruffians. On seeing me they high tailed it. I have no idea who they were, aside from one having a flat sounding accent'

I found David in a very poor way and calling for help. Whoever his assailants were, they had clearly been very thorough in their work. I intended to help but had worked myself into such a state of anger that I decided, with David prone, I would tell him how badly I believed he was letting sweet Mavis down and how he clearly did not love her as I did myself.'

'I am not too sure what I had been expecting David to say, hopefully an acceptance that I was right. Instead of which I was treated to his usual pompous nonsense about fighting for moral rectitude, but never once did I hear him say he loved Mavis. The more pompous he became and the more he pleased for assistance, the angrier I became and when he started defending that wastrel Hastings, I completely saw red and struck him with the gold knob of my cane. To my horror he reeled back clearly dead.'

'It was cold wet, and I am none too proud to say that I panicked. I rolled his body into the ditch and removed the note I had sent him and returned to the hotel. So now you know the truth what do you intend to do then John?'

Before I could say anything, almost forgotten by those in the room, the steward stepped out smartly from behind the drinks bar to say 'I am sorry Sir Carlton but the decision on what to do no longer lies with Mr Astley, I am Detective Sergeant Proudfoot of Scotland Yard, and I am arresting you for the murder of Lord David Coggles on the 21st May 1867.'

Almost exactly on cue the doors to the next-door box opened and out strode Inspector Richard Tanner with two burly officers.

If Tanner was surprised at this turn of events, it was not easy to tell, his whole demeanour gave off a reassuring level of Sang Froid. 'Thank you, Proudfoot, and I would be grateful Sir Carlton, if you would kindly accompany us back to London to discuss this matter further' Not that he had much choice.'

It was difficult to be sure what Sir Carlton was thinking. Most likely shock as to how his world had imploded in the space of little more than half an hour.

As he was being escorted from the room, Carlton seemed to have regained a little of his previous bluster turning to say 'In all honesty John, I considered the idea of you as a detective positively ludicrous. I had merely been looking to humour you and your slightly brighter associate. Strange how the police are outwitted by a buffoon and his mate!'

And with that charmless and less than witty goodbye, Sir Carlton was taken from the room. Hardly I reflected the way in which one member of the Bullingdon Cricket Club should speak to another!

After a moment of stunned silence, Jem jumped up and shook both Jimmy and I by the hands, damn neigh wrenching my arm out of its socket' Well done Mate, I'll be quite honest I too had a few doubts about your new life as a detective, but you've well and truly proved me wrong. Did you see the look on Carlton's face, you're no buffoon you and Jimmy are a couple of marvels.'

Whilst very touched by Jem's generous remarks I had to say' Honestly Jem I would have been lost without your help. There is however one man, to whom I owe more than I can ever repay and that is my friend and accomplice Jimmy 'The Flying Tailor' Patterson.'

'It's been a pleasure Mate and an honour to work with a real gentleman, true friend and someone who can now add to their talents that of detective.''

'Apologies for breaking up this touching orgy of well merited self-congratulation' Jem interceded' but I need to get back to the stables. 'As for Carlton's explanation of his actions, I'm not sure I entirely buy all he said. He may very well have set out that evening without any intention to murder Coggles, but the fact remains, he lured him to a quiet spot and when his opportunity came, he was willing to simply dispatch him to the next world with, of all things the family crest. I've also no doubts that the suggestion to write to subjects of all three dossiers was intended to put us further off the scent.'

'Whilst on my way to join Bloss, I will keep an eye open for Miss Enderby. It will not be the first time that Mavis has been left by herself at the races.' Jem added archly and with handshakes all round, Jimmy and I were left alone in the Box. All of us no doubt reflecting on Mavis having advised me about David's non-existent overnight disappearances.

I am not sure if any of us really wanted to dwell on the question of exactly what Mavis may or may not have known about Sir Carlton intentions and with his admission of guilt, perhaps it was best to let things lie there. I also decided it best not to mention, the close resemblance that Mavis bore to Sir Carlton's late wife..........

With all that had been happening over the past hour, proceedings on the course had been completely forgotten, but from the noise outside it was clear that racing was about to start. We used our vantage point to watch Black Diamond stroll to victory in the traditional opening race, the Queen Anne Stakes.

For once however, my heart was not in the races and we soon made our way to Ascot Station, to catch an almost empty train back to Waterloo. From where we made our way to see Messers Lewis & Osmotherly and give then the good news.

By the time we had finished with the legal chaps, leaving them to secure Harry's rapid release, it was early evening and we headed across to The Strand and that wonderful British institution 'Simpsons Grand Divan Tavern. From the Bill of Fare we chose Master Chef Thomas Davey's sumptuous roast beef, carved at the table, washed down with a bottle of Romanée-Conti 1858 Burgandy followed by a very fine House of Delamain XO Cognac.

As ever there were plenty of bright chaps playing chess, with the restaurant being an unofficial centre for world chess. Amongst the players there was a young Mancunian named Joseph Blackburne, apparently known as 'The Black Death' on account of his playing style!

Later in the evening Jimmy paid his two shillings to take on Blackburne, in one of ten games he was playing simultaneously. Jimmy damn neigh beat him, albeit Blackburne was playing all the games blindfold. For my part I find the game difficult enough at the best of times without not being able to see the blooming board!

We finished the evening around 11.00pm by which time we were both beginning to feel the effects of an extraordinary day. I was finally able to return to my own bed and slept in long and late.

Next morning, over a leisurely breakfast, mixed in with profound feelings of relief that Harry would soon be free, I still found it difficult to believe that none of our suspects, who I found loathsome to a man, were the guilty party. Instead, I was left with a deep sense of sadness that the culprit had been an old and I thought trusted friend.

Post breakfast I finally opened the envelope that David Coggles had given me in Stockbridge. Inside was the promised photograph of Buffy Utterby and I, together with a short note advising me to 'look out for the three envelopes I have sent to Elsham Hall for safe keeping'. I really had learned a lesson about opening my post promptly!

And so, Joesph, that concludes how, to my continuing surprise, I became a detective!

'What a marvellous tale Sir John and I'd have put my money on that arrogant young man Tobias Bracklesham. I would never I have thought of Sir Carlton.'

'I'm afraid Joseph, being highly unpleasant is clearly not a pre-requisite for being a murderer' Sir John chuckled

'What happened Sir John to the dossiers on Viscount Zeals and Tobias Bracklesham?'

''Well Joseph I would gladly have put them into the public domain to expose the behaviour of both the crooked and duplicitous braggarts. We were however, required by Scotland Yard to hand them over, since they apparently formed a part of the overall case against Sir Carlton. Damned if I could see how they had any bearing on the case. Much I don't doubt, to the relief of the parties involved and their families nothing formal was ever heard about them again. You can I am sure draw your own conclusions from that Joseph.'

'Was there any clue Sir John as to who the ruffians were who attacked Lord Coggles before Sir Carlton arrived on the scene?'

'We will ever know for certain' Sir John replied 'but you may recall my saying that there was quite a likeness between David Coggles and Viscount Bowlhead, both victims of similar attacks, undertaken by someone with a flat accent. You may also recall my mentioning that on the afternoon of the Derby, Parker's normally immobile features registered an obvious look of surprise on seeing a fresh-faced Viscount Bowlhead. My guess is that David was attacked by the Merry Men, thinking in the gloom he was Bowlhead, who they had intended teaching a lesson to for talking up the prospects of their employer's horse.'

'Can I also ask Sir John' did you ever have to pay the Danebury Confederacy back the £3000 you owed?

'Well,' Sir John replied'' it had not been requested by the time Padwick went, I don't doubt downwards, to meet his maker, in 1879. And neither Pedley nor Hill have shown a strong interest in keeping in contact, which is just as well since heaven knows how much I'd owe now at their rate of interest!'

'One final thing I had been wanting to ask Sir John?'

'I think I can probably guess this one Joseph'

'Why did you and Jimmy not become famous for solving this case?'

'That would certainly have been amusing but I'm not sure it would have helped in the tight knit world of racing, where I might have been seen as being in league with the Boys in Blue!

In any event, I don't think the police were any too keen for it come to light that the case had been solved by a couple of amateurs, nor would Sir Carlton have been either!'

'I should' Sir John continued' look upon this as an opportunity, with your ever-increasing literary skills, to one day become a real-life Dr Watson. The case book of The Mate and the Flying Tailor should provide a very nice financial sinecure' he chucked once again. Before asking me to pour us each a small glass of his treasured Tres Vénérable Delamain Brandy. Sir John observing, 'my book will need to produce a fair few noncies to afford another bottle of this stuff!'

And that is the way I will always remember Sir John, a true sporting English gentleman, someone always willing to do whatever it took to help his friends, even when the odds seemed stacked against him.

Epilogue – In The Mate's own words

It was Friday 7th June 1867 and the third and last day of Royal Ascot. Just like Derby Day, 25 days before it was cold and a little overcast but unlike that fateful day, the resemblance to a Siberia was much less marked. Jimmy and I were standing on the balcony of Harry Chaplin's box looking out over the course,

By half past twelve and with the first race not until 2.00pm the place was packed to the gunnels, a sea of gentlemen's top hats and colourful and elaborate headwear for the ladies. The bookmakers were already hard at work, if that term could be accurately said to describe their activities, taking bets on the races to come. Just like Epsom, I also had no doubts that the pin-prickers and pickpockets, would also be 'hard' at work plying their dubious professions!

From within the box, I could hear the clatter of plates as a mighty spread was being laid out for lunch. Standing to my left was Jimmy and my right Harry Chaplin, back where he belonged. The authorities, doubtless highly embarrassed by what had happened, had whisked Harry back into Court on the Thursday, allowing him to be here in time to hopefully see Hermit win that afternoon's St James Palace Stakes.

We all three had in our hand's glasses of a most agreeable extra dry **Perrier-Jouët champagne**. Harry looked out across the course and said 'It is truly most wonderful to be back and whilst I always believed the truth would out, there were I'll confess, sitting in my dank, dark cell at Newgate, moments of doubt. I owe my freedom to the efforts or you both and, my excellent lawyers' he added, nodding across to young Osmotherly, who was representing Mr Lews, in court to defend yet another esteemed client.'

'As a very small token of my thanks you will all be joining me for dinner on Saturday night at The Langham in Upper Regent Street' Only opened in June 1865 by Bertie Prince of Wales, fine food and wine apart, I was keen to try out London's first hydraulic lift – what on earth will those engineers think of next!

Many of the guests present in the box, had been there for the Lincolnshire Handicap, with one rather notable absentee.

'I will admit John, I would never have thought Carlton as capable of such a deed.'

'Neither did I Harry, and I wish it had been otherwise.'

'What do we think will happen to Sir Carlton' Jimmy enquired.

'I don't doubt Jimmy' Harry responded 'that whilst certain sections of the general populace would gain a visceral delight in seeing a member of the nobility executed, I rather doubt the establishment will have the stomach for that. My expectation, from what our legal friends have advised, is that Sir Carlton will be declared mentally unfit to stand trial. He may well find himself not far from here at Broadmoor Lunatic Asylum where, unlike Newgate, the rooms provide a view over trees but no more country house weekends, hunting or visits to the casinos of the South of France.'

At that moment, we were interrupted by a large cheer from the bookies below. Sauntering into the ring was the Marquis of Hastings, looking like a man without a care in the world, rather than one who had recently lost £120,000 and had to sell his fine Scottish Estate, to cover the debt.

Noticeably he was not accompanied by either Zeals or Bracklesham as one would have expected, hopefully he had rid themselves of them but trailing a little in his wake was the great follower Viscount Bowlhead and behind him in his usual daze Lord Woldingham

'I see the Marquis has, unlike last year, been having quite a successful Ascot' I commented.

'I think you could go as far as to say very successful' Harry replied, 'he may well have won back much of his losses, albeit I don't doubt it will all happen again.'

'Have you received your £10,000 from Hastings yet?' I enquired.

'I think it's best to say the cheque is probably still in the post' Harry responded with remarkable good humour' For today I am just grateful to no longer be in that hell hole Newgate and if I ever go into politics, it will be top of my list to close!'

From the back of the box a voice boomed 'Hello Chaps' before Jem joined us on the balcony. After the usual exchange of friendly felicitations, Harry could not resist asking Jem' So what was it like working as a junior detective for the Mate!'

'A pleasure to work for Harry, but he could be a bit of an old woman at times' added with a wink in my direction'

Seeing Harry looking a little confused I quickly chipped in 'Private joke Harry which I might be persuaded to explain when we get to the bottom of the large decanter at the Langham.'

With Harry back in harness and Lady Astley having forgiven me for not reading my post in a timely fashion, I knew that, for the first time in weeks, everything was right with the world. All I had to do now, was work out how I was going to get a profitable winner of my own next week at Brighton Races!

Principal Characters (Real)

Harry Chaplin (1840-1923) – The year after Hermit's victory, Harry Chaplin was elected to parliament as MP for Mid-Lincolnshire, remaining in the House of Commons until 1916, when he was raised to the Lords as 1st Viscount Chaplin. A devoted follower of Benjamin Disraeli he rose to become Cabinet Member for Agriculture. His genial personality ensured that he remained popular with the voters and able to make fiends across the political divide. On entering Parliament, he reduced his racing interests but managed to win the 1872 Lincolnshire Handicap with Guy Darrell and ran a successful stud operation based around Hermit. He continued to enjoy entertaining his friends on a grand scale but combined with a succession of poor harvests, he was obliged to sell the Blankney Estate. Despite expanding to 20 stone in weight he continued to enjoy riding to the hunt until late in life.

4th Marquis of Hastings (1842-68) – Notwithstanding the success he enjoyed at Ascot in 1867 it was sadly all downhill from there. With debts mounting, he soon found himself in the hands of Henry Padwick and company. He had the chance to win the Derby in 1868 with his colt The Earl. However, with Harry Hill standing to lose a considerable sum on The Earl, Lord Hastings was instructed to scratch the horse from the race. Never blessed with a particularly robust constitution and with his fortune and almost all his fair-weather friends gone, Lord Hastings passed away on 10th November 1868. Shortly before he died, he remarked 'Hermit's Derby broke my heart. But I didn't show it did I?'

Marchioness of Hastings (1842-1907) – After the passing of the Marquis of Hastings, the Marchioness married Sir Geroge Chetwynd Bt in 1870. Sir George had inherited a sizable estate in Warwickshire and like her first husband also owned a large string of horses and gambled heavily. The marriage produced two children but was not a happy one and the couple eventually split up, on the positive side Sir George avoided losing all his money!

James Merry (1805-77) – In addition to his racing and business interests, Merry was also Liberal MP for Falkirk. First elected in 1857, he was removed from office just four months later. Re-elected in 1859, he continued in parliament until 1874. His racing fortunes reached their peak in 1873 with Doncaster's Derby victory. However, with his health beginning to fail, he sold his horses in 1875. Somewhere along the line Merry and Buchanan fell out in a dispute about money!

Hermit (1864-1890) – After the Derby, Hermit remained in training until 1869 but never again achieved the same level of success and was by the end, running in lower value races. He did however achieve exceptional success for his owner at stud, siring the winners of some 864 races. He passed way at Harry Chaplin's Blankney Stud and to this day, his skeleton is still used for anatomy lectures at the Royal Veterinary College in Camden.

Captain Octavius James Machell (1837-1902) – Like Harry Chaplin, Jem Machell was the son of a vicar but unlike his friend, he did not inherit a large estate whilst a young man. Instead, he joined the army and after being involved in the suppression of the Indian Mutiny, spent seven years stationed in Ireland. Whilst there he developed a flair for judging races horses, putting that to very good use in the betting market. Finding that the army was getting in the way of his gambling, he resigned his commission and went onto win eleven classic races for his wealthy clients. He was eventually able to buy back the family estate in Westmoreland.

Henry Padwick (1805-79) – Whilst by day a well-known member of the legal profession, as referenced in this book, his main source of income was money lending. He also won a reputed £80,000 from his horse Virago's victory in the 1854, but also suffered large losses on the stock market. Whilst his activities were widely known, neither he nor his associates were ever 'brought to book'.

George Payne (1803-78) – Never the luckiest of racehorse owners, Payne was one of the most popular racing men of his day and a man trusted by many when help or good advice was needed. A fine card player he was a witness in the case of Lord de Ros v Cumming, where the former was unmasked as a notorious upper-class card sharp.

Sir George Lewis (1833-1911) – Articled to his father, Lewis went on to become one of the most prominent solicitors of the 19th Century, involved in many of the most prominent cases of his day. His reputation for discretion led to his being 'name-checked' in this regard by no less than Sherlock Holmes in 'The Adventure of the Illustrious Client'.

Jimmy Patterson – Referenced in Sir John Astley's 'Fifty Years of My Sporting Life', beyond their running exploits there is not too much biographical detail. He struck me however, as being a resourceful chap and I hope he will not have minded a small amount of embellishment as to his activities!

Lady Eleanor Astley – Sadly Lady Astley passed away just three years after her husband in 1897 aged 57 and is buried, together with her husband and son Jack who died in South Africa in May 1896 aged just 22, at All Souls Church, Elsham, Lincolnshire.

Inspector Richard Tanner was one of Scotland Yard's leading detectives of the era. He was the senior detective investigating the brutal murder of Thomas Briggs by Franz Muller, referenced by The Mate on his train trip to Lewes. Tanner pursued Muller across The Atlantic Ocean, eventually arresting his man in Manhattan!

Tass Parker was a well-known Black Country bareknuckle fighter of the 1830's and 1840's. Originally a second for the English Heavyweight Champion William 'The Tipton Slasher' Perry (1819-80), he subsequently became his opponent. Whilst unable to beat The Slasher in any of those fights, he managed in an 1844 bout in the Surrey town of Horley to last an incredible 133 rounds!

Joseph Lewis – Unfortunately I have not been able to find any more out about what happened to Joseph post his spelling working for The Mate but like to hope, that it proved to be the springboard to a rewarding career!

Principal Characters (more imaginary than the ones above!)

Viscount Bowlhead – Out admiring the spring flowers in St James's Park in London one April morning in 1868, Viscount Bowlhead found himself reminded of the battering he received a year before on his way to meet The Mate at Boodles Club. Very fortunately it was not the two ruffians who had set upon him but rather Mademoiselle Dupont also taking a break from her duties to admire the spring flowers. After contriving to 'run into' Madame a further ten times in the park, Mademoiselle thoughtfully suggested he might like to take her out for tea. They married two years later, after the Mademoiselle asked Bowlhead for his hand in marriage, a union that saw the birth of six sons. The Viscount succeeded to the Earldom and proving a fine custodian of the family estate, with a little 'guidance' from the Countess!

Tobias Bracklesham – Whilst never formally charged with any crimes, once the Bracklesham family came to learn of the existence of the dossier. Mrs Bracklesham being particularly concerned that the families 'good name' would be tarnished, Mr Bracklesham decided that what they needed was a new bottling plant in Uruguay. Bracklesham left England later in 1867 together with his new bride – Mavis Enderby! It also came to light, that John Gully's share in the family's firm had been acquired by none other than Henry Padwick!

Sir Carlton Scroop – After twenty years in Broadmoor, the Scroop family were able to 'negotiate' the release of Sir Carlton, on the grounds that he had fully recovered from the 'illness' which saved him from the gallows. In the meantime, the families' trustees had arranged for the family estates to be transferred to Sir Carlton' younger brother Jasper. Once ensconced in Scroop Hall, Jasper followed the example of fellow Lincolnshire estate owner the Reverend John King and married the Under Parlour Maid. Sir Carlton was 'exported' to Mandalay in Burma, centre of the world's Jade mining industry, together with a trusted family retainer to ensure he got up to no more 'mischief'. The family retainer being one Cuthbert Algernon Troutbridge.

Lady Amelia Irthlingborough – Soon after providing invaluable help to The Mate, Lady Amelia ended her engagement to Tobias Bracklesham. Wisely taking the time to come to terms with the untimely death of her true love David Coggles, she found herself drawn to the charms of the Honourable James Hydestile, who possessed many of his cousin's finest qualities. Married in 1869, the couple and their eight children settled happily into life on the Sussex estate her husband eventually inherited from his late father Lord Adversane.

Viscount Zeals – Like Tobias Bracklesham, Viscount Zeals was another who having not managed to obtain possession of his dossier, discovered a hither too unrecognised desire to go and live abroad. In his case Zeals made his way to the South of France where his proven ability to persuade other wealthy but foolish young men to part with their money, made him the ideal front of house manager for a large casino on the Cote D'Azur.

Lord Woldingham – On a visit to the East End of London one day in 1868, more befuddled than usual, Lord Woldingham managed to mistake a Christian Missionary training centre for his favourite Opium Den. Within a week Lord Woldingham had renounced all opiates and within six months had set off on a new life as missionary to the poppy fields of Afghanistan.

Printed in Great Britain
by Amazon